Malik whirled, his face frozen between fear and rage as he turned to see what had killed his ship. The thing hovered behind him, behind the disabled skimmer. It, too, was just a skimmer, much smaller than the *Lady*, but mounted on its prow was a strange device the likes of which Malik had never seen before.

There was a metallic dish whose inner surface was coated with a highly reflective substance that shone so brightly it hurt Malik's eyes. In front of the dish, at what could have been its focal point, was one of the crystalline flowers. The dish and the flower pointed right at Malik.

He thought how beautiful the crystal looked, then there was a pulse of light so bright that it burned his eyes out, and Malik Ferdenko was nothing more than vapor slowly dissipating in the cosmic breeze.

BUCK ROGERS®
Books

ARRIVAL

THE MARTIAN
WARS TRILOGY

Book One: Rebellion 2456
Book Two: Hammer of Mars
Book Three: Armageddon Off Vesta

THE INNER
PLANETS TRILOGY

Volume One: First Power Play
Volume Two: Prime Squared
Volume Three: Matrix Cubed

BUCK ROGERS

XXVc — THE 25TH CENTURY — BOOKS

The Inner Planets Trilogy, Vol. One

FIRST POWER PLAY

John Miller

Cover Art by
JERRY BINGHAM

FIRST POWER PLAY

First Printing: August 1990
Printed in the United States of America
Library of Congress Catalog Card Number: 89-51880

9 8 7 6 5 4 3 2 1

ISBN: 0-88083-840-4

TSR, Inc.
P.O. Box 756
Lake Geneva, WI
53147
U.S.A.

TSR UK Ltd.
120 Church End,
Cherry Hinton
Cambridge CB1 3LB
United Kingdom

To the memory of Philip Francis Nowlan

The Inner Planets

Earth

A twisted wreckage despoiled by interplanetary looters, Earth is a declining civilization. Its people are divided and trapped in urban sprawls and mutant-infested reservations.

Luna

An iron-willed confederation of isolationist states, the highly advanced Lunars are the bankers of the Solar System, "peaceful" merchants willing to knock invading ships from the skies with mighty massdriver weapons.

The Asteroid Belt

A scattered anarchy of tumbling planetoids and rough rock miners, where every sentient has the right to vote, and the majority rules among five hundred miniature worlds.

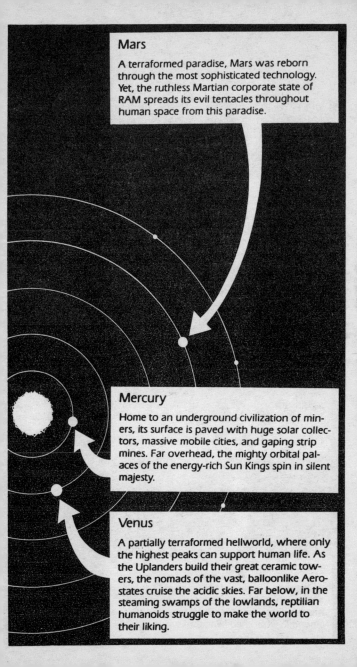

Mars

A terraformed paradise, Mars was reborn through the most sophisticated technology. Yet, the ruthless Martian corporate state of RAM spreads its evil tentacles throughout human space from this paradise.

Mercury

Home to an underground civilization of miners, its surface is paved with huge solar collectors, massive mobile cities, and gaping strip mines. Far overhead, the mighty orbital palaces of the energy-rich Sun Kings spin in silent majesty.

Venus

A partially terraformed hellworld, where only the highest peaks can support human life. As the Uplanders build their great ceramic towers, the nomads of the vast, balloonlike Aerostates cruise the acidic skies. Far below, in the steaming swamps of the lowlands, reptilian humanoids struggle to make the world to their liking.

CHAPTER ONE

Malik Ferdenko crouched in the black shadow, watching the light towers glittering like jewels before him on the plain below. According to the latest *Asteroid Almanac*, the small asteroid was supposed to be uninhabited. The lights, and the space-suited men scurrying to and fro between them, shouldn't have been there. It should have been a barren bit of rock whirling dark and untouched through the void, not a beehive of activity.

Malik smiled to himself as he watched the men rushing about before him like fireflies against the asteroid's dark surface. Such anomalies were Malik's livelihood. As an industrial spy, he'd spent most of his life prowling the wild anarchy of the Asteroid Belt, where almost anything could be found if one only knew where to look.

Malik had been searching for this particular opera-
tion for several months now. He'd first heard rumors
of an unregistered research station back on Ceres,
the largest asteroid in the Belt, and tracked its tortu-
ous trail to Barbarosa, the free-wheeling asteroid
spaceport run by the Rogues' Guild. On Barbarosa,
Young Bimwilly, the maitre d' at Club Noir, a posh
restaurant frequented by space pirates and other unsavory sorts, overheard a conspiratorial-looking trio
making plans to outfit and supply a bare rock located
on the outskirts of the Belt. Bimwilly, Malik's eyes
and ears at the restaurant, had passed on the information, and here Malik was.

Malik knew very well that of such whispers and rumors great fortunes were made. He'd made and spent
half a dozen of them himself in the past.

Below him, the last of the space-suited figures disappeared through a hatch leading into the asteroid's
interior. The rock was probably cored, Malik
thought, with living quarters, labs, and whatever
other chambers the unknown proprietors of this asteroid required.

"Activate log," he ordered, turning on the automatic sensor mike linking him and his private one-
man cruiser, the *Lucky Lady*. The ship waited for him
out of sight, beyond the asteroid's horizon.

"Acknowledged," flashed on the faceplate screen of
his space suit's helmet.

"Camera check," he replied, activating the camera
in the forefinger of his space suit's right glove. He

pointed it at the installation snuggled down in the small bowllike plain before him, and slowly swept his finger back and forth, recording a complete, panoramic view.

"Receiving," the ship's computer replied in the sexy contralto he'd programmed for it.

"All right," Malik said. "Nothing ventured, nothing gained."

He cautiously slipped out of concealment, using his space belt's thrusters to keep him near the asteroid's surface. He picked his way through the rough-edged rock formations, down to the smooth plain below.

"Sensor check," he ordered. "Sweep for security systems."

He waited on the plain's edge for the ship's computer to scan the area through the sensors in his suit.

"Negative," it said after a moment.

"No security." He frowned. "I hope this doesn't mean there's nothing worth stealing."

He polarized his helmet's visor nearly to black as he approached the brightly lighted field, but the light was so harsh that he could barely see through the terrible glare. He risked a quick glance toward one of the light towers, then turned away quickly, his eyes smarting and tears running down his cheeks.

"The lights are as bright as little suns. Temperature check," he ordered. He then glanced at the digital readout as it came up on the margin of his viewscreen. The temperature outside his suit was four hundred degrees and increasing. "Maximum reflection," he ordered.

The "smart" suit that he wore adjusted its reflective quality to the utmost, but the surface temperature continued to rise. Malik began to feel a little warm.

"Guess I'll have to work fast," he said. He held his right forefinger straight up, perpendicular to the asteroid's surface. "Zoom record," he said as he began panning it over the area before him. He continued the narration as he approached.

"I'm entering the light field now," said Malik. "There seem to be things growing in it. They look a little like flowers with big, angular petals that have sharp, flat edges instead of curves. There are three rows of the things, about ten in each row—thirty altogether."

He stopped before the first one, which was almost as tall as he. It looked like a flower, though up close it was obvious that the things weren't plants. They weren't even alive. They were huge crystals with a multitude of gleaming facets grouped like flower petals. The petals, though, were flat and hard and looked as sharp as flakes of obsidian. Malik let his finger camera linger on one, recording every detail of its structure and form.

"I've never seen anything like this one," he said. "It's dead black." He reached out to touch it, then drew his hand back, thinking better of it. Crystals were common components in the system, but these were unusual. "Almost as if it's supposed to absorb the light pouring down on it from all those high-powered floodlights."

He moved deeper into the crystalline garden, wondering what in the universe these fabulous creations could be and what they could be used for. They were certainly beautiful enough to be considered works of art, but no one built a secret base to guard artwork. His gut feeling—and he had learned a long time ago to trust his gut feelings—told Malik that the crystals had a dangerous purpose despite their fragile beauty.

He activated the finger camera and began a tight scan, making as detailed a record of the crystals as he could. Though he'd picked up bits and pieces of knowledge in many diverse fields through the years, Malik was no scientist. He did know a lot of eggheads who were for hire, though, and he wanted as much information about these amazing crystals as possible for future analysis.

He finished his scan and was debating the wisdom of breaking off a chunk of one of the crystals, to have some concrete, physical evidence, when the light towers flooding the crystal field with their painfully intense beams suddenly went off.

Malik froze in the sudden darkness. "Suit to black," he ordered immediately, and his space suit changed from reflective mode to the absolute blackness of his surroundings. He thought for one terrible moment that the station's mysterious proprietors had detected him. His mind seesawed between freezing and running, but he decided to stay in place, hoping to remain undetected in the darkness.

After a moment, when no alarms sounded and no one came after him, Malik began to relax.

at the crystals and noticed that some of them were changing. They had begun to glow in soft, vibrant colors. Light dripped like dew from their hard-edged petals, in all the colors of the spectrum and all shades in between.

"Temperature check," he said, aiming the finger with the proper sensor at the nearest crystal. It's temperature was rising, slowly but detectably, as it apparently released the light it had stored within its crystalline structure. Malik had read about thermoluminscent crystals before, but nothing with properties to this extreme. These crystals were a fantastic discovery with innumerable technological applications.

His introspection was suddenly interrupted by a strong, continuous vibration that Malik felt running up from the ground through the soles of his feet. The vacuum around the asteroid prevented Malik from hearing anything, but the heavy vibrations indicated that something big was approaching, fast. He turned around and let out a series of expletives in Classic Russian when he saw what was racing toward him from behind.

It was a dark, low-slung skimmer of some sort, with armor-plating and a large, nasty-looking gun turret swiveling around to get him in its sights.

Obviously, the crystal field's security system was so sophisticated that Malik's sensors hadn't detected it. He had underestimated his opponent, and in his business that could be a fatal mistake.

Malik knew that he was a sitting target. He wasn't

going to wait around to see if the skimmer's operator was the kind who shot first and asked questions later. He made his way carefully around one of the crystals, putting it between himself and the skimmer, and headed as fast as his thrusters could take him for the jumble of rocks and crags on the crystal field's edge.

"Unfriendlies on my tail," he told the *Lucky Lady*. "All systems on. Weapons ready. Come and get me."

Malik actually had something of the advantage in a race against the skimmer. The device that followed him apparently was designed for defense, not pursuit. It remained mere inches from the asteroid's surface and had to maneuver around the crystalline formations that stood between it and Malik.

Careful to keep his strides long and smooth, Malik glided over the asteroid's surface. In fact, he could hardly push off the surface at all. If he did, he'd shoot up into space, where he'd flap like one of the Martian ducks he was so fond of shooting on the wing.

The armored and modified skimmer rumbled after him but held its fire. He couldn't risk glancing away from the uneven ground to see if it was gaining on him, but he ordered his visor to go to "mirror" on its upper left quadrant, and he glanced up into it. Malik grinned. In the reflection he saw that he was losing the skimmer. He also was about to leave the open field and step into the jumbled cragginess of the natural asteroid surface. Once in cover, he could hide until his ship showed up and blasted the skimmer into nuts and bolts.

Malik's grin widened as he risked a glance back at

the skimmer. Its driver had miscalculated a tight turn as he tried to maneuver around the pedestal of one of the crystal flowers. The skimmer clipped the pedestal with the front of its right wing. The crystal teetered in near-zero gravity. Propelled by the wing's forceful blow, its enormous top rotated slowly and crashed onto the skimmer. It shattered, sending sharp shards billowing out in a scintillating cloud that clogged the skimmer's intake valves. The engine's vibrations increased and the skimmer shuddered on the asteroid's surface until the driver killed the engine.

Malik laughed aloud as he ducked into the jumble of boulders outside the light field. "Almost home now," he said aloud.

True, he had no idea what the mysterious crystals were, but at least he knew they existed. More importantly, he was escaping with his hide intact. With a little more judicious digging, he would be able to find out who had built this secret base and why, and how he could profit from it.

Impatient for his ship to arrive, he looked to the horizon. Malik then glanced at the readout line running on the base of his faceplate. Less than a mile away . . .

There it was! The *Lucky Lady* swept over the horizon and into view like a gleaming silver bird of prey. It was a small craft, but it was Malik's own and, ton for ton, was as deadly a bit of work as anyone would find in space. In times such as this, it was often all that stood between Malik and quick death, so he'd spared no expense in making his ship fast, deadly, and luxurious.

"Come to papa," he said.

"Ready for boarding," the *Lady's* computer replied in its sultry contralto. The brain running the ship may have been a digital personality, but its voice was that of a tri-dee movie goddess, full of sweet promise.

Malik had to scramble over about a quarter-mile of rough ground. "Be there in half a minute," he told his ship. "Prepare for departure and pour me a good, long drink."

"As you wish—" the *Lady* began, but its final word turned into a wail of static, surprise, and pain.

From nowhere a beam of intense energy burned through the black sky, clipping the *Lucky Lady* in the bow. Metal sublimated directly to gas at the center of the impact. At the edges, it ran like water, splattering like molten rain onto the asteroid's surface, where it cooled immediately into puddles of metallic tears. The *Lady* careened off into space, its computer brain vaporized, its controls locked on to whatever final orders the brain had put in the circuits before its demise.

Malik whirled, his face frozen between fear and rage as he turned to see what had killed his ship. The thing hovered behind him, behind the disabled skimmer. It, too, was just a skimmer, much smaller than the *Lady*, but mounted on its prow was a strange device the likes of which Malik had never seen before.

There was a metallic dish whose inner surface was coated with a highly reflective substance that shone so brightly it hurt Malik's eyes. In front of the dish, at what could have been its focal point, was one of the crystalline flowers. The dish and the flower pointed right at Malik.

He would have run, but he knew that there was nowhere to go. In a last, futile gesture, he held up his right hand and pointed his suit's middle finger at the vessel. The laser in the finger pulsed through the darkness. The tiny beam struck the skimmer but splattered harmlessly against its armored sides, as Malik had known it would. He hoped the camera in his other finger had picked up the image and sent it to his lost ship, but he had no way of knowing.

He thought how beautiful the crystal looked, then there was a pulse of light so bright that it burned his eyes out, and Malik Ferdenko was nothing more than vapor slowly dissipating in the cosmic breeze.

CHAPTER TWO

Kemal Gavilan took a deep breath of fresh air, held it in his lungs for a moment, then let it out with a long, satisfied sigh. It was a typical spring morning in Albukirk. The temperature was mild, the sun was bright, and there was a light wind. It was a beautiful start to a historic day.

Earth recently had freed itself from domination by RAM—originally Russo-American Mercantile—the huge, malevolent multiplanetary corporation that controlled Mars and had essentially run Earth for several centuries. Galvanized by Buck Rogers, the legendary resurrected hero from the twentieth century, Earth had bought its freedom with the lives of millions of its citizens. Its rebellion had succeeded. RAM finally had been beaten, and Earth had been left to rebuild itself.

The first session of the Planetary Congress was due to convene in less than a hour, and Kemal, who had fought on Earth's side during the Martian Wars even though he was Mercurian by birth, intended to witness the historic event from the start. The Congressional Hall was within walking distance of the prefabricated apartments that had been hastily constructed to house the congressional delegates, observers, and hangers-on—but then nearly everything in Albukirk was within walking distance of everything else.

A small town located in the southwestern part of what once had been the United States of America, Albukirk had been granted the honor of being Earth's preliminary world capital for several reasons. It was rather small and insignificant, so it had been spared the bombings that had destroyed the world's major arcologies during the Martian Wars. It also was located in a part of the world that had a relatively pleasant climate. This was no small consideration, since many of the delegates had to make due with rather flimsy temporary housing. After centuries of exploitation at the hands of RAM, the Earth was left a poor planet. Priorities had to be set in its reconstruction. In Albukirk's case, priority had been given to public buildings such as the Congressional Hall, where the world's business had to be done.

The hall was a moderately impressive edifice, but Kemal, used to the architectural wonders of Mars and Mercury, found it less amazing than the native

Terrans around him did. The domed design was somewhat familiar, and Kemal suddenly realized that it had been cribbed from another congressional building, the ancient United States Halls of Congress, destroyed sometime back in one of the minor wars of the late twenty-first century.

The hall's staircase of white pseudomarble was already crowded with delegates, observers, and hangers-on by the time Kemal arrived. He'd expected that. This was, after all, the beginning of the first truly free Earth government in several centuries. The Congress represented the culmination of months of sweat, blood, and tears, of strife, battle, and intrigue. It was bound to attract a lot of attention.

What Kemal hadn't anticipated was that he'd be the center of a great deal of it. He realized then that his dark bronze skin made him fairly conspicuous despite the Terran clothing he wore.

"Earth is for Earthers!" a man cried as Kemal mounted the lowest of the pseudomarble steps. He stepped in front of Kemal, blocking his way. A knot of men and women followed him, making it impossible for Kemal to simply walk around him. "Go back to space, where you belong," the man continued. "We don't need alien hands to help rebuild the Earth."

Kemal recognized him instantly, even though he'd never seen him face-to-face before. His name was Jeremy Clay. As the leader of the Purity Party, one of the newest, most popular political parties on the planet, his florid, handsome features had been beamed to every corner of the globe by the tri-dee communication networks. His mellifluous orator's voice continued ramming home time and again his party's message, "Earth is for Earthers! Aliens go home!"

Kemal took Clay's words and the congressional delegates' stares with apparent equanimity, though it was his bronzed skin color that prevented his embarrassed flush from being obvious.

Carlton Turabian, leader of the New Earth Organization—NEO—which had led Earth's rebellion, and Kemal's comrade during the Martian Wars, stood nearby. He'd apparently been waiting for Clay's verbal assault. Turabian spoke up in Kemal's defense.

"Kemal Gavilan was a friend of NEO long before it became fashionable to support Earth," he said. "He fought in NEO's name. He languished in prison because of our cause. He risked his life for us, and now you say there is no place for him among us?"

Clay allowed an insincere smile to curve his lips. "We acknowledge that Gavilan—or should we address him as Prince Kemal of the House of Gavilan, heir to the Mercurian Sun Kings?—has worked for Earth's cause. We can't forget, however, that his activities are bound up inextricably with the rather, well, complicated and uncertain politics of his home planet—which is, by the way, allied with RAM. We should be grateful for what Kemal Gavilan has done for us in the past, but the Earth has suffered centuries of abuse at alien hands. It is time for us to stand on our own, to make our own way in the system."

Thunderous applause and cheers arose from Clay's faction of the mob crowding the Congressional Hall's steps.

Kemal suddenly realized that the confrontation had been a setup. He suspected that Clay had nothing against him personally but was making Kemal's presence among NEO's executive councils a cause celebre for base, political reasons.

Clay wanted power. He wanted to head Earth's reconstruction, and he needed a cause to rally his forces around. There was a certain amount of xenophobia on Earth these days, and not, Kemal admitted to himself, without good reason. RAM had horribly exploited Earth for many centuries. It had raped the planet for its natural resources, leaving it a broken, polluted slum. When Earth, almost beaten to its knees, tried to rebel, the Martians had sent in their clone soldiers and long-range bombers, and almost smashed the planet back to the Stone Age.

Ultimately, Earth had prevailed in its desperate rebellion, thanks in no small manner to Buck Rogers and also the world's off-planet allies, particularly Venus and Luna.

Knowing that's Clay's attack was motivated by political reasons made Kemal no less angry. He had been used before as a political puppet by his uncle, Gordon Gavilan, the current Sun King of Mercury, and had hated and resented it. As the only well-known off-worlder still working closely with NEO, being so used a second time made him feel no better.

"Honorable delegates," Kemal said to the crowd standing around Clay, "Representative Clay is correct about at least one thing. I have labored long and hard for the NEO cause. I did it because it is always worthwhile to nourish freedom wherever it can be found. He also was correct that I am a Gavilan of Mercury, and it can never be said that Gavilans overstay their welcome when they discover that they are unwanted."

He turned and slowly walked away. At first, there was a stunned silence, then a mixture of cheers and catcalls, hand-claps and boos.

Kemal couldn't tell if the crowd's boos or cheers were being directed toward him or Clay, and at this point he was so angry that he didn't care. He had left his home world behind, risked his life in battle, spent time in prison when he'd been captured by RAM's allies, and for what? For a bunch of ungrateful louts. As far as he was concerned, they could keep their barbarous world. There were plenty of other places in the system that could use his talents. *Too bad I can't think of any offhand,* Kemal thought sullenly.

The day suddenly no longer seemed so beautiful and bright with promise. Kemal jammed his hands in his pockets as he angrily legged it over to his spartan apartment, which had been put up almost overnight and appeared like one of many mushrooms after a summer rain. He put his palm on the front door, deactivated the lock, and pushed the door open. He looked up in some surprise and frowned. "Oh. You here already?"

Dr. Huer.dos looked on with an expression of disapproval as Kemal paced angrily about the apartment. Huer appeared as a rather handsome, almost professorial, middle-aged man. In reality, he wasn't human at all, but was a living computer program, a computer-generated persona without body or substance. He appeared to stand in Kemal's apartment— and anywhere else he wished—by using an ingenious holographic projection device. The device allowed him to interact more easily with the flesh-and-blood creatures about him as well.

"I've been monitoring the opening of Congress—" he began.

"And saw my performance," Kemal interrupted. "Look, I know that I shouldn't have gotten mad and walked away like that, but Clay drives me crazy with his bigoted views. There are off-worlders who believe in Earth's cause, who have fought and bled for Earth's cause. I know. I'm one of them." He paused in his pacing and snorted. "Come to think of it, I never saw Clay around when there was fighting to be done. I think he just crawled out from under his rock when it became safe to be a politician again."

"You have every right to be angry," the digital personality told Kemal in fatherly tones. "Everyone knows you're a loyal NEO supporter and that you've risked your life time and again for the cause of a free Earth. Being mad is one thing. Showing it is another. You'll never become a successful politician if you're unable to hide your feelings."

Kemal shot the hologram an aggrieved look. "Who

says I want to become a politician?"

Huer looked closely at Kemal through the projector device's linked camera and microphone unit. "You are a Gavilan. Your father was Sun King of Mercury. Someday you may be in the position to take his place."

"I doubt it," Kemal muttered. "I'm sure that my Uncle Gordon would have something to say about that."

Huer fell silent. He knew that there was little he could say to console the young man. Gordon was the middle of three Gavilan brothers. He had taken the role of Sun King, the most powerful political position on Mercury, after Ossip, the oldest Gavilan and Kemal's father, had died suddenly. Kemal was only four then. Gordon had immediately packed the boy off to boarding school on Mars, where he'd be safely out of the way while Gordon solidified his grip on Mercury. Some twenty-odd years later, it was unlikely that Gordon Gavilan had any intentions of relinquishing his position.

That was partly why Kemal had thrown in his lot with NEO and the free Earth movement, Huer knew. Like his father, Ossip, Kemal was something of an idealist when it came to politics. He felt that there was no place for him in the intrigue-laden Gavilan family on Mercury. He wanted to go where his personal actions could make a difference, where the cause of freedom was clear-cut, where its plight was greatest.

Also, Huer reflected, Kemal was a young man full

of unbounded energy. He craved action and adventure like most people craved peace and comfort. He wasn't quite ready to settle down yet. Piloting a fighter through enemy armadas was much more exciting than the mundane and boring minutiae of hammering out a living political system, either on Mercury or on an Earth that had just gone through a ferocious life-and-death struggle to free itself from RAM's tyrannical grip.

Huer watched as Kemal resumed angrily pacing about his apartment. He truly felt for the young Mercurian, and not only because Buck Rogers had placed Kemal in his figurative hands before leaving to supervise Project Deepspace, a mission designed to probe the depths of the Solar System.

Rogers had known that Kemal would need watching in the political climate of Earth that was increasingly hostile to off-worlders, and Huer was just the one to play guardian angel to the young Mercurian. Huer's programming told him that Kemal was a valuable cog in the NEO machine. Not only was he a top-flight rocketjock, but Kemal's political ties to the top levels of Mercurian government could also prove important to the future of Earth. And because of his father's legacy, Kemal was personally one of the richest men in the system. That also made him a very valuable ally.

Besides all the obvious political motives, Huer also rather liked Kemal. The young man was hard-working, idealistic, and incorruptible. He was a true rarity, an aristocrat who believed in the right of all people to a decent, secure life.

Huer wondered what Buck would do in this instance, and Huer, who had been created to help Rogers adjust to his new life in the twenty-fifth century, knew more about Buck's thought processes than any being alive. He silently snapped his holographic fingers as an idea sparked through the electronic pathways of his programming.

"Don't worry about Clay and his band of xenophobes," Huer told Kemal. "They're just fanatics with loud voices. They're definitely in a minority."

"It's disturbing that they exist at all," Kemal muttered.

"Agreed," Huer said, "but how can we judge them too harshly? This planet has been through a lot these past few centuries, almost all of it instigated by offworlders. I'm not saying we should accept—or even excuse—Clay's xenophobia, but we can understand the reasons behind it."

Kemal flopped down onto his hard, uncomfortable sofa. "I guess so," he said. He squirmed about, trying to find a comfortable position. "One of the first things this world should do is import some decent upholsterers, so you can build some comfortable furniture."

Huer smiled. "There are a lot of things the Earth needs right now. Comfortable furniture is somewhere on the list, though I don't know if it's anywhere near the top. At any rate, I ran across something today as I was scanning the computer net that you might find interesting."

"What is it?" Kemal asked, his hazel eyes not exactly sparkling with enthusiasm.

"I'm not sure," Huer said slowly, baiting his line with care. "Two salvagers with NEO affiliations found a ship floating in a rather sparsely inhabited region of the Asteroid Belt."

"Floating?"

Huer nodded. "The ship had been abandoned. It'd also been through a battle. Part of it had been vaporized, and," Huer added significantly, "preliminary analyses on the remains indicate that the damage had been caused by an unknown type of energy weapon."

Kemal sat straighter. "Is that so?" He went to his computer console and thumbed it on. "Let me see."

Huer kept his smile to himself. He was getting Kemal interested despite himself. If this all worked out, he'd involve him in a little skullduggery, get him off-planet long enough for Clay and his band of fire-eaters to calm down, and immerse him in a little satisfying—but with Huer's oversight not too dangerous—adventure. As an extra tidbit, maybe these mysterious goings-on in the Belt would actually shake down to something that could be useful to NEO. Any way he looked at it, the plan was a winner.

"All right," Huer said, "but the really interesting thing is the ship's final log entry."

Huer sent part of his consciousness racing off into computer space and made the connections that would call the proper information up onto Kemal's computer screen. The first voice to log on was that of one of the salvagers who had discovered the derelict spacecraft.

"Log of the *Lucky Lady*," she said, "registered to Malik Ferdenko. Port of registry, Barbarosa, Asteroid Belt."

"Who's this Ferdenko?" Kemal asked while the log came on.

Huer's image shrugged. "I don't know. Indications from the log show that he was some kind of secret agent, perhaps an industrial spy."

"Any particular affiliations?" Kemal asked. "RAM, for example?"

"We don't know yet. I've been looking into his background a little, but with most of my attention centered on the reconstruction, I haven't given it top priority."

"Were his, uh, remains, discovered on the ship?"

Huer shook his head. "Not a trace of them."

A bleak asteroid landscape suddenly appeared on the computer screen. The voice-over account was in an accent that Kemal remembered well. He had spent sixteen years of his life on Mars attending school, and this Malik Ferdenko, the log's narrator, had a definite Martian accent. He might be living in the Asteroid Belt now, but he'd been born and educated on Mars! That immediately suggested RAM connections to Kemal.

The strange crystalline growths that appeared on the screen seemed to mystify Huer as much as they did Kemal.

"Ever seen anything like those before?" Kemal asked the digital personality.

Huer's image shook its head.

"Scan the computer net. See if they're tied to with any particular industrial use."

"That's quite an order," Huer said. "It may take some time."

Kemal only nodded, intent on the scene unfolding before him on the computer screen.

It was a stark, beautiful landscape. Kemal had to continually remind himself that this was not some taped drama. The events he was watching had really happened. He was viewing a crisis that soon would end, in all probability, in tragedy for Malik Ferdenko.

When Ferdenko suddenly shifted perspective to zero in on the pursuing skimmer, Kemal realized that things were moving to a swift conclusion. He could only admire Ferdenko's cool, matter-of-fact nerve as he ran for cover while calling on his ship. The spy calmly turned to look at the disabled skimmer. For a moment, Kemal thought that Ferdenko was going to escape.

His sleek ship appeared in what seemed to be the nick of time, then all hopes were dashed as part of it was vaporized in an eye-numbing flash of light. The shock stunned Kemal almost as much as it did Ferdenko, who whirled dizzily to face the death machine approaching him. There was time for a final comment, a final futile gesture of resistance, then there was a blaze of light so intense that it would have hurt Kemal eyes if the screen hadn't gone immediately blank.

"What in the world was that?" Kemal asked in a whisper.

"The new weapon," Huer said softly. As an electronic construct, he was always amazed at the continual invention with which flesh-and-blood beings designed ways to snuff out their lives.

"Run it back again," Kemal said. "Let's see what happens right before the . . . blast . . . or whatever it was that vaporized Ferdenko."

"All right," Huer said, "I'll slow it down, too."

"Right."

The death scene played itself out again with nearly balletic grace. Ferdenko whirled and imperfectly focused his finger camera on something. Kemal couldn't quite make it out.

"Freeze it," he ordered.

Huer gave the command, and the computer froze the action. Kemal peered at the scene intently, Huer's image hovering over his shoulder like an electronic ghost.

"It's a ship, a small skimmer, I think, with something mounted at the bow," Kemal decided.

"Enhance and enlarge," Huer ordered, and the image centered itself on the computer screen, blown up in size and sharpened in detail.

"It looks as if one of those crystals is serving as a focusing point for a parabolic mirror," Kemal said. "Have you gotten anything yet on the crystals?"

Huer consulted with the portion of his intellect he'd assigned the task of tracking down the crystalline structures. "Nothing," he reported. "Remember, the system is a big place, with a bewildering number of technologies to scan. If this is a new—or secret—development . . ."

Huer let his words hang in the air, and Kemal pounced on them eagerly.

"That makes sense," he said. "This Ferdenko is an industrial spy of some sort. He got wind of this secret project dealing with a new weapon of almost unimaginable destructive power—"

"And the weapon's creators," Dr. Huer interrupted dryly, "got wind of him before he could make his escape."

Kemal nodded. "This has to be run down." His mind racing, he had a sudden sobering thought. "No telling who might be involved with this weapon. If it's RAM, the entire system could be in peril." He looked at Huer. "Who knows about this log?"

"No one, really. Just members of the salvage crew that found it, and they're back in deep space again. I intercepted their report, thinking that this isn't the kind of thing that should be bruited about openly on the computer net."

"I agree," Kemal said. He shook his head. "I wish Buck were here. He'd know how to handle this."

Huer faced him squarely. "Well, he's not available, but I think I know what he'd say. I think you do, too."

Kemal nodded. "See a problem, find the solution." It was Buck's take-charge attitude that had galvanized NEO in its battle with RAM. Kemal looked at Huer. "We have to discover exactly what's going on before we drop this into NEO's lap."

Huer nodded, keeping his smile to himself. He had hoped that Kemal would react this way, and the lad wasn't disappointing him.

Kemal leaned back in the chair, fingers steepled, an expression of deep thought on his face. "Ferdenko was Martian, a potential connection with RAM, of course." He looked at Huer. "That might be the place to start the investigation."

"What about the Belt?" Huer asked. "That's where the *Lucky Lady* was found adrift, probably near this secret research station."

Kemal nodded. "Then I'll start there." He pushed away from the computer console and stood. "Will you be able to help in the investigation?" he asked the digital personality.

"Somewhat," Huer said. "I have extensive duties on Earth, what with the ongoing reconstruction and all. Take your portable uplink unit with you," the digital personality said, gesturing at the device that allowed him to travel nearly instantly, as well as project a holographic image. "You can call on me if you need emergency help."

"Thanks. Can you get clearance for my ship for immediate takeoff?" Kemal asked. "It's going to take a few days to reach the Belt. I want to start the investigation right away."

"We do have certain connections in the Belt," Huer reminded him.

Kemal smiled. "Of course. Find Black Barney. I think he might be interested in this."

CHAPTER THREE

Better things to do," Black Barney growled
from the bridge of his ship, the *Free Enterprise*, in the depths of the Asteroid Belt, "than
chase phantoms around the Belt. Business to think
about."

"I'm sure you do," Huer said smoothly, "but a new
weapons system—"

"Got all the weapons I need," Barney said stolidly.

"Yes, but to help Kemal—"

" 'Mercurian pup?' " said the enormous genetically
engineered warrior.

He had the same opinion of Kemal as he had of
everyone—except Buck Rogers, of course—total indifference. Both Barney's genetic engineering and early
training had stripped him of all casual human emo-

tions. He could neither love nor hate, unless someone happened to be between him and something he wanted. Then it was cold, emotionless destruction for whatever or whoever was keeping him from his goal.

His feelings toward Rogers were complicated and difficult to analyze, especially for a being who wasn't very introspective. His genetic programming made him obey those stronger than him—and Rogers had proved himself stronger by defeating Barney in hand-to-hand combat, something no other being in the entire Solar System had ever done.

Beyond his genetic makeup, Barney suspected that he had developed a grudging respect, even a liking for the resurrected hero from the twentieth century. But that would mean that Barney was becoming humane, and he didn't like to think about that.

"Well," Huer said, trotting out his trump card, "Buck would want you to help out. You know he told you to accept my judgment on things like this before he headed off on Project Deepspace."

Huer could almost hear the gears grinding in the pirate's head. He could certainly hear the low growls rising from the gennie's throat as he considered Huer's words.

"At least take a look at the log," Huer urged. "Who knows? You might see something to pique your interest."

There was a long, inarticulate growl, then Barney said, "Put it up on the screen."

Huer was careful to keep a poker face as he transmitted the files to the *Free Enterprise*'s computer. It wasn't smart to let Barney think you'd put one over on him. The pirate didn't like to lose, and he held grudges for quite a long time.

And he was a dangerous man to have for an enemy. With nearly seven feet of bone and muscle backed by an enhanced nervous system that doubled his reflex speed, Barney was a clone-warrior designed for destruction. He was pitiless in combat and ruthless in action. He had few loyalties or sympathies with any being in the Solar System, except Buck Rogers. The only ones who understood him, or whom he fully understood, were the few remaining living clone-brothers from his lineage. He was as grim, vicious, and dangerous a being as could be found anywhere in the system.

He waited impatiently on the bridge of his ship, a RAM heavy cruiser that he'd liberated from the Deimos spacedocks, while the computer files crossed the void between Earth and the Belt. When the log began, he watched with lidded, bored-looking eyes that nevertheless took in every detail. He just wasn't much interested in them . . . until the skimmer bearing the laser device flashed across the screen.

Barney suddenly sat straight up in his command chair and barked, in his deep, forbidding voice, "Freeze! Enlarge and enhance!"

"Ah," Huer said, materializing at Barney's side via a holographic projector on the ship's bridge. He'd accompanied the computer transmission to the Belt. Without the limitations of a flesh-and-blood body, a digital personality could travel at light speed. "It does pique your interest, as I predicted."

"Silence, ghost!" Barney ordered with a roar.

The pirate stared at the computer screen as the skimmer bearing the laser device leaped into top magnification. It was a recent model skimmer with registration numbers clearly visible on its side. Near the serial number was the corporate logo of the company that had built it, a depiction of a winged dragon holding a globe in one clawed hand.

"Dracolysk," Barney whispered in a voice that dripped hatred and venom.

Huer frowned. "Can't be," he said.

"Magnify logo," Barney growled in the same low, dangerous voice.

There was no denying it, Huer saw. The corporate logo was definitely the distinctive, trademarked Dracolysk sigil.

"An old ship—" Huer started to suggest, but Barney cut him off with a shake of his mohawk-crested head.

"New. No more'n a year old. Dracolysk," he repeated, grinding his teeth as if he were gnawing men's bones.

Dracolysk . . .

The name took Barney back more than twenty years, to his first conscious memories.

Newborn, right out of the vat along with a squad of clone-brothers, Barney had been dumped from the warm, placid waters in which he had been grown to fall naked and shivering against a hard, cold metal floor. He had already reached full growth and physical maturity. He was six feet, eight inches, with the body of a gladiator and the empty mind of a newborn, totally without knowledge or experience, though he gained both quickly.

His first memory was that of racking pain. As he lay naked on the cold steel floor, the overseer beat him and his clone-brothers with a neurowhip—a modified sonic stunner—sending showers of agony through their nervous systems as he taught them their first and ultimate lesson: Pain is life, life is pain.

The Dracolysk Corporation, the company that had created and reared them, was their master. Intended to be a new line of clone-warriors, with implacable wills, nearly indestructible bodies, pitiless souls, and total obedience to the company, Barney and his hundred and fifty clone-brothers and sisters went through a year of training hell on Gorgon Station, the Dracolysk research center where they had been created.

The training killed forty-eight of Barney's lineage and broke the minds of another score, but Barney survived the pain and terror thrust on his newborn soul. He emerged from the fire burned free of soft human emotion, but—unfortunately for Dracolysk—burned free also of the conditioning they had installed to keep their killing machines loyal to the Dracolysk name.

Barney led others to the same freedom he had found, and as he helped the clone-warriors break their conditioning, they swore a solemn and terrible vow, a vow on blood and steel, that when the time was right they would rise against their masters and blot the name "Dracolysk" out of existence if it took every one of their lives.

The time had to be right, though. Barney and the others had waited as patiently as they could. They pretended to be docile, ignoring the further pain and humiliation heaped upon them by the Dracolysk overseers, psychologists, and physical trainers, until—as it was called—Graduation Night.

That night, Hugo Dracolysk, chief executive officer of the corporation that bore his name, was to demonstrate Black Barney and his clone lineage to visiting executives from RAM, Dracolysk's parent company. That night, Barney led the others as they burst their bonds and, in a horrific demonstration, showed Dracolysk exactly how productive its bioengineering and harsh training methods had been.

Many clone-warriors had died in the revolt, but the Dracolysk Corporation had been wiped from existence in a night of carnage and terror that saw Gorgon Station's destruction. Everyone connected with the company had been sacrificed, and the surviving clone-warriors had dispersed to every nook and cranny of the Solar System.

At least, Barney had always thought that Dracolysk had been wiped out of existence, but here, twenty years later, the name appeared again like a nightmare rising from the black pool of Barney's subconscious.

"Scan," Barney told Huer with a voice like gravel

grating on sandpaper. "Find out about Dracolysk. Find out—" and here his voice became even harsher, as bleak and deadly as the hiss of a poisonous serpent striking in the dark "—if Hugo Dracolysk still lives." He stared into the computer screen.

"All right," Huer told him.

Barney glared at the Dracolysk sigil still emblazoned in the center of the ship's screen. "Send Kemal," he said.

Well, Huer told himself, I've succeeded in bringing Barney into the affair. He wondered, though, if the gennie would be as easily controlled as he had initially thought. Somehow, he doubted it.

CHAPTER FOUR

The trip from Earth to the asteroid called Barbarosa took Kemal almost a week.

Kemal considered himself lucky. It could have taken a lot longer, but cosmic coincidence put the Earth and Barbarosa on the same side of the sun, relatively aligned in their respective orbits.

The Asteroid Belt was a loosely associated collection of rocks sharing the same general orbit between Mars and Jupiter, approximately three times farther from the sun than the Earth. No one knew how many asteroids there were in the Belt. All the rocks with diameters greater than fifty miles had long since been discovered, mapped, inventoried, and colonized. There were two hundred thirty-three of those, but tens of thousands of smaller rocks. No one knew exactly how many of these smaller asteroids there were, or which of them were inhabited, because "Belters" were notoriously independent, strong-willed entities who tended to pull up stakes and move frequently. They rarely left forwarding addresses when they did move.

This led to the Belt's rather peculiar political structure, which was formally called the Free Asteroid Democracy, but more commonly—and perhaps more accurately—was known as the Belter Anarchy.

The Belters were perhaps the least prejudiced people in the system. They extended citizenship to every sentient creature in the Belt: true humans, gennies, mutants, and even computer-generated personae.

There was no congress or parliament, president or prime minister to run things in the Belt. The Ruling Council, currently a group of digital personalities inhabiting the Ceres Cooperative mainframe, ran the Belt's mundane, day-to-day affairs. Whenever an important issue arose that affected the entire Belt, the whole population had the privilege and duty to vote on it.

This led to many interesting political debates on the Belter computer net, as every sentient was entitled to express its opinions, no matter how bizarre.

This wild state of affairs led to the Belt's anarchistic reputation, and the most wild and anarchistic rock in the Belt was Kemal's destination, Malik Ferdenko's main hangout, Barbarosa.

Gas station, pleasure palace, brokerage firm, pawn shop, gambling den, hospital, drug store, and gymnasium, Barbarosa was all these and more. A hundred-mile-long dumbbell-shaped rock spinning amid the clutter of the Asteroid Belt, Barbarosa had been built and was maintained by the Rogues' Guild, a loosely organized confederation of privateers, freebooters, assassins, and thieves who thrived on the Belt's unfettered anarchy. Because of their reputation, they also were sometimes called the Black Brotherhood.

The station was built both on the surface and deep within the core of the asteroid. The surface portion consisted of two domed life-support systems placed on opposite ends of the oblong rock. Kemal landed his craft in the spaceport dome, which consisted of docking, fueling, and repair facilities. The other dome, connected to the docking facilities by a ninety-mile-long monorail system that had been built through Barbarosa's core, was devoted to the pleasures and entertainment of the space travelers, miners, and rogues who stopped there.

Kemal, eager after what seemed like a nearly endless trip out to the Belt, threw some extra clothing into a small handbag and headed for the monorail line that connected Barbarosa's two domes through the heart of the rock. The ninety-mile trip took less than an hour, but Kemal counted every second.

"Slow down," he told himself as he disembarked with a flock of eager passengers headed for the Fun Dome. "You can't go zooming around like some fictional Space Ranger out to foil the villain, save the day, and marry the heroine all in the space of a two-hour tri-dee drama. First things first."

He looked around. The monorail station had all the bustle of the great Pavonis Spaceport on Mars, but in miniature, of course. The station was smaller, and the crowds were smaller, but the people here seemed to have an incredible eagerness that the masses thronging the Pavonis Spaceport usually lacked. They were mostly spacemen, miners, and rockhoppers, hitting civilization—or at least what passed for civilization in these parts—for the first time in a long time. They were headed for fun, high times, fast living, and probably empty wallets.

Kemal needed a hotel. He picked one at random—the Ben Bow Inn—and went immediately up to his room, where he sat down at once at the computer terminal and tapped in the key words that let Huer know he'd arrived and was ready to start his investigation.

He then sat back, put his feet up, and waited. It didn't take long. One of the benefits of having a computer-generated persona as a sidekick was that it took Huer minutes rather than days to receive Kemal's call and appear in holographic form next to the terminal.

"Sorry for the delay," he said cheerfully. "Just making sure that the Barbarosa security computers didn't notice me sneaking through. No need to let everyone know I'm here."

"No problem," Kemal said, taking his feet down and sitting straight in his chair. "Any word from Barney yet?"

Huer's image shook its head. "He's been digging around for a few days but has reported nothing yet. I've discovered that it's best not to rush the big fellow. It only irritates him. He'll contact us when he discovers something of interest."

"All right. What's our next step?"

Huer gestured at the computer. It was a totally unnecessary flourish, but the digital personality liked to cultivate an aura of mystery and magic. He thought it made him more effective in dealing with humans, and to a certain extent he was right.

"I've fixed the computer so that anyone monitoring it will get the impression there's a boring stream of stock and commodity futures information flowing on it—can't be too careful in this spy business." He paused dramatically. "What we're really scanning—"

"Is a detailed inventory of Malik's business dealings of the last year or so," Kemal said with interest, "at least as reported by the Barbarosa mainframe." He leaned forward and intently read the lines scrolling on the screen before him.

"Exactly," Huer said. "Spying is considered an honorable business on Barbarosa, as long as you file your income honestly and pay the proper taxes on it. Of course, there's some very interesting security locks on this information to keep out busy-bodies like me, but anything that's locked can be unlocked, given the proper amount of ingenuity," Huer added with no hint at false modesty.

"This Malik's been a busy fellow," Kemal commented. "He's spied on RAM for Ardala Valmar and on Ardala Valmar for RAM. He's even spied on parts of RAM for other parts of RAM! It's a wonder he lived as long as he did."

"Like Valmar, he was a very good 'information broker,'" Huer said, "though things did catch up with him in the end."

"He worked all over the system," Kemal summarized, "but, according to this, not lately in the Asteroid Belt. Strange. We know he was here. We know he *died* here."

"Here's something even more interesting," Huer said.

"What?"

"While you've been reading his files, I took the liberty of delving deeper into the background information. I've cross-referenced his office address with a surveyor's plat of Barbarosa and discovered that it's only a postal drop."

"Too bad," Kemal mused. "I'd like to check it out. There's bound to be more detailed, more substantial information there."

Huer struck a pose as if he were deep in thought. "Well, I know of someone who might know where we can find Ferdenko's home."

"Who?"

"A fellow named Carp, Carassius Carp. He runs a gambling establishment known as Dead Man's Hand. He also happens to be the most knowledgeable information broker on Barbarosa."

"Oh?" Kemal asked.

"He knows everything that goes on in the station, most things that go on in the Belt, and a lot of what occurs in the system. He sells the information to anyone who can meet his price."

"I can meet it," Kemal said. "I'm a Gavilan."

Huer shook his head. "His price can be very steep. Sometimes he won't take money, just other information."

Kemal shrugged. "We'll see," he said.

"One more thing," Huer added as Kemal rose from his chair and headed for the door. "I've noticed something while checking the more routine items in Ferdenko's mundane accounts—utility bills, bank records, credit charges, docking fees, that sort of thing. From this data, it's obvious that he has a black box in his apartment, wherever that may be."

"Black box?"

"Yes." Huer sounded as excited as a digital personality could be. "It's a sophisticated computer system with a self-contained power source that's isolated from the rest of the net. It has no connection with the external world, no linkage with any system nets."

Kemal frowned. "That would make the computer kind of useless, wouldn't it?"

"We might think so, today," Huer said, "but in the old days, before the computer network was established, it was rather common for computers to exist in isolation from each other. In that case, of course, they could only use their own individual capabilities and whatever data the operators chose to give them, but they did have an enormous advantage over computers linked into the net."

"They'd be difficult to tamper with."

"Exactly. Computer viruses—or human spies—have no way to access them, unless they can be physically introduced through infected software."

Kemal rubbed his chin thoughtfully. "A unit like that might have some pretty interesting information locked up in it."

"Pretty sensitive information," Huer agreed. "Information you wouldn't want anyone else to see."

"It would be difficult to hack into," Kemal mused. "It's probably locked up tight with passwords and scramble codes and who knows what other safeguards."

Huer smiled. "Remember what I said? There's no lock that can't be unlocked given the proper amount of ingenuity."

"Okay. How do we unlock this black box?"

"Simple." Huer gestured at the computer terminal before them. "Insert a blank microdisk."

"All right." Kemal did so, sat back, and waited while the terminal blanked, then pulsed with green phosphorescent light. A few moments passed, then the screen stabilized again.

"There you are," Huer said, pointing at the disk. "A limited but very capable copy of myself, Huer.dos. Insert that disk into the black box, and all of its secrets shall be ours."

"Great!" Kemal said. "It's as good as done."

"Not quite," Huer cautioned. "First you have to see Carp and find out where Ferdenko was living. And watch out for this Carp. He can be a slippery fellow."

* * * * *

"First time in Dead Man's, mister?" a scantily clad young woman asked Kemal as he stood warily in the entrance to the main gaming room of Dead Man's Hand. The meaning of the casino's name had been lost in the mists of antiquity, but it did have a ring to it. A menacing ring, Kemal thought. That didn't seem to bother the multitude of rock-hoppers crowding the floor and spending their hard-earned credits with wild abandon, though.

"That's right," Kemal admitted.

The woman smiled at him. She was short, dark, and sleek with a tight-fitting, interestingly cut outfit that left only the best parts to the imagination. She was a change maker. Her job was to circulate around the floor and exchange the gamblers' money—dolarubes, credits, even precious jewels, dust, nuggets, or radioactive isotopes—for Barbarosa script, which was legal tender in Dead Man's Hand and throughout the Pleasure Dome. House rules required change makers to use the posted exchange rate, but how much of a tip they could badger from customers was left strictly to their own abilities.

"You look like a nice guy," she cooed in a voice designed to seriously impair the mental processes of most men. "Let me show you around," she added with a look and a smile that increased the power of her voice.

Kemal managed to tear his eyes from her charms, and glanced around the casino floor. There were tables set up for dice games of all sorts, card games, backgammon, three-dimensional chess, and half a score of games Kemal had never seen before and had no idea how to play.

"Actually," he said, "I've got business with Mr. Carp."

She nodded, obviously delighted that Kemal was of such fine, upstanding character and immense importance that he had business with Mr. Carp.

"I'll take you to him," she said. "Just follow me."

She turned and walked slowly across the crowded floor, and Kemal had to admit that he would follow her just about anywhere. She went to an open, arched doorway at one end of the gambling hall and stopped before the curtain that hung in front of the archway. The curtain consisted of strings covered with flat, shiny, thumbnail-sized objects that flashed gold, silver, black, and orange. On close inspection Kemal realized that the things were scales from some kind of animal.

A man stood to one side of the archway. He was bigger than Kemal, and older, with a balding head and menacing, scarred face. He looked about as friendly as the average Delph fish rancher, straight from the ocean depths of Earth.

"Mr. Carp in?" the girl asked.

"The office," the man wheezed.

She turned and smiled at Kemal. "Just go down the hallway and knock on the door," she said and held her hand out.

Kemal fumbled in his pocket. Used to an electronic economy, he normally didn't carry much hard currency, but he sometimes had some for small purchases. He gave her most of what he had.

"Big spender," she said sarcastically and sashayed back onto the floor. Kemal, his head turned back to watch her retreating form, took a step forward and ran into something harder than a brick wall.

He turned quickly to see that the scar-faced man had moved more quickly and quietly than he'd though possible. The gargantuan blocked his entrance into the hallway.

"Any weapons?" the man wheezed.

Kemal shook his head, but the bodyguard insisted on patting him down anyway.

"Okay," he said in his shallow, whistling voice, and stepped back out of Kemal's way. Kemal went on through the unusual curtain and into the hallway beyond.

The corridor was thickly carpeted and lit by soft, strategically placed bulbs that gave off subdued lighting to showcase the artwork hanging on the corridor's walls.

It seemed that Carp was an art collector, one who specialized. The pieces were all prints of some kind, their age and place of origin unfamiliar to Kemal's untrained eye. It was obvious, though, that they all came from approximately the same geographic area and probably from about the same period. Although the styles of individual prints differed slightly, the people depicted in them all looked as if they were of the same race—similar to the bodyguard's—and all wore similar clothing.

The prints also had one other thing in common. Somewhere in each print, whether featured prominently or included as just a minor design element, was a fish. Moreover, they all seemed to portray a particular kind of fish. Kemal couldn't put a name to the species shown in the prints, but they all seemed to have colored scales, like those on the string curtain he'd just passed through.

The corridor ended in another doorway, this one with a solid wooden door blocking it. Kemal knocked, and a muffled voice called, "Enter."

The room beyond was an office, furnished in an elaborate, expensive style. The carpeting was three times as soft and deep as that in the corridor outside. The furniture looked old but well preserved and cared for. It seemed to be authentic wood. There were actual printed-page books in a glass-fronted bookcase that covered one whole wall. The framed prints on the other wood-paneled walls—all with that same type of fish in them—were bigger, and even to Kemal's untrained eye, more expensive-looking than those in the hallway.

A man sat at a desk in front of the wall of books. He was a thin man, pale-skinned, with ropy-looking muscles exposed by the short sleeves of his shirt. His neck was long and skinny, with a prominently bobbing Adam's apple. His face was horsey and thin, with sunken cheeks and vague, bulging eyes that reminded Kemal very strongly of some of the fish depicted in the prints hanging in the office.

"Mr. Carp?" Kemal asked.

The man inclined his head. "Carassius Carp, at your service, Prince Gavilan. Please sit down." He indicated a wood-and-leather chair placed strategically in front of his gigantic desk.

Kemal sank down into the chair. "How did you know my name?" he asked.

Carp smiled. "I'd be a very poor broker if I didn't recognize the scion of the House of Gavilan. That alone makes you noteworthy. The fact that you played an important, though not, shall we say, as visible, a role in the Earth rebellion, only adds to your luster."

"Well, I'm flattered, but call me Kemal. I don't use my Mercurian title anymore," he said.

"As you wish," Carp said. "How may I help you?"

"I'm looking for a man," he began, then amended, "not the man, actually, but his living quarters."

"His name?"

"Malik Ferdenko."

Carp smiled. "Ah, yes, a name I'm familiar with. Has he . . . offended . . . you in some way?"

"No," Kemal said carefully. He wondered how much he should tell Carp, then decided that the less the information broker knew, the better. "I just need to know his address."

"I see. Being closed-mouthed, are we?"

Kemal said nothing.

"We are. Well, I'm afraid that I won't be able to

help you."

"I thought you knew everything about Barbarosa," Kemal said.

"I do," Carp replied. "I said 'won't,' not 'can't.' "

Kemal nodded. "I see, I think. Well, what might help you to change your mind?"

Carp leaned forward and gave Kemal a toothy smile. "Information," he said.

Kemal thought furiously. "All right," he said, "we'll trade point for point."

"Agreed. You go first."

Kemal was about to protest, then thought better of it. Carp had the upper hand. This was his home territory, and he held all the cards. Kemal had to give in. "Malik Ferdenko," Kemal said slowly, "is dead."

"Interesting," Carp purred. He looked neither surprised nor aggrieved. "You're sure of this?" he asked.

"Positive."

"All right," Carp said. "I guess that's worth a bit of information on my part. Malik Ferdenko's apartment is above a bar he owns on Cheap Street. The bar is called Three-Fingered Jack's. The address in 11600 Cheap Street."

Kemal stood. "Thanks," he said.

Carp looked mildly surprised. "Is that all you wanted?"

"That's all," Kemal said. He actually wanted to know plenty more, but he figured he could uncover it all himself and not have to let Carp in on things. "Your prices are a little steeper than I care to pay."

Carp drummed his fingers on the desktop. "I've

been told that before," he said. "I tell you what." He swiveled around in his desk chair to face a computer terminal sitting on a handsome credenza set adjacent to his desk. He switched it on, typed briefly, and the printer spewed out a page of closely spaced type. "Take this, no charge. It's directions to Ferdenko's apartment."

"Thanks."

Kemal accepted the paper with an askance look that made Carp laugh. "Don't worry," he said, "I'm just figuring that it wouldn't hurt to have a Mercurian Sun King heir—even one who doesn't use his title—in my debt. At least a little bit."

Kemal nodded slowly, folded the paper, and put it in his pocket. "Thanks again, then."

Carp stood. He was fantastically tall and thin, and towered over Kemal by at least half a foot. "You must excuse me," he said. He glanced almost eagerly at a door set into the back wall of his office. "It is time for me to be . . . elsewhere."

He extended a hand, and Kemal took it. The broker's hand was large and bony and cold. Kemal suppressed a shudder.

"One last bit of advice," Carp said as Kemal turned to leave his office, "and don't worry. This is free. I like to see my customers return."

Kemal frowned. "What is it?"

"Cheap Street," Carp told him, "is not the best part of Barbarosa. All kinds of unsavory sorts hang out there. Take a weapon with you and don't be afraid to use it."

"Thanks," Kemal told him, but the mysterious Carassius Carp was already disappearing through the back door of his office, intent on whatever strange activity awaited him beyond.

CHAPTER FIVE

Barbarosa was as close to heaven as any rock in the Belt could get, but even heaven had a dirty underbelly. On Barbarosa, it was called Cheap Street.

It wasn't really a single street, but a series of jumbled, crowded, dirty thoroughfares that made up the poor quarter of the station and had Cheap Street as its main byway.

As Kemal walked through the squalid quarter, he began to wish that he'd taken Carp's advice to heart and brought along a weapon. Confident that he'd be able to handle any situation that arose, however, he hadn't armed himself with anything more than an industrial-strength laser that he figured he might need to break into Ferdenko's apartment.

Now mingling among the inhabitants of Barbarosa's poorest quarter, the bad men and heartless women, the renegade gennies and feral digital personalities who inhabited the quarter's cheap hotels, drank in its perilous bars, and hid in its unregistered computer nets, Kemal could almost taste the danger in the air.

It wasn't only the filth and poverty that got to him, though they were oppressive enough. It went deeper than that. There was a depressive air of hopelessness about the quarter that couldn't help but affect every man, woman, and gennie in the place.

Cheap Street was Barbarosa's deepest level, built into the asteroid's hollow end, farthest from the spaceport. The byways were cramped and rusty. The air, which was pumped down from the cleaner levels above, tasted dirty and used. He felt the weight of the levels above his head pressing down. It seemed all inhabitants of Cheap Street did. They never looked up, never looked into Kemal's eyes. Kemal knew it would be a sign of danger if anyone did. They would be looking him over, trying to decide if he had anything they wanted and whether it would be worth the risk to try to take it from him.

So far everyone had decided to steer clear of Kemal, though he'd been eyed a few times by potential muggers. Once a group of renegade gennies, workers whose lineage might have been bred back to *Homo neanderthalensis*, watched as he strode past the street corner they'd staked out as their own. There were six of them, short, broadly built, hairy specimens with reddish skin and shiny, dark little eyes that looked as if they could see right through him. They all wore blue gennie overalls, which were patched and dirty and had a crude design drawn on the bib, a black outline of tools—they looked like a square-headed hammer and a curved sickle—crossed at their handles. The "cavemen" wore their clothes as if they were some kind of gang badges or tokens.

The workers looked tough and mean, and maybe just a little bit desperate, but Kemal somehow passed their test. He looked the leader in the eye as he passed, and the gennie was the first to break contact. Kemal went by unmolested but not without a tiny shiver of fear running down his spine.

Kemal knew danger when he saw it. He also knew that he'd have to handle things alone. Huer was great for finding out information in the computer net, but the problem of having a holographic sidekick was that he couldn't do much when it came time for action. Kemal was on his own when it came to that. He was ready, he hoped, for just about anything, but he was too level-headed to believe he could lick the whole world—or even this seedy little part of it.

Cheap Street was crowded. It looked as if it always was. Barbarosa worked on a three-shift schedule, so someone was always working and someone was always sleeping and someone was always looking for entertainment. It seemed, now, that there were a lot of someones looking for entertainment. Most of the denizens of Cheap Street weren't the type to sit home and watch tri-dee dramas.

Kemal made his way carefully through the meandering crowd, occasionally glancing at the sheet of paper that he kept hidden in his palm. Carp's directions were detailed but also convoluted. It seemed to be taking Kemal a long time to get where he was going. He began to think that Carp had sent him on a wild gennie chase, but finally he saw a sign blinking up ahead that marked the end of his quest. It was Three-Fingered Jack's.

The bar itself was on the ground floor of a dilapidated three-story building. The sign painted on the window was a gory hand missing its thumb and pinkie and still bleeding from the severed stubs of the missing digits. Horrible-sounding music wafted out through the doors, and horrible-looking people were going in.

The two floors above the bar presented blank windows to the street, without a clue as to what was behind them. Kemal looked up at the windows thoughtfully for a moment, then looked down as he felt something tug at the hem of his jacket.

"Got a dolarube to spare, mister? One small, thin dolarube for a veteran of the Martian Wars?"

Kemal saw half a man, cut off at the hip, looking up at him. The man's torso rested on a leather pad held to his body by a pair of crudely fashioned leather suspenders. His clothes were ragged and needed a wash. A patch covered his left eye; his right was bloodshot. His chin was covered with coarse bristles.

"Dolarube for a veteran?" he repeated. Before Kemal could say anything, the panhandler launched into his story. "I was a rocketman once, sir, but I lost my legs when a Venusian cruiser blew my ship to hell, sir, during the Earth rebellion." He spat on the sidewalk. "Lucky I got left what I got."

Kemal was about to ask him why he hadn't had reconstructive surgery, but then shut his mouth. Either the man was lying, in which case he'd just spin another lie, or else the obvious was true. He couldn't afford the reconstruction himself and RAM didn't care enough for its castoffs to pay for it either.

Kemal reached into his pocket and pulled out the handful of coins he had left. He found a five-dolarube piece and held it up for the crippled man to see.

"What's your name?" Kemal asked.

"Yuri, sir."

"Know this area, Yuri?"

Yuri's gaze went from the coin to Kemal's face. The veteran's expression turned calculating and shrewd. "Yes, sir. Yes, I do."

Kemal gestured at the building. "Know what's on the upper two floors of that building?"

The beggar scratched his head. "Big shot lives there, he does, named Ferdenko. Fellow owns Jack's, and other things about as well. Lives on two floors, he does, two whole floors." Yuri looked wildly envious for a moment. "Me, I just got a crate, a miserable little crate is all—"

"All right," Kemal said.

He flipped the coin at Yuri, who caught it in midair and touched two fingers to the side of his forehead in an informal salute.

"Thank you, sir," Yuri said, and started to hobble off, propelling himself forward by pushing his hands against the pitted, dirty sidewalk. He paused, then looked back at Kemal slyly. "There's a back staircase and entrance around the side, sir," he said.

Kemal nodded, and Yuri swung off, joining the line of customers pushing into Jack's.

Rear entrance, Kemal thought, just what I need.

There were a couple of unmoving bodies in the alley. Whether they were dead drunk or just dead, Kemal couldn't tell. He stepped past them and went to the base of the rickety-looking metal fire escape that zigzagged down the side of the building. He glanced around. There was no one in the alley watching as he went cautiously up the shaking metal ladder. The fire escape ended at a landing in front of a door on the top floor.

The door looked fairly strong, its lock fairly sophisticated. Kemal glanced around again and felt guilty about breaking and entering the apartment. Somehow, though, he had the feeling that Ferdenko wouldn't mind. Kemal quickly scanned the entrance for traps and electronic alarms. Finding none, he flashed the door open with the hand-held industrial-strength laser that he'd brought. It cut through the door's alloy like a diamond bit going through Venusian acid mud. He turned the knob and entered.

The building's upper floor was a single large room, simply, cleanly furnished with nice if inexpensive furniture that seemed largely to be Martian-made replicas of Earth-style antiques. In the middle of the top floor was a sunken conversation pit with a free-standing fireplace and comfortable-looking modular sofa. A hole in the floor in the middle of the pit opened on a spiral staircase that led to the lower floor. The lower level had been divided into bedroom, kitchen, bathroom, and study. It was in the study that Kemal found the black box Huer had discovered.

It was a compact Hawkins-17, a new model, quick and powerful, complete with its own independent fusion power source. It was expensive but well worth it for the security-conscious, since it was almost impossible to contaminate or invade—given, of course, that no one ever broke into the apartment to tinker with the machine directly.

It seemed, though, that someone *had* broken into the apartment—two someones, in fact: Kemal and the man in the chair in front of the box's terminal.

Kemal hunkered down to look at him closely. The man was dead, no doubt about it. Someone had drilled him between the eyes with a laser. The beam had cauterized the wound it made, making for a very neat, but still very dead, corpse.

Kemal was surprised to see that it was a corpse he recognized. It was the man from Dead Man's Hand, the scar-faced Delph who had guarded the hallway to Carp's office.

Kemal sat back on his heels. He suddenly realized why Carp had given him such convoluted directions to Cheap Street. The time-consuming trip he'd gone on had given Carp's own agent time to get to Ferdenko's place first to check on things.

Carp's man hadn't gotten very far before being killed. The computer was on, so Kemal leaned over the dead man and inserted the microdisk with the Huer copy on it. As he did so, he brushed the corpse, which was still warm.

Kemal looked around the room. The killers had vanished, but it was a good bet they were somewhere close by. He palmed his industrial laser. It wasn't very precise as a weapon, but it would have to do. He suddenly wished he hadn't been so self-confident and waltzed into Ferdenko's apartment practically empty-handed.

He knew that he had to work fast, but all he could do was wait for the Huer copy to penetrate the codes and passwords shrouding the information contained in Ferdenko's computer.

After a moment, the screen started to blip on and off at a furious rate, and Kemal leaned over the body to rummage through the computer work station's drawers, looking for anything that might help unravel the mystery.

He hadn't gotten very far when he heard a voice ask, "Find anything interesting?"

He looked up, startled, to see Yuri, the legless beggar, now standing before him on very shiny, very serviceable cyborg legs. Behind Yuri were three members of the gennie gang who had watched Kemal closely when he'd approached Jack's.

"Not yet," Kemal said calmly.

"Too bad," Yuri said, and aimed the sonic stunner he'd had in his palm.

Kemal stood straight up, a look of self-disgust on his face. The stunner's sonic waves enveloped the Mercurian prince in a net of shattering pain, and his eyes rolled up in the back of his head as he blacked out.

CHAPTER SIX

Kemal felt something smash into his rib cage, adding a sullen layer of blunt pain to the crawling network of fire ants that were eating away at his whole body.

"He's awake," a deep, heavy voice said, and Kemal opened his eyes.

That was a mistake. Pain lanced through his eyeballs, sinking directly into the center of his brain. He quickly shut them, but the throbbing sensation racking every nerve ending in his body wouldn't go away.

"Spotted you for an outsider right away," another voice said, a voice that Kemal vaguely recognized and, not so vaguely, hated. He forced one eye open, dully reasoning that if he kept one closed the pain would be only half as great. It was, but it was still almost unendurable. He groaned aloud and forced his rebelling muscles to push his body to a sitting position. He realized that he wasn't tied or bound in anyway, which was the good news. The bad news was that he couldn't make his body do anything more complicated then sit up. The sonic stunner had done a good job on his nervous system. Kemal knew that its effects would pass, given enough time.

He squinted at the speaker through a half-open eye. It was Yuri, the beggar who'd stopped him outside Jack's, who had later led the gennie gang—his gang, maybe?—up into the apartment to trap him. It had been easy, because Kemal had allowed himself to accept the obvious at face value. That was, he vowed to himself, the last time he would ever do that.

"I wondered," Yuri continued from the chair in front of the computer terminal, "what an outsider would be wanting at Malik Ferdenko's when Ferdenko wasn't at home." He leaned down for a closer look at Kemal's face. "I knew he wasn't at home, see, 'cause I know he's dead. Me and the boys are here to see who else knows about Ferdenko's passing."

Kemal grunted something unintelligible, his tongue still thick and stiff from the effects of the scrambler.

"That's all right," Yuri said with his sly smile. "Lots of folks underestimate me and the boys . . . once." He swiveled back toward the computer terminal, but continued to speak to Kemal as if he were still looking right at him. "I've been playing around with that program of yours while you were out in dreamland, and I gotta say its got me stumped." He glanced back over his shoulder at Kemal. "Some kind of worm, right? A code breaker?"

Kemal said nothing, and one of the gennies standing next to him drew back his foot and booted him hard in the ribs again. Pain blossomed like a skyrocket in Kemal's chest, and he panted hard to try to cancel it. In a way, it almost felt good. It helped dampen the fire still dancing on his scrambled nerve endings.

"I said," Yuri repeated, "you put a code breaker into Ferdenko's black box, right?"

"Tha—that's right," Kemal managed to get out.

"Good." Yuri nodded. "Now we're getting somewhere." He turned back to face the terminal and tapped a few more keys on the keyboard. "Looking for something special, or just fishing?"

Kemal thought hard. He tried to come up with a plausible lie, but his mind just wasn't functioning well enough to come up with a coherent but misleading story. He decided the best thing he could do, for now, was tell the truth, but tell it slowly. He had to string it out until he got his body and mind working again.

"Something sp—special," he admitted. He flexed the muscles in his arms and legs and felt strength and coordination slowly return.

"Something to do with his last trip to the Asteroid Belt?"

"That's right."

Yuri smiled. "And what do you know about that

trip?"

Kemal swallowed. "He's not coming back."

Yuri swiveled around, turning to face him. "We know that already," he said.

"Who's 'we'?" Kemal asked weakly.

Yuri smiled like a hungry wolf. "Let's just say that I represent some investors in the project Ferdenko was spying on, investors who want to make sure that word of their new . . . development . . . isn't prematurely leaked."

Yuri's expression was thoughtful, his voice softly menacing. "What do *you* know about it?"

"Just that he ran into a little trouble in the Belt," Kemal said, feeling increasing fluidity returning to his body as the pain receded to a dull ache throbbing in the background.

Yuri fixed Kemal with a hard, penetrating stare. "That's it?"

Kemal only nodded, marshaling what strength he could. Soon, he knew, he was going to run out of satisfactory answers and the time would come for action. He had to be ready.

"This code-buster program you put into his system—is it working?"

Kemal thought furiously. The microdisk he'd slotted into Ferdenko's computer had contained a limited and imperfect copy of Huer, but it certainly had something of Huer's cunning. Hopefully it was lying low in the system, still trying to open it up for Huer himself. If that was the case, if Huer was on-line or close to it, Kemal still had a chance.

He stood, or tried to. His legs were still weak and rubbery. He would have fallen over the body of Carp's man, which was slumped on the floor next to him, if one of the renegade gennies hadn't clamped a ham-sized hand around his upper arm.

"Let me get a look at it," Kemal said, tottering forward with the help of the gennie, who half-dragged him across the lush carpeting until he could look over Yuri's shoulder and lean against the back of the swivel chair for support.

The screen was still flashing what looked like random lines of data, or perhaps pure nonsense. Kemal couldn't tell if the Huer copy was lying low or still doggedly assaulting the safeguards Ferdenko had put in his system.

"Let me get to the keyboard," he suggested to Yuri.

Yuri shot him an annoyed look, then gave up the swivel chair in front of the keyboard. Kemal edged himself slowly into the seat. Motor control was returning, but he still felt as weak as a kitten.

"Huer: report" he typed with slow, clumsy fingers.

The screen accepted the message. The continual data flow ceased as a message appeared. "Huer.bkup reporting. Identify self."

Kemal hesitated. As Carp had already proved earlier, the name "Gavilan" was not exactly unknown throughout the Solar System. Still, he had not foreseen this contingency and adopted a code name that could be used when he needed to conceal his identity from thugs such as Yuri. It was another oversight he would remedy at the first opportunity.

He nevertheless typed "Gavilan" onto the screen, and the computer replied with the blinking message, "Working . . . working . . . working . . ."

Yuri snorted when he read the name Kemal typed, and glanced sideways at him. "Well, not too pretentious, are we?"

Kemal was momentarily puzzled, then he realized that Yuri was taking Kemal's real name for a code name! Kemal ducked his head, hiding a smile. "Well," he said, "one can always dream."

"If you're going to borrow someone's identity, I'd go for Holzerhein. Now, *there's* a guy with power. Look, your program's coming on-line."

Kemal held in a sigh of relief at not having to debate the relative merits of Holzerhein, RAM Chairman of the Board, versus Gavilan, Mercurian Sun King. The Sun King, though, did have one large advantage, as far as Kemal was concerned. He, unlike Holzerhein, was alive, not some computer-generated persona haunting dusty memory banks.

"Huer.bkup," appeared on the screen, "achieved penetration." There was silence, then a beep, then a flat, more machinelike version of Huer's voice.

"Summary," it said. "Malik Ferdenko discovered the existence of a secret research station on a previously uninhabited asteroid by researching inexplicable and unusual shipping manifests to that part of the Belt. Later, one of his informants (refer to Young Bimwilly) overheard men talking in a popular Belt restaurant (refer to Club Noir, Barbarosa). By checking the records of the transport and supply lines,

Bimwilly's information was associated with this secret base. From supplies delivered to the station, Ferdenko was able to deduce that it was being built to develop a new weapons system. He could discover nothing else concrete. Nothing else was added to these files before he left to investigate the base personally."

Yuri looked thoughtful. "Well, I guess that plugs up one leak." He looked at Kemal. "Now for another."

He looked over his shoulder and gestured at the three gennies looming in the background.

Still weak from the sonic blast, Kemal nevertheless decided that he wasn't going to face death sitting down. He forced himself to his feet as the smirking Yuri stepped aside and the gennies advanced, flexing their huge, callused hands and grinning like apes. They weren't going to use high tech to knock him out this time. They were going to beat him to death with their bare hands. Kemal could read it in their dark, shiny eyes.

He assumed a fighting stance, determined to give back as best he could, when a shimmering beam of light appeared between him and the approaching gennies, and Huer's image popped into existence.

"I wouldn't hurt him if I were you," Huer said menacingly.

The gennies pulled back, confused and momentarily frightened, but Yuri only made a noise of disgust.

"It's only a digital personality, you idiots," he snarled at his henchmen. "It can't harm you. It's not even real."

Huer smiled. "That may be true," he said, "but you can't say the same about my friend."

"Friend?" Yuri said with a frown.

"He should be here any moment," Huer said in confident, reassuring tones to Kemal.

Yuri laughed and shook his head. "A bluff! You must think we're fools! Take him!"

Huer, looking off in the distance, counted aloud to himself as the gennies advanced, "Five . . . four . . . three . . . two—"

There was a tremendous crash on the upper floor of the building that halted the gennies in their tracks, followed by a blood-curdling bellow like the war cry of a hound from hell.

"Ah," Huer said. "He's a little early."

There was the sound of heavy, tramping feet on the floor above, then a huge figure leaped down the stairwell and came crashing down among them with an impact that shook the furniture.

"Black Barney!" Kemal cried, never so glad in his life to see the space pirate.

He was nearly seven feet of muscle and bone, clad in black leather and shiny steel. His face was dark and sinister, gaunt and frightening, with wild, staring eyes and a mohawk crest of metal and plastic that bridged the hemispheres of his brain. He carried no visible weapon. It looked as if he needed none other than his huge hands, twice the size of the gennies', which he flexed open and closed like the jaws of an adamantine vise.

Yuri fumbled for the sonic stunner he'd stuck in his

waistband, finally managed to draw it, and fired point-blank at Barney.

The pirate took the charge right over the heart, and he laughed. Kemal realized that the pirate was immune to the stunner's current frequency setting. The pirate also wore smart clothes with a built-in electrostatic shield. It wouldn't stop slugs or flechettes, but it would neutralize hand-held energy weapons. Another good idea for future usage, thought Kemal.

Barney laughed. It was deep, rumbling, menacing laughter, like the sound of a bear grumbling in a dark cave. He stepped forward, grabbed the swivel chair in front of the computer console as he stepped by it, and swung it casually with one hand.

He struck the first gennie squarely in the chest. The chair's metal frame bent, and the gennie catapulted backward as if he'd been hit by a charge from a mass driver.

The other gennies were braver than they were smart. They charged Barney, trying to swarm him like Martian terriers worrying a full-grown wild stag. Barney swung right and left with the chair, one and two. The chair shattered, but both gennies he hit were out cold.

Yuri, meanwhile, had bolted for the staircase.

"No, you don't," Kemal said.

He leaped for the ersatz beggar and grabbed him around a metal-and-plastic ankle before he could get more than half a dozen steps up the stairway. Yuri tried to drag Kemal along, but the Mercurian prince clung tenaciously to Yuri's ankle with one hand and to the bottom of the stairway's banister with the other.

"Let go!" Yuri screamed as he drew back a silver-and-steel foot to smash Kemal's face.

"Barney!" Huer yelled.

The space pirate was staring in disappointment at his erstwhile foes. He turned at the sound of Huer's voice, dropped the chair fragment he still clutched in one huge hand, and moved faster than any normal human could hope to move.

He grabbed Yuri's metal foot before it crushed Kemal's face. He smiled at the cyborg, who twisted in his grip like a fish trying to avoid the gaff.

"Let me go!" Yuri shrieked. "Let me go, damn you!"

"All right," Barney rumbled. He stood straight up, forcing Yuri to hop for balance on the one foot still on the ground, then twisted the ankle he held as if he were flicking the cap off a bottle of beer.

There was a crackling sound as a shower of sparks rained from the cyborg thigh, where metal interfaced with flesh. Yuri screamed as Barney plucked the leg from his body like a drumstick from a roast chicken. Barney looked at the leg, then calmly tossed it over his shoulder. Yuri fainted from the pain and shock, fell, and skidded down the staircase, landing in a heap by a panting Kemal Gavilan.

Kemal looked up at Barney. "Thanks."

"Mrrr," the pirate said in his usual curt manner.

Kemal sat on the lowest step and took a deep breath. "Uh, what are you doing here, anyway?"

"Got Huer's call. Trouble. Came as quick as I could."

Kemal shook his head. "Not here, I mean. On Barbarosa."

"Oh." Barney's dark eyes were wide and serious. His face was menacing, despite its utter lack of expression. "I found out something. Dangerous."

Kemal sighed. He wasn't exactly sure that he wanted to know anything about something Black Barney thought was dangerous.

CHAPTER SEVEN

Barney wanted to go to a quiet little place to talk things over, but his idea of a quiet little place proved to be the wildest, loudest, darkest, most infamous dive in all of Barbarosa.

Although it was only midafternoon, the Spaceman's Rest Bar and Grille was so crowded that there was a backlog of customers trying to get in at the door. The bouncer stationed in the front was giving a couple of gennies a hard time, just adding to the confusion.

"No genetic trash in here," he told the two gennies. "We don't want you scaring off the real customers with your ugly mugs, so shove off."

It was unlikely that the bouncer's antigennie prejudice was bar policy. Even though he'd sunk to Cheap

Street, the bouncer had a classic genetically engineered body. Tall and leanly muscular, he had the graceful appearance of a trained athlete and the face of a tri-dee star. He undoubtedly felt superior to the gnarly, low-browed gennies and was the type to loudly demonstrate any superiority that he felt.

The gennies, who stood in panicked confusion in front of the doorway, seemed to be simple workmen out for a big city thrill. They obviously were out of their depth, frightened and bullied by the authority figure at the door.

"I told you to take off," the bouncer repeated as they conversed in quiet, bewildered tones, trying to figure out how to get out of the unwanted limelight. "We don't serve garbage like you here. Why don't you go find some place in the sewer plant where you can join your own kind? You test-tube freaks don't deserve to be among real people anyway."

Kemal watched the proceedings with a look of disgust. He hated prejudice in any form, but this display was particularly degrading. Like most of their kind, the harmless gennies were a little slow-minded, and the bouncer was taking obvious delight in bullying them. Gavilan glanced up at Barney, ready to suggest that they go elsewhere, when he saw Barney staring at the bouncer with a deadly, fixed expression. He didn't know Barney all that well, but he knew that that look meant danger. As the bouncer railed on against the quailing gennies, Kemal realized why Barney was regarding the bouncer so intently.

Barney shouldered his way to the front of the crowd without saying a word. A few people he pushed past started to protest, then saw who was pushing and fell silent. Barney soon was standing before the gennies and the bully who was abusing them. The bouncer looked up as Barney approached.

"Say," the oaf began, "you've got to wait your turn . . ." Barney's size and appearance made him change his tone remarkably quickly. " . . . sir, which is right now, if you'd care to enter."

"Mrrr," Barney rumbled with a meaningful look at the gennies, "and so do my brothers."

"Well, heh, any brothers of yours are welcome at the Spaceman's Rest, sir. That's for sure."

The gennies smiled uncertainly at their huge new friend. Barney looked at them steadily, without smiling, but somehow they seemed instinctively to know that he meant to help them.

The bouncer's smile was sickly. "Your brothers? This genetic scu—uh, these people? Surely you're kidding, sir."

Barney looked at him without smiling. "No," he rumbled.

"Sure," the bouncer said as Kemal fought his way through the crowd and reached Barney's side. "Sure, uh, whatever you say is all right with me."

"We go in," Barney said, his voice growling from the cave of his chest with subtle but definite menace.

The bouncer only nodded and stepped aside. Barney gestured at the gennies, and they went in with happy smiles to sample the delights within. Barney went to follow them in, stopped, and turned back to the bouncer. "One thing," he said. He held up a thick, muscular forearm, fist clenched, pointing straight at the bouncer's face. The bouncer, staring at Barney's huge fist as if he were afraid there was a poisonous reptile hidden in it, only nodded. "Never insult people . . ."

Barney flexed a muscle in his forearm, and a needle-pointed foot-long dagger extruded with the speed of a striking cobra from the sheath built into his arm. Its point touched the very tip of the bouncer's nose, breaking the skin. A drop of blood welled out, trembled on the tip of the man's nose, then fell onto his chest. The bouncer stood frozen and bug-eyed, apparently afraid even to breathe.

" . . . you don't know."

The blade snicked back out of sight, into the hidden sheath, and Barney went on into the bar.

"Nice trick," Kemal commented as he followed Barney inside. "I like how you just managed to prick his nose."

Barney's voice resounded from deep in his throat. "Aiming for one of his eyes," he said, deadpan.

The Spaceman's Rest was jammed and jumping. Kemal caught sight of the two gennies, happily belly-up to the bar already. For a brief moment, he thought that it might have been best if they'd been turned away, but, he reflected, they probably would have gone somewhere else and gotten into trouble. He couldn't police the world, not even a little part of it.

Black Barney and Kemal managed to find a table

that was almost free in one of the room's far corners. There, a drunken rocketman slept with his head in a puddle of Venusian Hard Water that had spilled from the bottle he'd been holding. Barney cleared the table by picking the drunk up by his shirt collar and using him as a rag to mop the table dry. He then dumped the rocketman on the floor.

A harried waitress scurried between nearby tables. Barney reached out a large hand. She ran into it, stopping as if she'd hit a brick wall. Annoyed, she looked at the table but became respectful when she saw the size of the customer who'd stopped her.

"Ginger beer," Barney ordered. "Boar's Head Brand. Bottle." He looked at Kemal.

"Yeah," Kemal said, "same for me." He waited until the waitress left, then looked at Barney. "Boar's Head ginger beer?"

The pirate nodded seriously. "Best in the system."

Kemal shook his head. "Whatever you say."

They waited until the waitress returned with two huge, two-liter bottles. Kemal wondered what he possibly was going to do with all that liquid but soon discovered that Barney drank more than enough for two. Actually, Kemal discovered, after taking a tentative sip, the stuff was pretty good. It had a lively fizz and a sweet yet tart taste that tickled his tongue.

Barney paid the waitress and added a more than respectable tip. Her eyes wide, she smiled broadly and said, "Whatever you two sirs want, just let me know."

Barney waved her off and finished his second mug.

"Now," Kemal said, "can we get down to business?"

Barney slammed the empty mug down on the table, then wiped the back of his lips with a huge hand and let out a loud, satisfied belch. He took his bottle, poured another mug, and began his story.

"Something big out in the Belt, something bad. Ships have disappeared, vanished."

"That shouldn't be so unusual," Kemal commented, "with all the pirates out there."

Barney shook his enormous head. "Not pirates. I'd know. Nothing for sale on the black market."

"I see what you mean," Kemal said, toying with his own mug. "Pirates don't hijack ships for the fun of it. They do it for profit, and there's no profit to be had by destroying something."

Barney drained his mug and poured himself another. "Right. This business is bad. Makes ship captains jumpy, harder targets. Worse," Barney said with a squint indicating his outrage, "some missing ships are pirates."

"Less competition for you, then," Kemal pointed out.

Barney brightened. "True. More to it than ships. Nirvana's gone."

"Nirvana?" Kemal asked, puzzled.

Barney poured the last of the ginger beer from his bottle and eyed Kemal's. The Mercurian prince pushed the ginger beer over into Barney's reach. The pirate took it with grunted thanks and topped off his mug. "Asteroid on the edge of the Belt. Cored by religious fanatics from Venus. Thought life there was too 'violent.' He harrumphed disgustedly, as if bewildered at the concept that anything could be too violent. "Built their own colony. Sat around looking at their navels and praying." Barney shook his head, as if baffled at such outrageous behavior.

"You say the asteroid is gone?" Kemal asked.

Barney nodded.

"How long have these disappearances been going on?"

Barney shrugged. "A month. No more."

Kemal thoughtfully pulled at his lower lip. "So there's a connection between the research station I asked you to check on and these disappearances?"

"Has to be," Barney said positively. "Device makes things vanish. Ships vanishing. Even an asteroid."

"Could be some kind of coincidence," Kemal said.

Barney made a strange sound, halfway between a cough and a bark. It took Kemal a moment to realize that the pirate was laughing.

Barney looked Kemal straight in the eyes. "No such thing. Start believing in that stuff, and you're dead."

"You're probably right," Kemal admitted, "but the connection is pretty weak. Why use this new weapon on innocent ships and peaceful asteroid colonies?"

"To see if it works," Barney said stolidly.

"What about the missing pirate ships? Surely those were armed."

"Pirates are always poking noses where they don't belong. Maybe they saw something they shouldn't have." Barney shrugged. The missing pirate ships were small, poorly armed and armored. "Owners wanted to test in a battle they could win." Barney shrugged his great shoulders again.

"We've got to stop them somehow," Kemal muttered, "but they've been very careful not to leave any witnesses. If only we knew where to start."

"We might," Barney said.

Kemal looked at him and quirked an eyebrow. "How?"

"Ferdenko's log. A clue."

"What?"

Barney looked at him, and Kemal could see something like hate move behind the pirate's normally unreadable eyes. "Skimmer carrying the weapon."

"Could you identify it?" Kemal asked with rising excitement.

"Special design. One company."

"You know what company?" Kemal asked eagerly.

"Dracolysk Corporation," Barney said, grinding the words out from behind clenched teeth.

"I thought you and your clone-brothers destroyed Dracolysk when you, uh, escaped from, uh, Gorgon Station," Kemal said, putting it as delicately as he could.

Barney shook his head. "We destroyed the station. Corporation lived on. Time to finish the job we started off Jupiter."

"Can you be sure that it's not just an old Dracolysk ship that someone bought secondhand and outfitted for this project?" Kemal asked.

Barney nodded.

"What do you want to do?"

Barney spoke in a deadly monotone. "Go to their headquarters. Discover their connection to this weapon. Crush them."

As if to punctuate his smoldering anger, Barney unconsciously squeezed his thick glass mug until it shattered in his hand with a startlingly loud popping noise. Vaguely surprised, he looked down at the remnants of glass littering the tabletop.

Kemal shook his head. "Look, if I've learned anything so far, it's that we can't just rush into things."

"Why not?" Barney asked in a menacing whisper.

"We need a *plan*," Kemal emphasized. "You may be right. Dracolysk may be involved with this. In fact, it sounds as if it might be something right up their alley. A war machine designed to snuff out life on a grand scale. But they've taken pains to keep this whole affair secret. They're going to have sophisticated safeguards at their headquarters, and they're going to be heavily armed."

"I'm armed," Barney announced. "We'll take *Free Enterprise*, swoop in fast, hit them hard, and clean them out before they know what happened!"

Kemal shook his head. "No. This has to be done carefully, subtly. We have to go in without their even realizing that we're there." He paused, deep in thought for a moment. "We don't even know where this Dracolysk headquarters might be. But I think I know someone who might."

"Carassius Carp," Kemal and Barney said in

unison.

"You know him?" Kemal asked.

"Dealt with him," Barney said shortly. "Useful."

"We can try to buy the information from him," Kemal said, "but he can be crafty. I know."

Barney grunted. "He owes me. He'll tell us where Dracolysk is."

"If he does," Kemal said cautiously, "you and I might not be enough to take them. We may need help."

Kemal spoke cautiously because he didn't know how the big pirate was going to react to such a suggestion. To his surprise, Barney only nodded.

"You're right. We'll need help." The pirate smiled. It was more a feral baring of teeth than an expression of good humor. "And I know where to find it."

"Where?" Kemal inquired.

"Some friends of mine will help us out," he said.

Kemal suppressed a sigh. He couldn't wait to meet Barney's friends.

CHAPTER EIGHT

The floor of Dead Man's Hand didn't look any different from the last time Kemal had been there. The individual customers crowding the various tables and games were different, but the change girls were just as pretty, the crowds were just as dense, and the noise was just as raucous.

"Hello."

It might have been the same change girl who had approached him during his first visit to the casino. Kemal wasn't sure, but if she wasn't the same woman, she was just as beautiful.

"Hello," he said, but Barney grabbed Kemal's arm and dragged him along before he could say anything else.

"No time for women," the pirate growled.

Kemal threw a smile over his shoulder. The change girl smiled back and shrugged, bemused, as Barney pulled the Mercurian prince away.

"Carp makes more money from selling information than from crooked gambling," Barney said. He glanced down at Kemal. "Say you like his fish. Sometimes he'll give a break to people who like his fish. Me, I hate the slimy suckers."

"Fish?" Kemal asked.

They had reached the open arched doorway with the string curtain. Another bodyguard was standing beside it. He was bigger, uglier, and meaner looking than the one killed by Yuri and his gang in Ferdenko's apartment. He and Barney eyed one another closely.

"Carp in?" Barney finally asked.

The other nodded. "Fish room," was all the guard said.

They went by him, through the arched doorway, and into the corridor beyond.

"Looked like you knew that guy," Kemal commented.

"I do. Ex-pigsmear champ. Now he's one of Carp's bodyguards. I beat him once. Bad."

As if that explains everything, thought Kemal.

The office beyond the corridor was empty this time. The door in the back wall was open a bit. Kemal could hear tuneless whistling coming from beyond it.

Barney looked down at him. "Remember," he cautioned, "say something nice about the fish."

"I'll try," Kemal offered.

Barney led the way through the door, with Kemal following.

"Hello," the pirate grunted. "Gordo said you were here."

They'd entered a large room, bigger than the adjacent office. It was approximately forty feet on each side. There was no furniture in it except for a few scattered chairs, isolated hassocks, and what looked like a couple of long workbenches. In the center of the room was a large ten-foot by ten-foot fountain surrounded by a waist-high marble wall. In the center of the fountain was a statue of a boy riding a fish. Water spewed from the fish's open mouth and trickled down into the pool bordered by the fountain's marble walls.

Set against the room's four walls, standing on benches and shelved on sturdy shelves five and six high, were dozens of rectangular glass tanks filled with water.

And fish.

Some of the tanks held only a few gallons and a few small fish. Others were huge, containing what must have been hundreds of gallons of water in which swam scores of fish, some of which were two or three feet long.

The fish seemed to be of the same kind depicted in the prints displayed in the corridor and office through which Barney and Kemal had passed. They sparkled with vibrant colors of orange and gold and silver and velvet black. Their tails were different shapes and lengths, from simple, straightforward fins to intricately flowing fantasies ballooning in the water like ornate bridal veils. Some of the fish had fantastic bulbous growths on the tops of their heads. Others had huge telescoping eyes or eyes floating in bubblelike sacs bobbing on either side of their heads.

"Good to see you again, Barney," Carp said. He was standing in front of one of the tanks, apparently siphoning water from it with a clear plastic hose into a large bucket on the floor at his feet. He set the hose aside and dusted his hands daintily. "You, too, Prince Gavilan. Are you buying or selling today?"

"Buying," Barney rumbled.

"Oh." Carp sounded disappointed. "I was so hoping that you had something to sell. Something like those specimens you brought me last year. Remember? The koi that RAM was taking to Mars to turn into bioengineered horrors for their terraformed lakes. I paid well for those." He seemed to reminisce fondly about the memory. "I'd pay *very* well for anything else like that you'd run across." The broker frowned, his Adam's apple bobbing frantically, as if his vague, watery eyes had noticed the expression on Kemal's face for the first time. "You didn't tell me that Barney was a friend of yours," he said to the prince.

"I didn't know that would make a difference," Kemal said.

"Well—"

"You mean," Kemal interrupted, "if you'd known Barney was with me, you wouldn't have sent me to Ferdenko's the long way, giving your own man time to check the apartment?"

"Uh, well—"

"Unfortunately, someone was already watching the place, someone who took out your man and would have gotten me, too, if Barney hadn't come along."

Carp frowned. "Who was it?"

"A cyborg named Yuri," Kemal replied. "He had artificial legs and a patch over his left eye. Know him?"

"Perhaps," Carp said defensively. "Look, I can see that you're disturbed. I tell you what. I'll make it up to you."

"You'd better," Kemal said warningly.

"Oh, I will. I most assuredly will. Tell me," Carp said, his voice sinking to a conspiratorial whisper, "ever see *goldfish* before?" He put an odd emphasis on the word, as if he were introducing his very favorite lover to Kemal.

The Mercurian, bewildered, looked at Barney. Barney made obvious gestures with his head, as if saying, "remember what I told you and praise the damn fish."

"I, uh, don't believe I have," Kemal said.

Carp beamed. "Come over here, then, where you can see better. Come on, come on. They won't bite." He laughed, as if at an oft-repeated favorite joke.

Carp stood before one of the larger tanks. An eerie thought struck Kemal as he looked into the tank full of the brightly colored little beauties. They were the kind with eyes bobbing in yolklike sacs floating on either side of their heads. They swam gracefully through the crystal-clear water of their enclosed environment, blissfully unaware of the hostile air surrounding them. Much like, Kemal reflected, the men and women of Barbarosa calmly walked around their own friendly, air-filled environment, unaware of the hostile vacuum that surrounded them.

The fish lived in a box within a box. Kemal wondered if there were a third box, if the Solar System and the universe that contained it also was contained within a closed box. If so, what possible kind of environment could exist beyond? The notion was more than a little unsettling.

"These little beauties are called Celestials," Carp crooned, running his hand lovingly down the side of the aquarium.

"Very nice," Kemal said, impressed by the fish if more than a little taken aback by Carp's obvious strangeness.

"And these," the fishkeeper said, suddenly twirling like a symphonic conductor and pointing an imaginary baton at the pool around the marble fountain in the center of the room, "are koi. Not the specimens supplied by my friend Barney, no, nice enough as they were, but real, honest to goodness koi born in Japan back on Old Earth." He leaned forward conspiratorially. "These fish are over three hundred years old!"

"Really?" Kemal asked. "That would make them—" He was about to say that they were the second oldest living creatures he'd ever seen, next to Buck Rogers, but suddenly realized that that might not be the most politic thing to say. "Very old indeed," he finished.

"Old," Barney echoed with a grunt. It seemed the

nicest thing he could think of to say about the fish.

"And these little beauties—" Carp said.

"Those are very nice, too," Kemal said firmly. "Perhaps we can look at them after you've answered some of our questions."

Carp sighed. "Very well. We can talk while I work." He returned to his abandoned bucket and hose, and began again to siphon water from the tank he'd been working on when Barney and Kemal had interrupted him.

"Ever hear of an outfit called Dracolysk?" Kemal asked.

"Certainly," Carp said. "It was about to make it big about twenty years ago when its—" he glanced at Barney "—when it had some trouble."

"But it's still around," Kemal insisted.

"Oh, sure," Carp said. "It's pretty insignificant as corporations go, but it still exists."

"Where is its headquarters?" Kemal asked.

"In the Belt. A rock called Dragon's Lair. All the location data on it is in the *Almanac*."

"Hugo Dracolysk?" Barney asked in a voice like glass grating on sandpaper.

"He still runs it, I think. He's a lucky man. One of the few to escape the clone uprising on Gorgon Station." Carp eyed Barney and Kemal fishily. "What exactly do you want with Dracolysk, anyway? Is it connected with this Ferdenko thing?"

"Old business," Barney said in a grave voice.

Carp stared at him. "Whatever you say." His gaze was coolly appraising. "One more thing you should know. The man named Yuri, the man who killed my bodyguard and ambushed you at Ferdenko's apartment?"

"Yes," Kemal prompted.

"He's Hugo Dracolysk's right-hand man."

Kemal and Barney looked at each other.

"Thanks," Kemal said. "That explains a lot of things. I guess that's what we needed to know for now," he said.

"How many of my clone-brothers in the Belt?" Barney added.

"I'll have to check my computer," Carp said. "Four, I think. And one of your sisters as well."

"Find them," Barney ground out. "Tell them to come to Barbarosa Station. Dead Man's Hand."

"They won't listen to a message from me," Carp protested.

"They will," Barney said, "if you tell them it's a matter of blood and steel. They'll come."

* * * * *

One Barney was pretty impressive. A roomful of them, Kemal thought, was damn near overwhelming.

All right, Kemal conceded, the private meeting room in the back of Dead Man's Hand wasn't actually full of Barneys, but three of Barney's clone-brothers and one of his sisters in the same place at the same time was still a sight to behold.

Black Barney was the biggest and grimmest-looking of them, but the others all shared a certain aura with the pirate, a sense of danger and menace that was the Dracolysk legacy to the entire clone lineage.

Carp had only been able to contact three of the males who'd been in the Belt for business or pleasure. The other, the inventor named Ochoa-Varilla, who owned his own asteroid, was deep in a new project and refusing all calls. The others had assembled, as Barney had promised they would, upon getting the word put out by Carp on Barney's behalf.

Quinto was the only one, besides Barney, who openly carried a weapon. Quinto was a courier, a messenger, a go-between who worked for any individual, corporation, or political entity who would pay his fee. The line he walked was a little more on the legal side than Barney's, but several times in his career he'd ignored questions of legality where profit was concerned. He was almost a physical duplicate of Barney, except that he wore his hair long and combed back from his high forehead, letting it falling down over his shoulders, and he needed a shave. He always needed shave.

Sattar Tabibi, rumored to hold a position high in the RAM hierarchy, wore a smart suit of the finest material, newest style, and undoubtedly deadliest design. He had a sleek, well-fed look about him. His face was missing the harsh planes of his clone-brothers, and his tunic and jacket were cut to conceal the extra padding he carried about his middle. But he was no less deadly than the others. Specially trained in cunning, stealth, and deception, Tabibi might have had the sharpest mind among the living Barneys. He certainly had the most treacherous.

Stalin Khan looked the least like the others of his lineage. He was just as tall and athletically built as the others, but the face he wore was not that of his fellows. It was unblemished by scars and unlined by worry. Khan was a philosophy professor at Coprates Central University and was currently on sabbatical in the Belt, where he was doing research for his new book.

He may not have looked like the other clone-warriors, but the bleakness of his heritage ran in him just as deep as it did in the others. His best-selling book, *Power and Darkness*, was built around the thesis that neither was possible without the other. It was a theory that guided his life as much as it did his fellow clones.

Kemal found the last of the Barney line the easiest to look at. The clone-warrior called Lilith was six feet, six inches of sleek beauty. She was slim, tan, and taut-muscled. Even the scar that traced her jawline, white against the bronze of her otherwise flawless skin, was sexy. She caught Kemal looking at her and smiled seductively.

He smiled back despite himself, and Lilith stretched like a cat, the short tunic she wore lifting and displaying lithe, muscled thighs. As trim as a tigress, she looked as passionate as one, as full of life, energy, and sensuality. And, Kemal realized, as full of casual cruelty. Out of all the Barneys, she was the one he'd least care to cross.

"Well," Quinto said, interrupting Kemal's reverie, "I'm sure we're all wondering why you called us here today, pilgrim."

His words were directed at Barney, who was eyeing his fellow clones with intensity. It must be strange, Kemal thought, to see yourself confronted by so many similar images, so many other beings so like yourself, yet so different. It was like staring into fun house mirrors. Each presented a distorted likeness, yet underneath the distortion were identical cores. What, Kemal wondered, must Barney be feeling?

Whatever it was, the pirate kept it hidden behind his usual impassive expression.

"Dracolysk," he said, and fell silent.

Quinto took a long pull at his drink, set it down, and smiled. "Hey, I like to reminisce about the good old days as much as the next guy, but I'm a busy fellow."

Lilith's smile broadened. Her incisors were as pointed as a cat's. "We paid them back for what they did to us. We ripped their guts out and left them crawling in their own intestines."

Barney shook his head. "Not all," he said.

"No one escaped Gorgon Station during the uprising," Khan said, fingering the down-curving swoop of his thick mustache. "We made sure of that."

"Perhaps not." Barney was looking directly at Sattar Tabibi as he spoke. "Some of our brothers left the station when the fight had been won. Before we slaughtered the slavers. We never checked our brothers to see if they left the station alone."

All eyes turned to Tabibi, who regarded them with calm equanimity.

"Some of us left, it is true, before the fight was over, not seeing the point in extracting childish revenge. And it is possible, to further their future life, that they took along, let us say, certain passengers for a certain promised fee."

"Among the passengers," Barney said in a voice like two chunks of flint colliding and throwing off sparks, "was Hugo Dracolysk, CEO of Dracolysk and head of the cloning project."

"Perhaps," Tabibi said with a nod.

There was a moment of silence in the room. No one doubted for a second that Tabibi's bland admission was proof positive that Hugo Dracolysk, whom they all thought dead for twenty years, was still very much alive.

"Hugo Dracolysk," Barney finally said in the same deadly voice. "Responsible for pain."

"And also," Khan put in, "our very existence. Let us not forget that. Hugo Dracolysk made us what we are through bitter pain and back-breaking work. We owe him something."

Lilith seemed to take Barney's position in the argument. "We owe the filthy pig a sharp stick through his eye," she said.

Kemal looked from Barney to his clone-mates. It was obvious that the space pirate and Lilith were for finding Hugo Dracolysk and stringing him up as soon, and as painfully, as possible. Tabibi had actually helped him escape from the Dracolysk holocaust, and Khan seemed to take a philosophical view about their past master. Only Quinto remained silent, his thoughts obscure behind his readily grinning face.

Barney turned to him. With the uncanny sense that existed between clone-mates, Barney seemed to anticipate what Quinto was about to say.

"Hey, pilgrim, I'm on your side. Kind of. I mean, he and the other Dracolysk bastards put us through hell, and then some. But that was over twenty years ago. A lot of ether under the rocket since then. I suppose I'd be willing to take him out. He sure deserves it. But where's the profit, you know? What'd we get out of it besides satisfaction?"

Barney chuckled, a grim, humorless sound. Kemal had the sudden feeling that the pirate was about to spill everything.

"Say, listen," Kemal said quickly, speaking aloud for the first time since the conference began. "I don't know if we really want to discuss—"

"Something's been happening," Barney said, his voice drowning out Kemal's as if it weren't even there, "in the Belt."

CHAPTER NINE

Kemal listened as Barney told his clone-mates all the information about the laser device and the connections to Dracolysk that they had uncovered so far. They all listened as patiently as anyone of Barney's genetic lineage could listen—which wasn't very patiently at all. After Barney was finished, there was a momentary silence as the clones looked around the room at each other.

"I'm afraid that my position hasn't changed," Tabibi said. "I still see no useful reason to challenge Dracolysk. The risks far outweigh the possible benefits."

Quinto let out a snort of laughter. "You're getting cautious in your old age, pilgrim. Or should I say even more cautious. We all know it'd be dangerous as hell to go up against Dracolysk, but think about it! Radically new weapons don't come around every day. Why, just the plans alone would be worth a fortune!"

"You want in?" Barney growled.

"You bet your gene-engineered butt I do," Quinto said. "Why, with a score like this I can retire and buy a bigger'n'better Belt rock than Ochoa's."

Kemal looked at Barney blankly, who took a moment to explain. "Ochoa-Varilla is one of our clone-brothers. Bought his own asteroid from the proceeds of his inventions."

"I see," Kemal said.

Tabibi stood up. "I don't." He looked around the room. "If there's nothing else you desire to discuss . . .?"

Barney shook his head. "Remember, this's under the seal of blood and steel."

Barney held up his right hand as he spoke. Kemal noticed for the first time a two-inch-long jagged scar that looped around the fleshy part of the base of his thumb. It was hardly noticeable compared to the more spectacular scars that adorned Barney's face and body, but Tabibi also held up this hand and revealed an identical scar around the base of his own thumb.

"I remember the oath our entire lineage swore before the Gorgon Station uprising, and will honor it as I always have. Our business is our own. No need for anyone else to know it."

He bowed to the group and dramatically swept out of the room.

"Can you trust him on that?" Kemal asked after he'd left.

Barney turned his bleak gaze on the Mercurian. "Never broken the oath before. None have."

Quinto laughed. "None of us have dared. We all know that you'd be on our trail like a hellhound, hunting us for the rest of our very short existence on this plane."

Barney only nodded and turned to Stalin Khan. "You out, too?" he asked.

Khan shook his head. "On the contrary. The academic life has its advantages, but it is a little lacking in some areas." As he spoke, the philosopher's eyes took on a gleam every bit as dangerous as Barney's. "It's been some time since I've felt the warmth of fresh blood spilling on my hands." He held out his right hand, palm first, to display an identical scar. "By blood and steel," he said. Barney looked at Quinto and Lilith. They, too, held out their hands.

"For the money," Quinto said, laughing.

"For the revenge," Lilith said, grimacing.

"Dracolysk headquarters," Barney said, "tonight."

"Wait a minute," Kemal interrupted, standing up. He fell silent when four pairs of Barney eyes fell on him. "There's a problem here," he began, uncertain how far he could push Barney and get away with it. Barney obeyed Buck Rogers to the letter, but Kemal wasn't Buck. All he had to rely on was a promise of cooperation, and Barney's sense of cooperation extended only as far as he wanted it to go. And from the look on the pirate's face, Kemal had just about found its limits.

Barney rose to his feet and towered over the prince. The pirate looked like an avalanche of destruction ready to fall at the slightest sound or gesture. Silence hung like a shroud in the room, stretching tension to the breaking point. Kemal knew he couldn't back down. If he did, he'd never have Barney's respect again.

He faced the angry pirate for what seemed an eternity but was, in reality, only a couple of heartbeats. The problem was, he could think of no way out of this impasse.

When Khan suddenly spoke, shattering the tension, Kemal almost could have kissed the professor.

"The boy has a point," Khan said calmly.

"He does?" Barney asked, rounding on his clonemate with a voice as dangerous as it was soft.

"Yes. There is a problem. Him."

Barney frowned, his forehead crinkling in concentration.

"He's been privy to our council," Khan continued, "but how do we know we can trust him?"

"Hmmm?" Barney seemed somewhat taken aback, as if Khan was questioning his judgment. "*I* vouch for him," Barney said loudly.

"Ordinarily," Khan replied, "that would be good enough. But not in this situation, with him knowing about our intention to assault a RAM subsidiary."

"Yeah," Quinto piped up. "How do we know we can trust the kid? I mean, I don't know him from Adam."

Quinto looked at Lilith, and she nodded.

Barney flared into anger so quickly that Kemal was thankful it had been directed away from him, but before it could burst into full mayhem, Khan cooled the pirate down with a placating gesture.

"Now there's no need for an uproar," he said. "There's a simple way to solve this."

"How?" Barney asked sullenly.

Khan held up his hand again. "By blood and steel."

Barney looked at him for what seemed like a full minute, then turned to look at the others in turn. They all nodded, and Barney finally turned to Kemal. "Blood and steel," he said. "Oath of the clone lineage. No outsider has ever taken it. None have ever been offered it."

"Well," Kemal said, "that sounds like quite an honor. What does it all . . . mean?"

"It means," Khan said, standing shoulder to shoulder with Barney, facing Kemal, "that you will never act in any manner against a brother—or—" he added, glancing at Lilith, "—sister, in the lineage. Under pain of expulsion and instant death at the hand of your clone-mates."

"I can live with that," Kemal said.

"And," Quinto noted, standing at Barney's other shoulder, "you will give your brothers—or sisters—any help they request, at any time, in any place. Under pain of expulsion from the lineage and instant death."

"I can live with that," Kemal said.

"Never divulge lineage secrets, plans, or mysteries," Barney growled. "Under—"

"—pain of expulsion and instant death," Kemal interrupted. "Sure, I can live with that."

Lilith snaked around her clone-brothers. She was shorter and lighter than the others but no less deadly, despite her beauty. "And to seal the pact," she said, "we share blood. And steel."

As she spoke, a dagger, razor-sharp and gleaming in the light, sprang out of the flesh of her left wrist. She took Kemal's right hand in hers. Her flesh felt warm, as if her body heat was higher than the human norm. Her hand was slim-fingered and very strong.

Kemal swallowed hard. "I guess I can live with that, but can you?"

Lilith stopped in surprise.

"Blood and steel is your oath," said Kemal, thinking fast. He had no wish to be bound to this gruesome brotherhood if he could avoid it. "It means nothing to me. Make me swear by something I hold dear."

"Death is a simple oath," said Khan. Anger flared in Barney's eyes at the insult.

Kemal faced the Barneys levelly, knowing a flicker of fear would mean his death. "As you hate the man who cloned you, as you hunger for the blood of Hugo Dracolysk, so I loved my father. Love is not an emotion you credit, but as strong as your hate is, my love equals it. I swear, on the blood of my father, that I will keep faith with you in this enterprise. By blood and steel," he said.

Kemal looked up. He was surrounded by Barney and his clone-brothers, hemmed in like a young sapling among the great trees of the forest. The prince looked at Barney. The pirate's colorless eyes told him nothing. Lilith still held Kemal, her grip like steel, her beautiful face interested, as if she approved his bravado.

Barney looked around at his clone-mates. "Blood and steel," he said, clasping hands with Kemal. His hand was the size of a bear paw, and his grip had a bear's strength in it.

"Blood and steel," Kemal replied.

Quinto was next. He grinned as he took Kemal's hand. "Blood and steel, pilgrim," he said, and started to squeeze.

Barney's grip was strong, but Quinto's was purposefully punishing. Kemal clenched his jaw into a smile and took it, giving back as best he could. He didn't seem to faze Quinto, though, being unable to match his gene-engineered strength.

After Quinto's grip, Khan's was fleeting and almost soft. His smile was sardonic, his recital of the vow almost mocking.

Lilith was last in line. She took Kemal's hand in hers and pulled him close. Surprised and overmatched by her gene-engineered strength, Kemal was astonished to find her pressing hard against him, her face only inches from hers.

"I have my own test," she murmured in sultry, silky tones, and she put her mouth on his. Kemal was too surprised to respond. She pulled away and smiled. "Not bad," she said, "but it's better when you help. Blood and steel."

Kemal muttered the ritualistic reply as she broke

away from the embrace. He looked quickly at Barney and the others, almost defiantly embarrassed, but no one seemed to pay much attention to Lilith's behavior. Only Quinto was smirking at Kemal, but that seemed to be his usual expression.

"Now," Barney rumbled, "objections?"

There were murmured denials.

"All right," Barney said.

Kemal flexed his hand. He looked up to see all the Barney's staring at him.

"I guess there's no question anymore. We take down Dracolysk tonight."

Barney's lip curled upward in a genial snarl that, for him, was a wide grin. "See?" he said. "Blood oath works wonders."

CHAPTER TEN

Being the largest and one of the brightest of rocks in the Belt, Ceres was the first asteroid to be discovered by the astronomers of Old Earth. Shaped rather like a bloated pumpkin seed, it was more than six hundred twenty miles on the long axis, and half that through the short.

It was also one of the first asteroids to be colonized and currently had the greatest population of any rock in the Belt, with more than twenty thousand humans, gennies, and digital personalities living on and in it. Tunnels honeycombed its interior like winding ant-nests, and pressure domes sprouted all over its surface like colonies of mushrooms.

Kemal and the Barneys sat in two skimmers behind a ridge overlooking the pyramid-shaped arcology that served as both business headquarters and living quarters for Hugo Dracolysk and the Dracolysk Corporation.

The situation reminded Kemal of the war games he'd taken part in while studying at the Ulyanov Academy. Only this wasn't a game. He had put aside the toys and stun weapons he'd amused himself with at the academy for the real thing. His companions were no longer the scions of the finest families in the system who had been sent to Mars for a military education, but rather a pack of disreputable killing machines created in test tubes. And their objective wasn't to capture Blue Team's flag, but to enter, loot, and destroy an interplanetary corporation while assassinating its head. Life, Kemal reflected as he smiled at Lilith, who sat next to him in the skimmer, had sure gotten strange lately.

It was cold in the back of the skimmer. Kemal turned up the temperature of his smart space suit. Barney and Quinto were up front in the other skimmer, awaiting the return of Stalin Khan, who had gone ahead to scout the huge, squat pyramidal structure sprawling on the plain below.

The pyramid had been built of Martian sandstone, with accents of glass and stainless steel polished so much that they gleamed even in the dark night. A mile on each side and a quarter-mile tall, the Dracolysk sigil—a dragon holding out a globe in one taloned paw—was etched deep into the sandstone near the pyramid's crown.

"A beautiful night," Lilith's sibilant voice whispered in the helmet speaker close to Kemal's ear. "The stars are so clear, so bright."

Kemal only nodded.

"It is a perfect night for killing," she continued.

"If you say so." Lilith was beautiful, but Kemal preferred his women to be less cold-blooded. Like Duernie. It had been a long time since he'd thought of the quiet, enigmatic Dancer girl whom he'd not seen since he'd left Mercury so many months ago. Something might have developed between them if the Martian Wars had not intervened. *He'd* certainly wanted it, though she was cool and cautious and hard to open up. Still, . . .

There was sudden movement in the rocks to the right of the skimmer, breaking Kemal's train of thought. He reached for his laser pistol, but Lilith laid a hand on his forearm.

"It is Khan," she said in a low voice.

A patch of darkness detached itself from the shadows and seemed to flow down toward them.

It never failed to amaze Kemal that such big creatures could move so effortlessly. And if Khan was this good, Kemal could only speculate on the abilities of Sattar Tabibi, whose specialty was stealth and cunning.

"Guard of Desert Runners," Khan said quietly over the radio as he floated back through the atmosphere. "Two on patrol outside the checkpoint, two on duty inside."

"Way in?" Barney grunted.

"Obviously the checkpoint—once we eliminate the

guards." Khan paused. "You know, I might be able to get a new graduate seminar topic out of this. 'Death-dealing: A Personal Perspective on Wielding the Ultimate Power.' What do you think?"

"I think you'd better get your mind off impressing coeds and back onto tonight," Kemal said.

Khan flashed a sardonic grin. "All right. Two teams. Barney and I will take out the guards on patrol. Quinto and Lilith, take those on the inside after Kemal distracts them by pretending to be a Draco-lysk exec pulling a surprise inspection. How's that for a plan?"

Kemal mulled it over, then nodded. "Not bad. Let's do it."

The clone-warriors cracked the two skimmers' bubble tops, climbed out, and used the jet packs mounted on their suits to move off into the night. There was a closeness between the members of the clone-lineage, a feeling that each almost always knew what the others were thinking. It sometimes left Kemal feeling a beat behind.

This was one of those times. He was almost ready to call out after them, when a dark shape materialized at his side again. It was Lilith.

"I know you feel like you don't really belong," she said, then paused. It may have been a trick of the starlight, but for the moment, through the faceplate of her suit's helmet, she looked like a vulnerable human. "That's really a good thing. No one should want to be one of us. No one." Then the moment passed, and she was the same old Lilith. "Come on. Let's go kick some Dracolysk butt."

She took his hand, and they moved down over the talus slope of the bluff to the plain below, staying as close to the surface as their thrusters would allow.

It was treacherous going. Luckily they'd brought along infrared spy-eyes. Otherwise, they'd never have made it in one piece down the steep slope littered with jagged stone. Quinto was impatiently waiting for them in deep shadow at the base of the bluff. The guardhouse, a small dome connected to the main base by a covered passageway, was a tiny oasis of light in the black desert of the deep night. Neither the patrolling guards nor the clone-warriors stalking them could be seen.

"About time," Quinto said, annoyed. "Stop for some kissy-face in the dark?"

"Don't you wish?" Lilith sneered back.

As volatile as the clone-warriors' tempers were, Kemal could see this exchange getting quickly out of hand. He yanked Quinto and Lilith back on track as forcefully as he could.

"All right, we'll sort out who gets to go out with who later. Right now, we've got some problems to solve. Khan came up with a dandy little plan, but it was short on a few details. Like exactly how do we convince the Desert Runners that I'm a Dracolysk executive?"

"Simple, pilgrim," Quinto said. He reached into a pouch on his suit's utility belt and pulled out a hand-sized rectangular slab of plastic. "With this."

It was a RAM Internal Affairs ID plate glowing a

deep, arterial red. Internal Affairs, a descendant of the dread KGB of Old Earth, was the shadowy secret police of RAM. Its main weapons were terror, murder, and intimidation. Its agents went where they wanted and did what they wanted, no questions asked. Their ID plates evoked unquestioned obedience from even high-level corporate executives.

"Where'd you get that?" Kemal asked. "I thought these badges were tuned into the life-force of each IA agent, making them impossible to forge."

"They are," Quinto said. "This is a sure-enough authentic plate, pilgrim. Picked it up before we went on this little jaunt. Thought it might come in handy."

"But the plates go black if they're separated from their agent for any length of time."

Quinto shrugged. "Well, it's not widely known—and understandably so—but there's a certain chemical procedure that can fool the plate into thinking it's still in contact with its agent—for a little while at least. Then, of course, it goes black and becomes useless."

"And the agent who owned it?" Kemal asked.

"Well, he sure doesn't have any use for it now."

Kemal decided not to press for details. "All right. Hand it over." He took the card and slipped it onto his suit's utility belt. "I'll be the agent. You be my loyal assistants."

Quinto bowed sarcastically. "Lead on, O great chief."

"Right."

They burst boldly out of the shadows and headed straight across the open space to the checkpoint. Before they'd covered twenty yards, a light bore down on them from the guardhouse and a voice speaking with the typical high-pitched whine of the species of gennie called Desert Runners boomed over their helmet radios.

"Restricted area! Identify self!"

Kemal held up his hand. His assistants, floating a respectful three paces to the rear, stopped.

"Krushcenko," Kemal said, using the name on the ID plate. He took the card from his belt and held it out. Its distinctive crimson surface flashed bloodily in the light. Mimicking the arrogance of the Internal Affairs section, he didn't bother identifying himself specifically as a member of the dread secret police.

There was a momentary silence from the guard hut, then the Runner barked out again, "Advance for positive identification."

Kemal made an arrogant gesture toward Quinto and Lilith, then manipulated his thrusters and moved forward without hesitation. The key to success for this caper, he told himself, was acting as if he were in command. Take it for granted, and the Desert Runners would, too.

There were two gennies in the hut, both in pressure suits, one of whom was waiting for Kemal in the open airlock to the guard post.

Martian Desert Runners were the oldest gene-engineered race in existence. Their mixture of human, canid, and feline ancestry showed in their generally human shape, short, thick fur, elongated incisors, and catlike eyes. Their bodies were long and lean, except for broad, powerfully muscled chests, which gave them a top-heavy appearance. Their basic fur pattern of deep red was broken by mottled bands of black and dark brown, giving them a calico appearance. The Runner in the doorway wore large, gaudy copper earrings that could be seen through his faceplate, and had little coppery bells braided in his fur. They gave off a tiny, continuous jangling that his suit mike picked up as he shifted his feet impatiently.

The Runners originally had been created to herd the migratory Martian meat-beasts as they followed the seasons on their annual rounds. Because of the high degree of loyalty bred into the Runners, many corporations and wealthy individuals raised personal packs, grooming them to be ferociously devoted guards and watchmen.

"Check the perimeter," Kemal snapped before the Runner could say anything to him. "Any problems here?"

"None, sir," the Runner said, responding to the command in Kemal's voice.

"All right," he turned to Quinto. "Log in on the computer inside the guard hut."

Quinto snapped off a credible, "Yes, sir!" and brushed by the Runner in the doorway. The one still inside was watching the proceedings with a disapproving frown and fingering the stock of his bolt rifle uncertainly.

"Uh, sir," the first Runner said. "I'll have to check your identification more closely." The guard had markings that reminded Kemal of pictures of the

Cheshire cat that he'd seen as a child.

"Oh, all right," Kemal said, a trace of exasperated annoyance in his voice. He turned to Lilith. "Show him your ID."

She smirked, in the manner of a vicious, ruthless secret policeman's henchman, floated close to the Runner, and fumbled with a pouch attached to her utility belt. The Runner leaned forward to look at the card she pulled out and offered him, and she sprung her wrist knife.

It tore through the Runner's suit and throat, right above the left ear. He gave a small, startled gurgle, and she yanked her wrist, slashing him from ear to ear. The Runner in the hut didn't even have time to aim his weapon before Quinto was on him. The clone-warrior didn't bother with his wrist knife. He just leaped on the Runner with superhuman quickness and broke his neck with bare hands. The Barney caught the body as it rebounded and placed it in the chair, closing its terrified eyes.

"Just in case anyone looks in on the monitor," he said over his shoulder, "they'll think this bozo's sleeping."

Kemal nodded unhappily. He was a warrior, but he didn't particular enjoy dealing in assassination. Lilith and Quinto seemed to have no such scruples. Their eyes sparkled with barely suppressed excitement as they waited in the guard hut for Barney and Khan to show up.

"What's taking them so long?" Kemal muttered.

"Relax," Quinto said, the excitement of the kill still

surging through him. "These gennies have delicate senses. Our brothers have to be careful when sneaking up for the kill. They can't let them alert the guard posts on the other faces of the pyramid."

"Here they are, now," Lilith said, pointing with a slim arm that showed no sign of housing a deadly weapon.

Khan and Barney emerged silently from the dark and joined them at the guard post. Barney glanced at the bodies, the one in the chair, the other stashed out of casual sight.

"Good," he grunted as he sealed the exit and pressurized the room. "Get to work."

"Right," Quinto said.

The would-be commandos stripped off their pressure suits, and the magnetized soles of their boots stuck lightly to the complex's floor.

Quinto sat down at the computer console as Kemal took out his computer uplink.

"Huer," Kemal said, "we need you. It's time to go to work."

A moment or two passed, then the digital personality blipped into existence inside the guard hut. "You called?"

"We're about ready to enter the dragon's lair," Kemal said, "and we need a front man to lead us in."

"What do you want me to do?" Huer asked.

"First shut down the security system in at least this section of the arcology," Kemal said. "We want to be able to move around without being spotted."

Huer nodded. "Got you."

"Also, we're going to need you to loot their computer net for information. We need to find out exactly what connection Dracolysk has with the research station that produced the laser device."

"And we need to know where Hugo Dracolysk is," Barney reminded them with a menacing grumble.

"Right," Kemal said. "Can you handle that?"

"No problem," Huer said, and his image disappeared.

"Now for our insurance policy," Quinto said as he enabled the guard hut computer and slipped a microdisk in the drive slot.

"What's that?" Kemal asked.

"Virus bomb," Quinto explained. He checked his thumbwatch. "It should make things very interesting in about twenty minutes."

Barney was already striding through the passageway that connected the guard post to the Dracolysk arcology. The others followed. The door to the main building was locked, but Quinto deactivated it with an ID card taken from one of the dead Desert Runners. He bowed sardonically as the door opened, and waved the others in.

They found themselves in a delivery area for raw materials used by the Dracolysk factories and research labs. It had been shut down for the night. The loading docks were dark and the conveyer belts leading off into other parts of the arcology were silent and unmoving.

Barney reached out and tugged on one of the belts. It was three feet wide and made out of hard rubber and plastic. He turned and looked at the others.

"Good idea," Kemal said. "We'll split up. With each of us taking one of the belts, we should be able to cover a good part of the station. We'll wait for Huer to loot the computer files—"

"Then we find the chairman," Barney rumbled meaningfully, and Lilith nodded.

"And take anything that looks valuable," Quinto put in.

"Whatever," Barney ground out. There was no doubt what he believed to be the most important aspect of this raid: repayment of what he considered an old debt.

"Where do we rendezvous?" Khan asked.

"Wherever the chairman can be found," Barney said.

Khan shook his head. "Not very precise, but I guess it'll do." He looked at Barney. "You know, you should see someone about your obsessive behavior. It would do you some good to relax every now and then."

"Relax after I finish crushing Dracolysk's skull."

"Let's not stand here talking about it," Lilith said. "Let's do it."

"Right." Kemal scanned the belts. There were only four of them. "I'll stay with Lilith." He looked at his thumbwatch. "We've got about ten minutes until the virus Quinto put in the computer activates itself."

"All right," Barney said.

Everyone had already turned away and was climbing upon belts that led to various parts of the compound. Lilith climbed up on the last belt, and Kemal followed her on hands and knees.

The belt ran slightly downhill through a slot in the wall and into darkness. It sagged under their combined mass, but, apparently used for transporting heavy material, was in no obvious danger of collapsing. As soon as Lilith and Kemal went past the wall of the shipping and receiving area, the conveyer belt became enclosed in a circular conduit. The air inside the conduit was stale but breathable. And since the conduit was not quite tall enough to stand up in, they continued to make their way on hands and knees.

Kemal glanced at his watch after what seemed an interminable time had passed. It had been only four minutes, but still there was no sign that they were approaching the belt's terminus. Caught up short, he suddenly bumped into Lilith, who had stopped up ahead. She turned, looked over her shoulder, and hissed in a low voice, "Opening up ahead. I'll check it out."

She disappeared through another slot in the wall. Kemal had an anxious moment or two waiting alone in the confined darkness, then the clone stuck her head back through the hole and gestured for him to come ahead.

He joined her at the slot and pulled himself through.

"Cafeteria kitchen," she said, gesturing around in the darkness. "Must be where they cook the slop that comes from the food vats and dish it up to their workers. Empty now. Good thing they're not on round-the-clock shifts."

Kemal nodded. The kitchen was full of large, vatlike heaters and ovens where workers prepared the processed food that was the staple of other workers and low-level executives. Now the chrome and steel vats bulked like silent sentinels in the darkness, maws gaping open to receive the containers of mushy, doughy gunk that would be delivered in the morning via the conveyer belt Kemal and Lilith had just negotiated.

"I want to find a computer and check on Huer," Kemal said, looking at his watch. "We've got just about six minutes left before the virus is scheduled to kick in."

"Find the cafeteria manager's office," Lilith said. "We'll be able to tap into the system from there."

Kemal nodded. They separated and were soon hidden from each other by the immense kitchen accoutrements that looked more suitable to mixing chemicals than preparing food. Come to think of it, Kemal realized, the processed food served here *was* mostly chemicals.

From off in the darkness to the right he heard a low whistle. Hoping it was Lilith, he approached cautiously, his laser pistol out and ready. She was standing before a little room that was closed off from the rest of the kitchen by thick glass walls. Even though it was dark, the pair's infrared goggles revealed a ghostly desk piled high with magnetically held papers and a computer terminal sitting off to its side.

Kemal and Lilith looked at each other.

"There we are," she said, excitement dancing again in her dark eyes.

They went in. Kemal slid into the chair in front of the computer terminal and flicked on the little desk lamp. He took off his infrared goggles, set them aside, and turned on the power to the computer.

First there was nothing but a slight humming of cooling fans as the computer came to life. A questioning prompt came up and kept blinking off and on at a steady, metronomic rate, saying, "Please identify self . . . Please identify self . . . Please identify self . . ."

"Where did Quinto get that virus?" Kemal asked Lilith, who was leaning so closely over his shoulder that he could feel her warm breath on his ear.

She shrugged. "Some computer whiz out in the Belt. Guaranteed to—"

"I think it's starting to work," Kemal said, pointing at the screen.

The prompt speeded up its stately pace until it was flickering so fast that it appeared continually visible on the screen. Then the image imploded, shrinking to a black dot that immediately blossomed into a shower of stars and sparks of every color and all the shades in between. Stamped in bold black letters over the explosion of color appeared the words, "We don't need no stinking badges! HAHAHAHAHAHA-HAHAHAHA!!!!!"

"What's happening?" Kemal asked.

"I guess the viral program is declining to identify itself," Lilith said.

"Who wants breakfast?" the screen asked as lights

suddenly flared on in the tiny office as well as the huge kitchen outside. The automated cooking devices all turned on. The lids to the warming vats clanged shut with a deafening clamor, then immediately sprung open, then shut again, then opened, creating a cacophonous rhythm of steel on steel.

"Identify self?" the computer asked almost timidly, Kemal thought.

"Up your entry port with a live wire," the virus replied. "I'M TAKING OVER!"

The lights started to flicker off and on as the programs fought for control of the kitchen facilities. They switched on and off so rapidly that the room looked as if it were being lit by a madly cycling strobe. It was an unpleasant effect that hurt Kemal's eyes.

"We've got to figure out how to find Huer," Kemal said as he knuckled his aching eyes.

"Try a search command," Lilith suggested. "Either the resident program or the virus might answer."

"It's worth a shot," Kemal said as his fingers flew over the keyboard.

"Invalid search," the computer replied. "Classified information."

"Says you," the virus countered. "Paging Dr. Huer. Dr. Huer, please pick up the white courtesy phone at the front desk. Paging Dr. Huer. There is an emergency at the hospital. Please pick up the white courtesy phone."

"Is that virus crazy?" Kemal asked, turning to look at Lilith, startled to see her face close to his. Her tanned skin was flawless, her lips large and inviting. She seemed to realize the effect her closeness was having on Kemal, even in the midst of the madness in which they found themselves.

"So I understand," she said with a smile. "It's been written with an internal 'logic' designed to blow its hosts' circuits with calculated weirdness." She licked her lips, leaving them moist and inviting.

This really is madness, Kemal thought.

Kemal turned quickly and cleared his throat, but before he could say anything, a message flickered on the computer screen.

"I'm in the mainframe core," the message read.

"That's got to be Huer," Kemal said excitedly. Lilith wound a finger in the hair at the nape of his neck, and nodded. "Let's see if we can get him some help."

"Allow Dr. Huer access to all classified information," Kemal typed.

"Cannot comply," the virus program replied. "Invalid parameters to request. Cannot comply. CAN. Cannot. CAN. CannotCANcannotCANCANnot- CANCANNOTCAN CANCAN—"

Light bulbs blew in their fixtures. A weird, thin wailing that soon resolved into odd music came from the loudspeakers placed about the kitchen.

"Bagpipes," Kemal mused. "They used to play them at the Ulyanov Academy." He shook his head. "I wonder what's going on in other parts of the station."

"Chaos," Lilith surmised. "Pure and simple chaos." There was a sudden shimmering in the air before them. A holographic form of Huer's handsome, middle-aged persona appeared, then flickered out of existence before it could solidify.

"Huer!" Kemal exclaimed.

It appeared again, rippled like a mirage on a desert wind, then solidified before them. Huer smiled at the clone and the prince.

"The secret research base that Ferdenko gave his life to discover," Huer announced, "is called Rising Sun Station. Dracolysk doesn't seem to run it, but has been exclusively supplying it with supplies and raw materials since it was built."

"Well, who does own it?" Kemal asked.

Huer shook his head. "I haven't discovered that yet. There's a lot of information to go through."

"You didn't by any chance discover the location of Hugo Dracolysk?" Kemal asked. "I'm afraid that Barney is going to insist upon the information."

Lilith poked him from behind. "Not only Barney," she said.

"I don't know," Huer said with a frown. "I digested an awful lot of data. Let me check my memory circuits." Huer looked off into the distance for a moment. When he turned his attention back into the room, there was a smile on his face.

"Oh, yes," he said.

"Where is he?" Lilith asked, an edge as sharp as a razor in her voice.

"He lives," Huer replied, "in a private suite at the apex of the Dracolysk pyramid." His image pointed up. "Right over our heads."

CHAPTER ELEVEN

No one paid much attention to Kemal and Lilith in the chaos that had engulfed the Dracolysk headquarters. The virus bomb had won the battle for control of the Dracolysk computer, and madness reigned in what once was an utterly airtight, totally controlled environment.

Crazed, conflicting orders were shouted over the loudspeakers and booted up on the terminals throughout the system. Confusing things even further was the fact that the Dracolysk computer, though beaten, wasn't yet down for the count. It, too, was issuing orders to countermand those issued by the virus. The virus itself, growing in mastery and subtlety, was issuing nonsensical commands using the style and format of the Dracolysk computer. No

one knew which orders to follow. The fact that the
Dracolysk employees had been conditioned from
birth for unquestioning obedience didn't help matters any when they found themselves in the position
of having to choose between conflicting commands.

Some latched onto orders and followed them single-
mindedly, even if the command was something as
nonsensical as painting walls with toothbrushes.
Some were reduced to states of near catatonia by the
conflicting orders bombarding their brains; they simply wandered about in a daze, doing nothing.
Others—their comfortable, orderly lives torn apart
before their very eyes—slipped into states of psy-
chotic tension resulting in firefights exploding all
over the complex.

The virus also was playing havoc with the physical
environment. It raised the temperature in some
parts of the complex to heights that would have made
a Mercurian uncomfortable and lowered it in others
so that frost started to appear on the carpeting and
furniture. It turned on fire suppression systems, creating rainstorms and snowstorms, and turned on and
off and on again all manners of alarms, bells, and
whistles, which reduced the security staff to a state of
weeping hysteria.

Kemal and Lilith watched the pandemonium from
a little nook next to the elevator bank leading to the
pyramid's upper levels, while Huer zipped off to various part of the compounds to round up Barney and
the others.

Khan was the first to arrive, looking as suave and

unperturbed as usual. Barney showed up next, and then they had to wait for several long minutes for Quinto. When he finally arrived, he had a bundle of loot slung in a sack over his shoulder and a nasty-looking gash on his forehead that was already healing as he joined them.

"Leave that behind," Kemal said, gesturing at Quinto's bag.

"Hey, pilgrim, there's some good stuff in there," he protested.

Barney turned a face to him that brooked no opposition. "Leave it," he said flatly.

"Besides," Kemal added, "there'll be better loot where we're headed." He pointed up to the top floors.

"All right," Quinto said with a sigh. "I'll stash it here, where I can recover it on the way down."

Barney growled impatiently. "Get your program to work these elevators."

"No problem, pilgrim," Quinto said. He took out his tool kit and jimmied open the door to the elevator's control panel. Within moments he had needle-nose pliers deep into the control box's innards. "This thing is wired with a special security system, but I think we can bypass it."

"Is Dracolysk home?" Kemal asked as Quinto worked on the guts of the control box.

"He's home," Barney replied. "We checked with the computer."

"And you believed it?" Kemal asked.

"It may be crazy," Quinto said without looking up from his task, "but I know its control functions. I know how to get a straight answer out of it."

"The problem isn't with Dracolysk being home," Kemal said. "It's with the company he's likely to have."

"Company?" Barney said impatiently.

"Security guards," Kemal said. "Apparently he's got his own personal pack of Desert Runners. The ones out front were just a small part of the pack. If Dracolysk raised them to be his bodyguards, they'll be loyal, tough, and as mean as they can get."

"Not tough enough," Barney growled.

"How many Runners in a pack?" Quinto asked as he probed the elevator control box.

"Twenty warriors, maybe thirty," Kemal replied.

"Twenty or thirty?" Khan said.

Barney turned a cold eye on him. "What's the matter? Odds too small?"

"Got it!" Quinto exclaimed. The elevator doors swooshed open to reveal an enclosed cage the size of a small room.

"The elevator landings will be guarded," Kemal warned as the clone-warriors piled into the lift.

"We'll have to chance it," Khan said. "Our best chance is to get in fast, hit them hard, and run."

"I'd hate to see our worst chance," Kemal muttered as Lilith grabbed him by the arm and pulled him inside the elevator.

"Come on," she urged. "Want to die in bed a feeble old man?"

"Do I have a choice?"

She flashed him a smile that was almost human.

As the elevator rocketed up to its destination, strange, insipid music began to sound from its speaker grills. The virus said in an ethereal voice, "Top floor. Cosmetics, lingerie, notions—"

"What's 'notions'?" Quinto asked.

Before anyone could answer, the elevator abruptly stopped and its doors opened to show a vestibule the size of a small house. There was a very large, obviously very old, and very, very valuable rug attached to the vestibule's floor. It had been woven in an intricate pattern that suggested entwined serpents—or dragons, Kemal realized—and dyed in a dozen rich shades that had faded with age to muted pastel colors.

Set against the vestibule's walls were dozens of plants ranging from miniature orchids to fruit-bearing trees potted in vases taller than Kemal. In the middle of the vestibule was a squad of heavily armed Desert Runners. They were turning toward the open elevator with surprise on their furry faces.

"Down!" Barney roared from the rear of the elevator, and Kemal was slammed hard on his face by a heavy weight. The moaning cry of a bolt rifle operating on full automatic sounded from behind him.

The silver slivers of death whispered over his back, and caught the Runners as they were turning and aiming their weapons. The particles stitched through them and the plants beyond, shredding flesh and stripping leaves and even cutting completely through the trunks of some of the smaller trees, setting them adrift in the zero gravity. The magnetized boots held the guards fast, and the Runners' free-floating blood stained the exquisite carpet in a most appalling manner.

"—and assassinations," the virus finished in the same sing-song voice. "Have a nice day." The Barneys and Kemal exited, and the elevator doors closed.

Kemal twisted his neck to see Lilith's face inches from his. She had tackled him to take him out of Barney's line of fire, and not an instant too soon. His slower human reflexes wouldn't have gotten him out of the way in time.

"Thanks," he said.

"Any time."

Her eyes were dark, reflective pools that Kemal felt he could drown in. Her weight pressed down on him not unpleasantly. Her body heat radiated from her like the light from a sun gone nova. She lithely stood and offered him a hand up. He took it, and their grasp lingered, their fingers entwined.

"Come on," Barney said impatiently as he brushed past them. "Haven't got all day."

"Four more down," Khan said, referring to the gory remains of the Desert Runners, blown nearly to pieces by Barney's deadly bolt rifle. "Sixteen to go."

"Approximately," Quinto said.

"Precision," the philosopher said, "is the hobgoblin of little minds. What matters in the long run if there are sixteen, seventeen, or indeed only fifteen—"

"It doesn't," Barney growled as he took the lead. "They're all dead meat."

"My point exactly."

Kemal followed, shaking his head. Whatever else it entailed, being a companion to Black Barney had certainly introduced him to some exciting times.

"Fan out or stay together?" Quinto asked as they passed from the entrance hall into a huge room that was bigger than most Belters' entire living quarters.

"Stay together," Barney asserted. "Bunch our firepower."

It was difficult to figure exactly what the spacious chamber was used for. Kemal supposed that it could act as a gathering room or simply a display hall for the various works of art attached to its walls or held by magnetized pedestals scattered about its floor.

Kemal was hardly an art historian, but he was heir to the Sun Kings. Even though he'd spent most of his life off Mercury, he could still recognize authentic masterpieces when he saw them.

There were pieces done by many of the finest artists of the last four or five centuries, including paintings, sculptures, mobiles, and collages in myriad styles and materials. The real strength of the collection, though, lay in the Old Earth pieces.

Kemal wandered through the gallery, realizing that it displayed a thousand years of Earth art. Dracolysk wasn't one of the great powers, so the really classic names and works were missing, but there was the minor Picasso, the odd Matisse, the lesser-known Frazetta.

Kemal fought the urge to linger over the paintings. He reminded himself that he was still in the midst of a very dangerous situation, where it wasn't smart to let his attention wander, when he passed a bright alcove holding a rather unusual sculpture. He passed, stopped, and turned back again.

"Huer!" he called into his uplink, and the living program appeared almost instantly before him. He pointed at the sculpture.

"Good lord!" Huer said emphatically.

Lilith, who had turned around impatiently to drag Kemal back to reality, looked at the piece that was the center of their attention and frowned. "What's the problem?" she asked.

"The sculpture," Kemal told her.

Her frown deepened. "What about it? It's pretty enough, but I've seen better," she said, unimpressed.

"So have I," Kemal replied, "on the log of the *Lucky Lady*. That's one of the crystals that Ferdenko discovered on the research station in the Belt."

Kemal couldn't imagine something so beautiful serving as the focal point for such a deadly weapon.

It was as tall as he was and intricately, delicately faceted with an almost uncountable number of crystalline petals that seemed to drink the light pouring down on them from floodlights above. The crystal transformed the light it absorbed into a shimmering, iridescent aura that sparkled in subtly different shades from petal to petal, flowing and rippling like living color impossible to duplicate with paint and brush. As they watched, the quality of the light from the floods changed, creeping up in intensity, and then gradually lowering. As the light changed, so did the crystal's colors. It was a living light show, changing from moment to moment, an enthralling, mesmerizing display of color, form, and shadow. More than that, Huer's analysis of Ferdenko's records showed the crystal to be extraordinarily dense. He had cross-referenced its structure and found it to be unique in the solar system. Chemical analysis showed that the unusual configuration was due to an element that did not exist within the parameters of his programming.

"We must be on the right track," Kemal said to Huer. "We have to find out where Dracolysk acquired this crystal. It'll put us on the trail of the others."

"There's an acquisition number engraved in the pedestal," Huer said. "I'll see if I can find the collection catalog in the computer banks."

"All right," Kemal said, "but be careful."

"I will," he promised. "Besides, the computer's got a lot more to worry about than a worm poking through some unsecured catalog files. You know, I ran across that viral program, and it's *weird*." Huer shuddered and disappeared.

"If you want to question Dracolysk about the crystal," Lilith pointed out, "you'd better find him before Barney does."

Kemal looked at her. "What about you?"

"Me? I'll let you question him. I can wait that long."

"Why . . ." Kemal hesitated, then decided that he had to ask the question. "Why so vengeful? Was Dracolysk really that terrible?"

Lilith stared at him, nothing at all of humanity in her face or expression. "You can't imagine what Hugo Dracolysk and his people did to us. They created us to be slaves to enlarge their personal fortunes. They tortured and killed us by the score to train us. And the females of the lineage—there's a reason why so few of us survived. We were bred to be warriors, but some of us were also taken as toys, playthings, by men who liked to play rough." There was the closest thing to anguish in her eyes that Kemal had ever seen. "I belonged to Hugo Dracolysk personally for nearly a year, and I intend to take every terrible, horrible second of that year out on him before I allow him to die."

Kemal looked down, unable to bear the suffering he saw etched on Lilith's face. He reached out a hand to touch her shoulder and she started like a frightened animal.

"I'm sorry," he said.

She straightened, then smiled crookedly. "We'd better find Barney," she said, "before he robs us both of what we want."

They hurried through the gallery, past a fortune in ancient and modern art without so much as a glance one way or the other, and tried to find a sign of the clone-warriors who had gone on ahead of them.

At the end of the gallery was a set of great metal double doors, one of which gaped open. As they approached, they could feel warm air spilling from the doorway, warm air laden with moisture and odors unlike any Kemal had ever smelled before.

They rushed through the doors and pulled up, astonished, on the brink of a room so large that walls and ceiling were lost to view.

"What in the world," Kemal wondered aloud, "have we stumbled into?"

Like the vestibule off the elevators, this room was also filled with plants, but here the plantings were cunningly hidden so that they seemed to be growing naturally out of soil. The plants grew straight, he knew, because of the light sources above them. There were trees adorned with flowering vines and creepers, bushes and shrubs, and tall, concealing grass that, for some reason, Kemal was reluctant to pass through. Kemal still could feel his boots held by a magnetized floor, even through the soil, which itself must have contained iron to keep it in place.

The air tasted moist and smelled heavily of rich soil, humus, animals, and their by-products. A flash of moving color caught Kemal's eye, and he looked up in astonishment to see a small flock of brightly colored birds wheeling through the air—an odd sight in an environment without gravity. They landed and disappeared among the sheltering branches of a large tree.

"This must be an eco-chamber," Kemal said.

Eco-chambers were common in many arcologies set up in inimical environments such as the Belt. It was a psychological necessity for humans to be able to wander in something other than a sterile, artificial environment of steel and plastic and conditioned air.

Eco-chambers served the same functions as parks

and zoos did in the Old Earth open megalopolises of steel and concrete. They gave a person a necessary taste of nature, a reminder of the way humans had lived for millennia before encasing themselves, like Carp's goldfish, in artificial little worlds.

"It's a big one," Kemal said with some wonder. He looked around. "If Barney and the others stumbled in here, they could be just about anywhere."

The calm of the eco-chamber was suddenly shattered by a long, moaning burst from a bolt rifle and answering staticlike hisses of laser fire.

"Especially near the sound of weapon fire," Lilith quipped.

"It came from that direction," Kemal said.

Lilith nodded and headed off through the thick, tall grass at a run.

Kemal hesitated. There was something almost sinister about the lush greenery that made him wary, but, he realized, wariness was never going to get him anywhere with this crowd. Laser pistol in hand, he plunged into the grass after Lilith.

The grass blades were thick and rough, and they seemed to catch at his smart suit as he moved between them. If it had been tearing at flesh instead of smart clothing, he would have been full of scratches and cuts within moments as he followed Lilith.

He was tempted to cry out for her to slow down but decided to keep his breath for running. Even though the prince was running in low gravity, Lilith's gene-engineered body was uncatchable as she was spurred on, Kemal thought, by the idea that Barney and the others might be cheating her out of her revenge.

Within moments she was out of sight behind a tall, thick stand of bamboo. If not for the trail she'd made beating through the chest-high grass, Kemal would have lost her.

Kemal floundered on alone. He thought of skirting the bamboo, but Lilith's trail led right through it. He pushed into it determinedly and fought his way out into an open area that was so unexpected that he would have stumbled from lack of resistance if he hadn't run right into Lilith. She was standing on the edge of the clearing, her back to him, her feet braced wide.

She glanced over her shoulder at Kemal. When she spoke, her voice was curiously soft and calm. "I hope," she said, "that you're prepared to die."

Kemal looked beyond her. A tall man was standing in the center of the clearing. He had the Martian look about him, a sure, winning handsomeness that came from generations of breeding and more than one trip to the cosmetic surgeon. He wore a beard, which was rather unusual for a Martian, and a full suit of body armor. He carried a laser assault rifle. A dozen tall, lean creatures who looked as if they were ready for dinner surrounded him. Kemal and Lilith were to be the main entree.

The man didn't seem to notice Kemal, but rather stared at Lilith almost as hard as she stared at him.

"My dear," he finally said in a silky voice that was as menacing as Barney's deepest bluster. "How nice to see you again after all these years."

At that moment, Kemal had no doubt that they'd just found the master of the house and the CEO of the Dracolysk Corporation. It was Hugo Dracolysk himself.

CHAPTER TWELVE

Thinking quickly, Kemal reached into his belt pouch and drew out the RAM Internal Affairs ID plate.

"Internal Affairs, sir," he said, trying to sound respectful and authoritarian at the same time. "I've been on the trail of these space pirates for some time now—"

"Quite," Dracolysk said with a little smile of polite disbelief. "Your story would be more credible if your ID plate hadn't gone neg on you."

Kemal turned the plate's face toward him. Dracolysk was right. The damn thing had turned black, quite the opposite of a functioning ID plate. Whatever technological magic Quinto had worked on it to keep it alive had obviously run out.

There was a stirring in the pack of animals that had gathered around Dracolysk. Kemal had never seen their like before, but he realized immediately that they deserved his fear.

They were long, slender bipedal creatures, reptiles with a dash of bird about them. Most were about ten feet long from the tip of their powerfully jawed snouts to the end of their sinuous tails. They stood five feet tall on the average, and most looked as if they weighed between a hundred and a hundred and fifty pounds. Their skin was leathery like a reptile's, yet they also had feathery crests on the tops of their birdlike heads. They carried their small, weak fore-limbs folded close to their chests. Their hind legs were thick and powerful-looking, tipped with huge, razor-sharp sickle-shaped claws that looked as dangerous as anything Kemal had ever seen on an animal. Around their claws were cinched metal devices that must have kept them on the ground.

"Ah," Dracolysk said, "you're admiring my beauties." He reached out and put a gloved hand on the feathered crest of the creature nearest him and stroked it gently. It never took its unblinking eyes off Kemal. "They are something special. They were created by our genetic research branch." He looked at Lilith. "Something you should be familiar with, my dear."

Kemal saw her tense. He realized that she was about to throw herself at Dracolysk despite the fact that his reptilian hunters were ready to tear both intruders to bits. Kemal knew that they had to stall and hope that Barney and the others were somewhere close enough to come to their rescue.

"What are they?" he asked, winding a fist in the material of Lilith's suit, behind her back and out of Dracolysk's sight. Kemal doubted that he could hold her back if she really wanted to go for him, but he hoped that his touch might somehow calm her down. It might have worked. At any rate, she didn't go after Dracolysk. Not just yet.

"*Velociraptor antirrhopus*," Dracolysk said. He saw the blank look on Kemal's face. "One of the most feared predatory dinosaurs of the Early Cretaceous period of Old Earth," he explained.

"Those things are dinosaurs?" Kemal asked. "I thought dinosaurs were big, clumsy animals, slow and stupid—"

"You thought wrong," Dracolysk interrupted. "Dinosaurs came in many shapes, in every conceivable size. They were smart—especially the predators—sleek creatures, supremely adapted for survival. The *velociraptor* species existed relatively unchanged for fifty million years. Fifty million! That's over a thousand times longer than modern man. And *considerably* longer than *your* personal survival rate is likely to be.

"But, you," Dracolysk said, turning his attention to Lilith, "you, my dear, I still remember with a certain . . . fondness. It is good to see that you survived the troubles at Gorgon Station. And the intervening years have been good to you. It's hard to believe how long it's been since I held you in my arms."

Goaded beyond endurance, Lilith let out a long, keening wail of hate and leaped at her tormentor, dragging Kemal, who still had a hold on her suit.

Dracolysk, still smiling his sweet, hateful smile, extended a hand with a small electronic device in it. The thing was the size and general shape of a remote control unit for a tri-dee show viewer. He fingered a series of switches.

The velociraptors suddenly broke the bonds that had held them motionless, and with eerie, savage cries hurled themselves at Lilith and Kemal.

Lilith screamed back. It was hard to tell whose cry was more savage, hers or the predators'. As she sprung, she unsheathed her own wrist knives, longer and as deadly as the sickle-shaped claws the velociraptors carried on their hind legs.

In a flash of insight, Kemal realized that those hind legs were the creatures' main weapons. The tiny forelimbs folded up at their chests were puny compared to the powerful pistons of their rear legs. The size and shape of the forelimbs suggested that they were meant to grasp and hold while the great hind legs did all the damage.

Lilith crashed among the pack, ducking under the dinosaurs forepaws as they reached out for her, slashing at their soft underbellies and then moving out and away with the speed of a whirlwind. Then the rest of the pack engulfed Kemal, and he had no more time to worry about Lilith. He had his own survival to worry about.

The creatures were fast. They came at him bobbing

and weaving like boxers crazed on amphetamines. They were quicker than he was and probably stronger. The only thing he had going for him was his superior brain. He had to use it, or die.

He leaped straight up as they charged at him. The extremely weak gravity pulled feebly at him as the killer dinosaurs gaped stupidly at where he had just been standing. Prey had never acted like that before. They didn't know what to do.

Pushing off a tree trunk, Kemal finally came down, landing right on the back of one of the creatures. He encircled its rough throat with one strong arm, clamped his knees tightly to its side, and held on for dear life. The creature raised its short forepaws and waved them futilely in the air. It couldn't reach back to grab him with either forepaws or mouth. He was safe as long as he managed to hold on.

He drew his laser pistol with his free hand and snapped off two quick shots, drilling two of the dinosaurs neatly through their heads. Both stalked about jerkily for a few moments, not yet realizing they were dead despite the blood that gushed from the holes in their brains. Both finally fell as a third beast puzzled things out as well as its limited intellect allowed it to. It leaped upon Kemal's captive mount, flailing and kicking with its disemboweling hind claws.

Kemal's beast responded to the challenge with a roar and a flurry of kicks of its own, and Kemal decided that the best strategy might be to get off this particular creature and capture another. He slid off the predator's back just as it and its opponent crashed to the floor, rolling and kicking and tearing great gobbets of flesh from each other's unprotected stomachs.

Kemal spared Lilith a glance. She was surrounded by the beasts and covered in blood. Kemal couldn't tell how much of it was hers and how much of it belonged to the dinosaurs she was trying to cut through in a berserk attempt to get at Hugo Dracolysk.

Dracolysk was watching Lilith with fascination, as if utterly captivated by the violence that had erupted before him. Lilith, meanwhile, was battling with dogged determination to get through to him, as if equally captured by the thought of buying his life at the cost of her own.

She was, Kemal realized, never going to make it. Twice he watched velociraptor claws slice through her body armor and the flesh beneath, and it became all too apparent that not all the blood splashed on her body was her enemies'.

There was only one thing Kemal could do. Taking a running start, he leaped and launched himself on one of the beasts battling Lilith. He landed high on its back and pressed the muzzle of his laser pistol in its ear pit. He pulled the trigger, and the beast stiffened, turned, and crumpled to the ground, held there by the metal cinches around its claws. Kemal tried to get off but couldn't manage it in time.

The velociraptor crumpled heavily to its side, pinning Kemal beneath it. He kicked and struggled to get away as another of the predatory creatures loomed over him. He shot it in the belly, but that only seemed to make it angry. It trumpeted in rage and kicked at Kemal. He hid behind the body of the dinosaur he'd shot, which rocked at the power of the other's kick. It finally rolled over and freed Kemal, but it also knocked the pistol from his hand.

Kemal crouched on the ground. The dinosaur loomed over him like an avalanche of death ready to fall. Kemal knew he had no way to escape, knew he was dead as the predator came at him, huge jaws grinning wide with row upon row of sharp, gleaming teeth.

Then, somehow, Lilith was between them. She had broken through the circle of killers that surrounded her. Dracolysk stood to her right, fear contorting his face as he realized that Lilith now had a clear run at him. Kemal was to her left, crouched before the angry predator that was about to steamroll him. She had less than a second to decide what to do.

With a keening wail of hatred and frustration, she flung herself between Kemal and his nemesis.

The dinosaur changed targets as it pounced, and landed on Lilith instead of Kemal. She screamed as it ripped at her with its razor-sharp claws, tearing through her body armor as if it were tissue paper, scoring deeply into the flesh and organs underneath.

Kemal echoed Lilith's scream. He looked around desperately for something—a weapon, a stick, a rock, anything—to beat the dinosaur away from Lilith. What he saw was Hugo Dracolysk, staring at the horrific scene unfolding in front of him, a line of drool running unnoticed down the corner of his chin as he was mesmerized by the destruction he witnessed.

Kemal let loose a maddened howl of his own and sprung at Dracolysk. His muscles drove him far and hard against the nonexistent gravity. He struck his target full in the chest. Dracolysk catapulted backward, dropping the device that controlled the dinosaurs. He scrabbled for the laser pistol in the holster at his belt.

"You fool!" he screeched at Kemal. "I'm not invisible to them outside the suppressor field!"

Thanks, Kemal thought, that's all I needed to know.

He dove after the control box as Dracolysk snapped off a shot at him. A bolt of energy burned across Kemal's forehead and, for a second, everything went blank. He struck the ground with numbing force. But then his eyes came back into focus. He reached out and grabbed the control device as another energy beam seared the air before his face.

Worry first about the dinosaurs, Kemal told himself, then Dracolysk. He staggered toward Lilith and dove over her prone body. The velociraptor had drawn back to nurse the belly wounds Lilith had inflicted with her wrist blades, and as Kemal cradled her bloodied form, the dinosaur suddenly lost interest in them. It was almost as if they weren't there anymore.

That left only one immediate and visible target for the four remaining velociraptors, and they closed on Hugo Dracolysk like the fearsome hunters they were.

Dracolysk screamed and turned his pistol from Lilith and Kemal to his pets. He managed to bring one of them down, but the others were ready to swarm over him like ants at a picnic.

With a final curse, Dracolysk holstered his pistol and jammed his hands into the pockets of his smart suit.

"You'll pay for this, damn you!" he screeched, as he rose swiftly in the air above the snapping jaws of the dinosaurs.

Damn! Kemal thought. Dracolysk was wearing a jet pack. Now all he had to do was hover out of reach of his rapacious pets and pick off Lilith and Kemal at his leisure.

Dracolysk seemed to realize that as well. With a sneer on his handsome features, he drew his laser pistol and ignored the capering predators snapping futilely at his feet. "Good-bye, whoever you are," he said, and rose higher into the air to get a better aim at Kemal.

Kemal drew Lilith closer. A lush artificial jungle seemed a strange place to die for one born on Mercury, but it would do. It would do all too well.

Kemal stared defiantly at Dracolysk, but the sudden, shuddering moan of a bolt rifle caused Dracolysk to lose aim and concentration. A stream of projectiles battered him, tossing him in the air like a bird buffeted in an unexpected windstorm. Dracolysk's armored smart clothes blocked the slivers of steel, causing them to splatter harmlessly away, but Dracolysk knew that he was an easy floating target for whatever other weapons his other assailants had.

With an angry howl, Dracolysk decided that discretion was the better part of valor. He shot Kemal a look of pure hatred, jammed the thruster on his jet pack, and disappeared in a blur, leaving another stream of bolts to splatter harmlessly in his wake.

Lilith, breathing heavily, looked to the sky. "I can't see very well," she said in a husky voice. "Did they get him?"

"Yes," Kemal lied, cradling her head on his chest. He couldn't bear to look at the awful wounds on her abdomen, afraid to even try to staunch the flow of blood bubbling up from them. "Dracolysk is dead."

"Good," she said. She looked up at Kemal, though he wasn't sure that she could see him through the haze clouding her eyes.

"You'll be all right," he said. "Barney will be here soon."

She laughed, then choked on the pain. "I've been around death long enough to know when it's come for me." She raised a hand to touch Kemal's face and frowned at the gory dagger protruding from her wrist. She sheathed it, then gently put her hand on Kemal's cheek, leaving bloody fingerprints on his skin. "It's only what I deserve," she said. "Sorry . . . sorry I never got the chance to know you better. I would have liked that."

"So would I," Kemal whispered, but he didn't think she heard.

Her hand became limp in the air, and he gently closed her staring eyes. He sat in the dirt and blood and held her. This was so unlike the death he was used to, the clean death in space, where opponents were blown to sterile molecules by a blast from energy weapons. This was dirty and a lot more personal. He looked down at Lilith, remembered her kiss and the warmth of her lithe body. Now she was dead.

He held back tears as he cradled her cooling corpse, waiting for Barney and the others.

They arrived within moments. The combined firepower of the three clone-warriors blew the milling velociraptors to pieces in no time.

The three surveyed the scene wordlessly. They looked a little battered themselves, the result of their battle with Dracolysk's Desert Runner bodyguards in another area of the eco-chamber, but nothing like Kemal. Or Lilith.

"Dracolysk?" Barney rumbled.

Kemal nodded. "He got away."

The space pirate booted a severed velociraptor head like a soccer ball deep into the jungle. "He'll rot in hell forever, when I'm done with him," he said as the beast's head arced away to float in the foliage.

Kemal stood stiffly. "Help me with Lilith," he said.

"Leave her," Barney responded brusquely.

Kemal turned on him, but Khan caught his arm.

"Leave her," he said, a trace of gentleness in his voice. "This place will be her pyre."

He nodded to Quinto, who kneeled and placed half a dozen powerful explosive charges about her, enough to take out the entire top of the pyramid.

Kemal saw that this would be a just ending for the clone-warrior, and he nodded. "All right," he said.

Huer blipped into existence via Kemal's uplink unit. He took in the scene but said nothing about Lilith. Instead, he reported to Kemal, "I've found the skimmer pad. It's a straight shot from here. Should be no problem to get there. I opened the other dinosaur pens and everyone is now . . . occupied."

"Let's go," Kemal said.

"And one more thing," Huer added. "I finally tracked down the catalog entry for the crystalline flower on display in the gallery."

"And?" Kemal prompted savagely, in no mood for further games.

"And," Huer said, "it originated on your home planet. It came from Mercury."

CHAPTER THIRTEEN

C haos engulfed the Dracolysk arcology like an
unstoppable tsunami. Kemal and the others
were hardly noticed in the wild anarchy
through which they passed. The crazed viral program had battalions of workers roaming through the
halls, painting furiously, moving furniture, tearing
down walls, and generally creating an uproar that
the wild-eyed supervisory personnel had no chance of
reining in. Firefights broke out as squads of security
men were given conflicting orders, or their ser-
geants, rightfully suspicious of the orders issuing
from their heretofore reliable computers, tried to
take things into their own hands—and only made
matters worse.

Kemal and the Barneys weren't the only ones

heading for the skimmer pad. Many of the top executives had decided to run for it, deserting the arcology like rats fleeing a foundering ship.

The confusion at the pad provided more than enough cover for the party's escape. Kemal and the others found new pressure suits and put them on, then patiently waited their turn for a skimmer among the increasingly panicked crowd. No one questioned their right to be there. No one was about to question such a grim-looking, heavily armed party.

Kemal took the controls as they piled into a skimmer and rolled out of the airlock. Barney, sharing the front seat with Kemal, turned and looked at Quinto, who was crammed into the back with Khan.

"Blow the explosives," Barney said.

"Way ahead of you, pilgrim," Quinto replied. He was already holding the detonator in his hand, thumb poised above the protruding red button. He depressed it just as they cleared the airlock.

They couldn't hear the explosion that took the top off the Dracolysk arcology, but the concussion waves caused by air blowing out into the surrounding vacuum buffeted the skimmer for a few moments. Kemal fought for and gained control of the vehicle, then turned back and looked over his shoulder.

Khan, Kemal reflected, had been right. The pyramid made a fine funeral pyre for Lilith. It looked like a Viking ship on its way to Valhalla. Wherever Lilith was going, heaven or hell or a special purgatory reserved for clones—which, after all, many eminent

theologians argued were nothing but soulless autom-
atons anyway—she wasn't journeying alone this
night.

Kemal swooped over to where they had parked the
hidden skimmers that had brought them to the arcology. He landed. "Well," he said, "what now?"

"I'm afraid my part in this little play is finished,"
Khan said. "Not that it hasn't been very entertain-
ing. It's also given me ideas for several very interesting articles that scores of scholarly journals will be
clamoring to publish once I write them. But I'm
afraid the new semester starts within the week. My
sabbatical's nearly over and it's back to explaining
the fine points of Nietzsche to a pack of dullards." He
clapped Barney on the shoulder. The space pirate
spared a moment from his intense scrutiny of the
burning Dracolysk arcology.

"Farewell, brother," Khan said. "Call me again if
you ever throw another party like this one."

Barney only grunted. He had no patience for fine
speeches or farewells. Besides, he was still enthralled by the spectacle of Dracolysk's downfall.

Khan nodded at Quinto, who grinned back, and
then turned to Kemal. "Farewell, little brother," he
said. "Don't mourn long for Lilith. She died a fitting
death, pursuing her heart's desire. Who could ask for
more?"

Kemal shook his head, not quite convinced. "If you
say so."

Khan grinned, popped into the skimmer's airlock,
and exited. He boarded the first skimmer and fired

up the engine.

"Quite a fellow," Quinto said. He rummaged through a rucksack stuffed full of ancient, valuable, and portable pieces of art he'd managed to snatch from the gallery as they made their escape from the doomed Dracolysk arcology. "Well, pilgrims, I'm off, too. Can I drop you anywhere?" he asked as he hefted his bag of precious masterpieces.

"No," Barney said, without looking at him.

"Okay," Quinto said. He turned to Kemal. "I hate these mushy good-bye scenes," he said, and exited to the other skimmer they'd arrived in. Both flew off into the night.

Kemal and Black Barney watched Dracolysk burn for a little while longer until the emergency crews succeeded on cutting off the atmosphere to the damaged area. Kemal was warm in his heated smart suit, but he still felt cold inside at the thought of Lilith's death. In the short time he'd known her, he'd realized that beneath the plastic and steel there had been a warm and sensitive . . . person.

The arcology's summit was all ashes now, drifting away on the sterile solar winds.

Kemal had been acting out of an abstract belief in justice and right. Now he wanted to see the creators of the laser device pay for their crimes. It all suddenly had become very personal to Kemal.

"It seems to me," Kemal said thoughtfully, "that we've got two choices. Huer said the crystals came from Mercury. We could go there and investigate. Or, now that we know its name, we could go to this Rising Sun Station. . . ."

He let his voice run down as he thought about it. He hadn't been on his home planet in quite some time. And even then, it hadn't seemed like home since his father's death. It particularly hadn't seemed like home during his last visit, when his uncle Gordon had introduced him to one of Mercury Prime's least-known dungeons.

Kemal realized he was glad, in a way, that the trail also led away from Mercury. He didn't like being there. He didn't like what was left of his family, and he didn't like thinking about what it might be like if his parents were still alive. And the old saying was true. Out of sight, out of mind. When he wasn't there, he didn't think about it.

Still, it was difficult to keep turning his back on the place he was born. And it was nearly impossible to stop thinking about all the people—friends, foes, and even those totally indifferent to Kemal Gavilan and his fate—who lived there.

"Hugo Dracolysk?" Barney asked. "Where?"

Kemal considered the question. "Well, I don't think he'd flee to Rising Sun Station. On the other hand, it's the only lead we have that seems remotely possible. It's *really* unlikely that he would go to Mercury."

Barney growled, showing his teeth in a savage grin that was anger unslaked by the carnage at the Dracolysk arcology. "We go to Rising Sun."

* * * * *

Kemal discovered that the shortest distance between two points often was not a straight line. In this case, the line between Ceres and Rising Sun Station took a jag, leading them back once again to Barbarosa and Dead Man's Hand.

Nothing but the players had changed in the casino. Kemal followed in Barney's wake as the pirate pushed impatiently through the crowd. Gordo, Carp's bodyguard, was ensconced in his usual place.

"Fish room or office?" Barney growled.

"Office," the guard replied, and Kemal and Barney went to the end of the hall, where Barney knocked loudly, once, on the closed door, and pushed it open.

Carp was seated at his desk, admiring a new print that he'd apparently just acquired.

"Just in time," Carp said, holding it up to be admired. It was a print of a small boy standing on a rock and looking down into water that held a very big fish. "It's from Old Earth, nineteenth century Japan. It was done by a master woodblock artist named Yoshitoghi and was part of a series of woodblocks called *Thirty-Six Ghosts*—"

"Nice," Barney said. "Not here to look at pictures."

Carp sighed. "Always the impetuous one. Well, what do you want this time?"

"Ever hear of a Belt research station called Rising Sun?" Kemal asked.

Carp pursed his lips and shook his head. "Not offhand, but that's not really very surprising. There are tens of thousands of small colonies, businesses, and scientific stations in the Belt."

"This one has connections with Dracolysk," added Kemal.

"Dracolysk, eh?" Carp commented. "This affair wouldn't have anything to do with the Dracolysk arcology on Ceres burning two days ago, would it?"

"No," Barney said, deadpan.

"Hmmm," Carp said. "What exactly do you want with this Rising Sun, anyway?"

"Oh," Barney said with what he fondly believed was great casualness. "We want to get him inside." He nudged Kemal and sent him staggering. "Let him have a look around."

"Well," Carp said, "I'm sure I'll have some information on Rising Sun in my files. Perhaps we can discover who's been delivering supplies to the station, and get your man on the ship's crew. Then it would be up to him."

Barney and Kemal looked at each other. Kemal nodded. "Sounds like a good plan."

Carp glanced at his thumbwatch. "Almost dinner time. Tell you what. If you want to stay and relate any slight details you may have heard about Dracolysk's demise, I'll have one of my men go through my files. If this Rising Sun Station is operating in the Belt, I should know something about it. We should have results by the end of the meal."

"Okay," Kemal said. "Sounds good."

"Fine." Carp carefully placed his print in a desk drawer and stood.

"What's for dinner, anyway?" Barney asked.

"Broiled fish?"

Carp looked at them aghast, while Barney made grinding noises deep in his throat that indicated he'd made one of his rare—and always so successful— jokes.

* * * * *

Dinner turned out to be fresh—irradiated, not frozen—real beefsteaks imported all the way from Earth and served with fried Venusian bog potatoes. It was quite tasty, though Barney was more than a little annoyed that Carp didn't stock the pirate's favorite brand of ginger beer. After Carp first pumped them about the destruction of the Dracolysk arcology, he regaled them with goldfish stories. Interesting at first, monotonous by desert, they made Kemal glad when one of Carp's servants interrupted. He came in, placed a sheaf of papers by Carp's elbow, bowed respectfully, and left them to finish their multiflavored balls of sherbet banded with different colors to resemble miniature Jupiters.

"Success," Carp said, leafing through the papers left by his steward. "A shipment of supplies is due to leave Barbarosa tomorrow for Rising Sun Station on the contract hauler *Merry Widow*, captained by owner-operator Captain Quillan." He read farther down the sheet. "Even better news. Captain Quillan has apparently hired a new pilot for the trip. His name is Con Smythe."

"Where is this Smythe?" Kemal asked.

Carp leaned back in his chair and patted his full stomach. "Well," he said, "I *may* be able to track him down for you, but it seems to me that you're getting a little more information than you've traded for."

Barney leaned forward. "We'll owe you," he said between clenched teeth.

"Ahem. Well, I suppose you're good for it. Smythe's playing Planetary Roulette in my casino at this very moment. And," Carp added, frowning darkly, "he's winning heavily."

Barney pushed away from the table and stood up with a stomach full of beefsteak and bog potatoes. "We'll do something about that."

"Nothing too permanent," Kemal cautioned the space pirate.

"Few days of amnesia," Barney growled.

"All right."

Carp stood with them. "Now that we've eaten, perhaps you'd—"

"We'll look at fish some other time," Barney said. "Too busy."

"Too busy," Kemal echoed to a disappointed Carp as Barney dragged the prince away.

"Good thing we got out of there," Barney said. "Next thing we knew, he'd have had us feeding his slimy things worms. Ugh." The space pirate shivered at the thought.

Con Smythe looked like a veteran Belter. He wasn't much older than Kemal, but his face was as craggy as the surface of an asteroid and he was deeply tanned from unshielded exposure to radiation. His sparse hair was a pale, whitish blond.

Kemal and Barney had shadowed Smythe as he played at the Planetary Roulette table at Dead Man's Hand. Smythe's luck was good, and he left the table with his pockets bulging. Kemal had been about to follow him when he felt Barney's steely fingers on his shoulder.

"Snatchers," Barney said in a low voice.

Thieves. They would wait until Smythe was done playing, until he had cashed in his chips, then follow him into some dark corridor and take his loot. The Belter's attackers were indeed quick and smooth. Kemal, who knew what to look for, saw that one had emptied Smythe's pockets before the other had eased the pilot's limp body to the concourse floor.

"Those guys stole Smythe's money," said Kemal.

Barney looked down at him. "So?"

"So we're going to let them get away with it?"

"Why not? They did us a favor. Besides," Barney added as he strode on, effortlessly carrying the pilot over his shoulder, "we're going to steal his ID papers."

A crowd had gathered by the time Barney and Kemal had reached the pilot.

"Make way!" Barney said, and when Barney spoke, people listened. "What happened?" he growled, kneeling down by the fallen pilot.

One of the snatchers glanced up into Barney's eyes and didn't like what he saw. "Well, I don't know, sir," he said, the "sir" automatically coming to his lips at the sight of Barney. "This fellow just collapsed, and I caught him. Uh, do you know him?"

"Shipmate," Barney said briefly as Kemal also knelt, then felt for Smythe's pulse. It was there, sluggish but steady.

"Well, uh," the snatcher said, realizing that something was wrong but not quite understanding what, "you'll want to be taking him to the doc's then?"

"Good idea," Barney said. He stood, reached down with one hand, and casually slung Smythe's limp body over his shoulder. "Thanks," the pirate said in a voice as cold as a Plutonian snow field.

"Uh, sure," the snatcher said, then melted into the surrounding crowd that already had claimed his partner.

"Let me through," Barney said lowly, and the crowd parted before him like the Red Sea before Moses.

Barney had picked off the pilot as easily as the snatchers had lifted his purse. Kemal trotted by his side as the pirate strode off.

CHAPTER FOURTEEN

They spent the time they had left on the *Free Enterprise* disguising Kemal and preparing him for his role as Con Smythe, Belter pilot.

They dyed Kemal's dark skin darker and his hair lighter, fitted him with a light-colored false beard, and gave him a prominent cheek tattoo in semipermanent ink. The tattoo was a skull transfixed by a lighting bolt, the sigil of the Hell's Belters, a noted gang of toughs and hellions scattered throughout the asteroids. No one, figured Barney, questioned a Heller too closely about his past, and the fewer questions Kemal had to answer, the better.

The whole disguise had been Barney's idea. Kemal wasn't exactly Buck Rogers, famous throughout the system, but he had been somewhat prominent during the Martian Wars and he *was* a Gavilan.

After being caught in Ferdenko's apartment, Kemal decided that at times it was better to be cautious than overly self-confident. He didn't want to be found out before he could discover anything meaningful about Rising Sun Station.

"The *Free Enterprise* will be on your trail," Barney said gruffly. "But calling us in will blow your cover, so if you yelp to us, it had better be for something important."

With Barney's warm send-off still ringing in his ears, Kemal made his way through the Barbarosa spacedocks, where he was to report to Captain Quillan of the *Merry Widow*, which was docked at Berth Ninety-two.

The slip was easy to find in the well-organized chaos of the docks. In fact, it wasn't far from the *Free Enterprise*. Kemal, at Berth Ninety-two, stopped and stared in dismay at the thing docked there. Even though Kemal had fought with NEO—an organization not known for having the most modern equipment—in the Martian Wars, he had never seen such a disreputable pile of rusty junk in his life.

The *Merry Widow* looked at least eighty years old—which was about fifty years longer than the average Belter ship lasted. And it looked as if it had gone through a *hard* eighty years. The hull was dented and battered by collisions with stray rocks and pitted with rust and cosmic ray damage. More than one repair plate had been welded to the hull, and some of the exposed pieces of communication and astrogation gear looked older—though that seemed hardly possible—than the main body of the decrepit tub itself.

Well, Kemal told himself, welcome to the Belt. People out here weren't rich. They used things until they wore out. Sometimes they continued to use them even after they wore out.

He went to the open entrance hatch and shouted, "Ahoy the ship! Permission to enter."

He heard his words echo eerily up the hollow central axis of the craft and there was a long silence. For a moment he thought no one was at home, then finally a deep voice bellowed, "Come on in! Wipe yer feet first!"

Sure enough, there was a battered and worn welcome mat, stained with the dust and grime of an unknowable number of planets, moons, and Belt rocks, placed right before the entrance hatch.

Kemal hitched up his space-duffle, obediently wiped his feet clean, and started to climb up the central shaft, balancing his bag over his shoulder.

The interior of the *Merry Widow* was completely opposite its outward appearance. It was old-fashioned but spotless, with everything carefully mended and precisely put in its proper place. It almost could have been a museum dedicated to the space-faring life of the last century. Although it cheered Kemal somewhat that he wouldn't be trapped in something that smelled like a garbage scow and looked worse, he still was disconcerted by the patched appearance of the antique instrumentation he passed as he made his way up to the control room, the craft's foremost cabin.

"Con Smythe, reporting for duty," he announced formally at the entrance to the control room, standing laxly at half-attention.

"Come in, come in," said a low, gravelly voice, the same one that had bid him enter the ship and wipe his feet. "We don't stand much on ceremony around here," it added.

"Yes . . . sir," he said, crossing into the room and staring at its only occupant.

"Call me Captain Quillan," she said, "or call me Mom if yer want. It's all the same with me."

She—Kemal guessed that she was a she—sat at the astrogation table, figuring a course. She was so short that her stubby legs swung several inches clear of deck. She was so wide that her broad behind fit snugly in a chair built big enough to seat behemoths. Her hair was mostly hidden under a battered captain's cap. What little Kemal could see was gray. Her face was—to be kind—chubby, with round, apple-red cheeks, multiple chins, a pug nose, and more lines and wrinkles on it than a folded astrogator's map. The stub of a cigar was clamped firmly in the corner of her mouth.

She looked about three times older than her ship.

"Shut yer mouth, sonny," she said, glancing up at him. "Yer gonna catch all the flies if yer leave yer jaw hangin' open like that."

"Yes, Mom," Kemal said, calling her by the first name that popped into his head.

"Now, I'm not gonna have trouble with yer, am I, sonny?" she said, scrutinizing him.

"Trouble?"

"Yer not the type has trouble takin' orders from a woman, are yer?"

"Uh, not at all," Kemal said hastily.

"Good. Last pee-lot I had was an ornery cuss. Always questionin' my orders. Had to beat him across the chops a few times jus' to show him who's boss on the *Widow*."

Kemal must have goggled, because she looked at him severely. "Don't think I could do it, sonny?"

"No, it's not that exactly—"

"Wall, I've buried seven husbands already. Lookin' fer number eight right now." She squinted, looking at him closely. "Say, yer not too bad on the old eyes. Interested?"

"Uh—"

She waved it off. "Wall, don't worry about that now. We got plenty of time to get to know each other. It's four days to the Rising Sun."

She hopped down off the astrogator's chair. She was, Kemal saw, less than five feet tall and as broadly built as a weight lifter. Her cigar smelled worse than a Venusian acid bog. She waddled forward with the spacer's habitual rolling gait, her sturdy magnetized boots clicking against the deck, and stared closely at Kemal, focusing on the tattoo seared into his cheek right above the beard line.

"Say, Hell's Belters, huh?"

Kemal drew up to his full height and put on his best

sneer. "You got something against the Hellers?"

Mom Quillan shook her head. "Nope. Third husband was one. But he got kicked out fer bein' too mean." She shook her head in fond remembrance. "He was a real darlin', he was. Cute as a button. Like you."

"Uh, thanks."

She nodded. "Yer bunk's on next level down, port side." She went by, patting his rear as she did. "Yer know, we're gonna get on jest fine, I think. Jest fine."

Kemal sighed. Good thing the trip to Rising Sun was only going to last four days.

* * * * *

It was a long four days.

Mom—that is, Captain—Quillan ran a tight ship despite its shabby outer appearance. She was the captain and astrogator. It was an unusual shipboard combination, but apparently she'd inherited the ship from her first husband, who had been the *Widow*'s original captain-owner. She'd been astrogator first mate and approximately fifty years younger than her husband, who hadn't outlasted their maiden voyage together. She renamed his ship, took over the hauling business, and embarked on a long but not very successful career punctuated by a series of short, not very successful marriages to a number of younger and younger men. It wasn't that she was getting rid of her husbands in any criminal manner. She was just extremely unlucky in her choice of spouses. They seemed to expire with amazing regularity under all kinds of incredible circumstances.

Number two died of a heart attack after striking the million-to-one hand at the Rocket to the Stars game in Dead Man's Hand. Unfortunately for Mom, a whole army of creditors and tax men immediately arrived on the scene, leaving her just about enough dolarubes to bury him.

Numbers three and four both died when the ventilator units on their spacesuits jammed, leaving them stranded outside the ship as they tried to make repairs.

Number five was drilled between the eyes by a micrometeorite as he was sprucing up the hull's paint job during a slow afternoon when he had nothing better to do, hence Mom's continuing superstition about not maintaining the outside of the ship.

Number six, her first non-spaceman husband, a writer, had an electrifying accident in the bathtub with his lap-top computer.

The stories all had blended together by the end of the first day, when Kemal had heard each of them five or six times. By then, he was just nodding and mumbling and avoiding the captain's roving hands as best he could.

The other crew members were longtime *Widow* sailors. They all were used to Mom's eccentricities and functioned fairly well as a crew. They had to in space, or else they wouldn't last very long. They weren't surprised to see a new pilot, either. Apparently most pilots, a congenitally headstrong lot to start with, were either driven crazy by Mom's odd habits or driven off by her continual proposals. It seemed that Mom still had a soft spot in her heart for husband number one, and she hit on rocketjocks whenever she had the chance.

The eccentricities of life aboard the *Merry Widow* all were calculated to drive Kemal nuts, from Mom's checking behind his ears as they sat down to dinner, to the ancient though well-maintained equipment he was forced to deal with, to Mom's continual romantic suggestions.

Add to all this an increasing inner tension, which Kemal couldn't afford to show, as they approached Rising Sun Station, and it became a nerve-racking journey through the Belt that Kemal would just as soon never repeat again.

Rising Sun Station itself was a big disappointment, but Kemal kept an eye on it as he maneuvered the antiquated *Widow* through its docking procedure with the rock. His initial visual inspection revealed nothing of interest. The station seemed to be drilled into the heart of a smallish, barren, and totally dull rock floating in an eccentric orbit out on the very edge of the Belt. The crystal farm revealed by Ferdenko's log was nowhere to be seen. The installation itself, if Kemal could judge from the brief glimpses he got while maneuvering the *Merry Widow* into one of its two docking platforms, was like hundreds of other small, nondescript research stations scattered throughout the Belt.

There was nothing to indicate the sudden death

that had struck the industrial spy so unexpectedly, so violently, only a few weeks before.

"Good job," Mom Quillan told Kemal after he'd nudged the *Merry Widow* into its berth without a noticeable jolt. "Yer got good, strong hands."

"Thanks," he said tersely. Terseness was the newest defense he'd adopted against her continual compliments, suggestions, and indecent proposals.

He stood, yawned, and stretched like a cat. Now that the ship was docked, his job was done. His apparent job, that is. Now his real work could begin in earnest.

"Think I'll take a spin around the rock," he informed Mom, the only other member of the *Merry Widow*'s bridge crew, "and see what there is to see. I'd like to feel solid ground under my feet again, not metal."

The captain shook her head. "Can't," she said.

Kemal looked at her and raised an eyebrow. "Why not? They doing something secret on this godforsaken piece of dirt whirling around the middle of nowhere?"

She shrugged. "Guess so," the captain said. "They've asked us not to leave the ship."

"Haven't you wondered what's going on out there?" Kemal asked.

"It's none of my business," Mom said. "They want to keep secrets, it's fine with me. Say, I ever tell you 'bout the time me and my fourth husband—he was the pigsmear pro—tried to open up a pigsmear franchise on Venus?"

"Only five or six times," Kemal muttered under his breath.

"What'd you say?"

"I have to go to the head," he lied, and scooted off the control deck.

Besides escaping Mom Quillan, Kemal realized that this was also the perfect time to try a secret reconnaissance of Rising Sun Station. It was also the only time he'd have to try it, because Mom had told him right before docking that they were scheduled to lift off in four hours.

The *Widow*'s other two crewmen, Graystock, the engine man, and Simpson, the freighter, were busy unloading the supplies—foodstuffs, mechanical parts, and an asteroid tractor—that Mom was ferrying to Rising Sun. Kemal easily sneaked through one of the hull access ports on the side of the ship opposite the freight bay and moved off unseen into the darkness of the poorly lighted dock. His boots kept him securely on the ground.

From his vantage point deep in the shadows Kemal could see that freight handlers from Rising Sun were helping the *Widow*'s crew with the unloading, but two men also stood, laser rifles in hand, supervising.

Kemal figured they also were keeping an eye out for anyone—like him—trying to sneak off the ship. But security was lax. Supply ships probably had landed scores of times on Rising Sun without incident, and what once had been vigilant security had grown careless until the men were only going through rote, meaningless ritual.

Kemal scuttled off without a sound. Now, if he only had some faint idea of the station's floor plan. Carp hadn't been able to help in that regard.

Rising Sun apparently had been built by workers imported by Dracolysk, or whoever was running the research group. No outside help had been used. Neither were any outsiders currently manning the station. In that regard, security remained tight. Whatever was going on was definitely an in-house project. Ferdenko had found out the hard way just how much they wanted to keep things to themselves.

Kemal had a sudden thought. From the *Widow*'s viewscreens he'd had a long-range view of the asteroid within which Rising Sun was built. They'd been so far away that Kemal hadn't been able to discern any distinguishing details, but like many rocks, the asteroid had a bloated pumpkin-seed shape. They'd flashed over one of the long surfaces before docking, and Kemal hadn't seen anything remotely resembling the crystal farm depicted in Ferdenko's log. The bright light towers, for example, would have been immediately obvious.

Therefore, it had to be on the opposite surface of the asteroid.

Ferdenko had approached the farm from the surface and that approach had spelled disaster for the industrial spy. Kemal decided to try to go through the rock's interior and come at the farm from underneath.

He was bound to run into more people using that route, but, in the long run, that might even be for the best. He could hide among people. On the surface, he'd be alone and isolated, like an insect crawling on a blanket, just waiting for an obliterating fist to come down and squash him.

Just like Ferdenko.

CHAPTER FIFTEEN

Kemal moved away from the docking area using poorly lit service corridors that, luckily for him, were devoid of traffic. It was evident from signs all about him that Rising Sun had been built recently. In this part of the station, little attention had been paid to the finishing details. Wires ran up near the ceiling side-by-side with undisguised conduit. The corridors themselves, most cut through the rock of the asteroid, had a rough, unpolished feel about them, with blast marks and chisel gouges still quite obvious. All in all, it seemed that Rising Sun had been thrown together in some haste, and there were few indications that the builders intended it to be a permanent facility meant for years and years of use.

Adjacent to the docking area Kemal stumbled into a locker room apparently designed for the use of dock personnel. There was a large hamper net of greasy, dirty coveralls, and—much to Kemal's delight—another hamper full of clean, folded coveralls identical to the ones worn by the station personnel that he'd seen helping the *Widow*'s crew unload supplies.

Kemal quickly stripped off his pilot jumpsuit, balled it up, and stashed it at the bottom of the hamper net containing the dirty coveralls. He found a clean pair in his size, climbed into them, and was just sealing the crotch-to-chest zipper when he heard the locker room door bang open. Half a dozen men sauntered in, grousing tiredly among themselves about work, boredom, work, bosses, and work.

Kemal glanced around the room, but there was nowhere for him to hide. He silently fingered the small laser pistol that he'd transferred into the coverall's pocket along with his uplink unit. The workers were sure to realize that he was an outsider. A station this size had no more than a hundred crew members, all of whom had to know each other at least a little. Kemal had no stomach for wholesale slaughter, but it looked as if he might have to kill everyone if he wanted to escape the locker room with his cover intact. He took a deep breath and waited, the hand in his pocket clutching the butt of the laser gun.

The workers came into the main body of the locker room in a loose knot. All looked tired and dirty, smudged with grease from packing cases and the residual construction dust that tended to gather in outer tunnels and corridors, which had little or no air-conditioning.

The man in the lead was complaining about the poor quality and minute quantity of beer that the *Widow* had brought this trip. He saw Kemal standing in the middle of the locker room floor, stopped, and nodded.

"Who're you?" he asked wearily as he slumped on a bench in front of a locker.

He didn't seem very alarmed at Kemal's presence. Maybe, Kemal thought, just maybe he'd be able to bluff his way through this.

"Smythe. Con Smythe," he said, starting toward the door.

The man reached into his overall breast pocket and pulled out a pack of cigarettes. He put one in his mouth, inhaled sharply, then more smoothly as the self-igniter lit.

"You one of the new boys just come in on the *Glory Bound*?" the freight handler asked.

"That's right," Kemal said, somehow managing to keep the smile off his face.

The freighter grunted. "An eager beaver," he said to his companions. A few laughed, but most just slumped wearily in front of their own lockers.

Kemal did not reply. Instead, he walked past the bored and tired men. He could feel every pair of eyes following his progress, most listless, but one or two bright with interest. He breathed a sigh of relief when he had put a bank of lockers between them. He went through a door and found himself in an anteroom. To the left were two cubical offices, the desks piled high with papers and tapes. One office was dark, but a light shone in another, and the click of computer keys told him someone was hard at work. To the right was a single door. Kemal turned the handle carefully, to find pitch blackness inside. He did not search for the light.

He stepped inside, checked the lock to be sure it did not engage automatically, and closed the door as carefully as he had opened it. Then he fumbled for the manually operated light. For an instant the glare blinded his eyes. He then saw that he was in a storeroom—perfect for his purposes.

"Doc!" he said softly into his uplink unit.

Huer popped into existence, appearing to lean casually against a shelf. "You called?" he asked.

Keman nodded. "I need readouts of the station. Access routes to the crystal beds."

Huer smiled. "You don't ask for much, do you? This place has enough security blocks to choke a mainframe, especially on the administrative levels."

"All I need is a physical layout of the station and your best guess," Kemal said.

"That's possible." Huer's eyes went vague, as they always did when he was probing a computer system for data.

Minutes ticked by and still Huer's face was blank. Kemal, more and more nervous, kept one ear to the door. The longer he stayed in one place, the greater his chances of being discovered. Finally Huer blinked.

"You're going to have to run some tough security, but I think I can breech it . . . one step at a time."

"Where to?" asked Kemal.

"First we've got to clear this level. We can communicate through the uplink's viewscreen. It's too small to display complicated messages, but I should be able to guide you left and right, up and down, and the like. I show a corridor in front of this sector. Turn left." Huer winked out of sight.

Kemal, glad for action, opened the door.

". . . two days a week off on-station, but no one gets to leave the rock for the whole year. No one with our security clearance, anyway."

Kemal froze, leaving the door open in a hairline crack. Hastily, he killed the lights.

"Security around here is tighter than a Lunan with a dolarube, Keppel. You knew that when you signed on."

"I'm sick of it. Nothing to do but work, nothing to eat but synthetic slop, and nothing to drink worth drinking."

"Good pay, though."

"Sunflowers!" snarled the first man. "Hoo-ha over a bunch of crystals . . ."

The voices faded and were cut off abruptly as the two men went into an office and closed the door. Kemal slipped out of the storage closet and entered the corridor turning left, his blood racing. Sunflowers! He was on the right trail.

Kemal checked his thumbwatch. There were still three hours until the *Merry Widow* was scheduled for lift-off, but Mom could notice that he was missing at any time. He reached the end of the corridor. "Now where?" he hissed into his uplink.

"Right," said Huer, his voice muted.

Kemal followed Huer's directions, trying to look as if he belonged to the purposeful throng. This corridor was busier. He nodded curtly to a man who waved at him as he passed.

"There he is," the prince heard a voice say.

Kemal turned to see the voluble freight handler from the locker room pointing at him. The freighter was accompanied by two men with sidearms in button-down waist holsters.

"—looked strange," Kemal heard him say. "He said he came in on the *Glory Bound*, but her workers are all assigned."

The security men started toward Kemal. He was in for it now. There was only one thing to do. He ran.

"Hey!" one of guards shouted, but Kemal already had bolted through the door in the rec room's far wall.

He skidded down a corridor and raced past a pair of astonished men in lab coats. Alarms suddenly started blaring in the corridor from unseen speakers, followed by a shockingly familiar voice that almost stunned Kemal.

"Security alert! Security alert! This is Commander Gavilan. There is an intruder loose in the station! Repeat! There is an intruder loose in the station! He is tall, bearded, and dressed in orange workman's coveralls. Repeat, orange workman's coveralls."

It was his cousin, Dalton Gavilan! Was his planet—his *family*—involved with the development of the laser device? He knew that the Sun Flowers had originated on Mercury, but he had never suspected his own family of involvement in this weapons factory. The thought of his uncle Gordon—and worse, Gordon's son Dalton—with all that power made Kemal sick. Gordon was a despot, but he was relatively unambitious and seemed satisfied by his role as Mercurian Sun King.

Dalton, on the other hand, was a merciless, sadistic maniac who would like nothing better than to have the entire system goose-stepping to his tune. What he would do with a weapon like the laser device was almost unthinkable. Gordon, of course, was now around to control him, but Gordon wouldn't last forever. Dalton was so ambitious that Gordon, in fact, might even have an accident someday.

An accident. Like Ossip . . .

The thought struck Kemal like a thunderbolt, making his stomach flip around like the first time he'd done a complete loop in a skyplane when he was eight. He'd never thought of it before. He'd been so young that he'd taken the explanation of his father's death for granted. An accident, they'd told him.

An accident that had cleared the path for Gordon to take the position of Sun King, because, after all, little Kemal was so young. But even after Kemal had reached his age of majority, Gordon was still Sun King, with Dalton smirking in the shadows.

Damn, Kemal thought, a thousand million damns!

He'd been so blind, so unsuspecting, even when he should have known better.

But he had to put all such unsettling thoughts about his father's demise out of his mind.

He had a more immediate problem to deal with. If he was caught and brought to Dalton, his cover would certainly be blown. Despite his disguise, there was no doubt that Dalton would recognize him.

Which wasn't good. To say that the two of them didn't get along was something of an understatement.

The last time Kemal had been on Mercury, he'd been a prisoner of Gordon and Dalton. They'd tried to break his spirit and get him to turn away from NEO and wholeheartedly join them in their alliance with RAM. He had suffered through that torturous imprisonment in the deepest dungeons of Mercury Prime, but had finally escaped when Buck Rogers had captured Dalton in a space battle and exchanged him for Kemal.

Dalton had been in favor of killing Kemal then. Now, here, literally in the middle of nowhere with no one to constrain him, Kemal had no doubt that Dalton would do something drastic to him. Like send him for a walk out of the nearest airlock without a pressure suit.

Well, he told himself, don't get caught.

His best chance, he realized, was to make his way back to the *Merry Widow*, or maybe even the *Glory Bound*, and then get off the rock. He could offer explanations, apologies, and compensation later. Now he just had to get away from Rising Sun.

Fortunately the description of him being broadcast wasn't exactly precise. There were dozens of tall, bearded men dressed in orange workman's coveralls on the station. But that hardly made it safe for him. The first thing he had to do was make the description even more inaccurate. He had to lose the coveralls.

His jumpsuit was back in the freighters' locker room, but that was half a station away. There must be other clothes somewhere on the station that he could find and change into. If only he had someone to spy for him who could help him plan his moves.

He stopped and slapped his head in frustration. There was someone. Huer, of course. The perfect spy. Smart, sly, and invisible. He couldn't ask for anything more.

There were numerous supply closets and storage hutches off the main corridors. Kemal dove into the nearest one and pulled the door shut after him.

He flicked on the overhead light. It sputtered, flickered, and finally hummed fitfully into life, and Kemal saw that he was in a maintenance closet stuffed with brooms, mops, wheeled garbage bins, and other equipment needed for janitorial work. It was cramped and more than a little smelly from half-used containers of disinfectant and detergent, but he probably was safe there, at least for the time being.

He pulled out his uplink unit and thumbed it to life. "Huer," he said, "I need help. Immediately."

Perhaps half a second went by, then Huer's image, projected through the holographic eye in the uplink unit, was shimmering in the air very close to Kemal in the small closet. Another good thing about sidekick computer personae, Kemal thought, is that they don't take up very much space.

"What's wrong?" the digital personality asked.

Kemal filled him in.

"So you want me to scout for you," Huer said, grasping the essentials at once, "and help you avoid the search parties?"

"You got it."

Huer smiled. "Consider it done."

"Right," Kemal said. "First find me some different clothes. The orange coveralls are a dead giveaway."

"Certainly," Huer said. "How about those hanging on the hook right behind you?"

Kemal turned around. There, hanging behind him, was pair of dull gray coveralls. Kemal took them down off the hook and reflected how easy it was to overlook small details during a time of crisis. They smelled terrible, but they had to do.

Kemal changed quickly, struggling a little in the close confines of the closet. "Okay," he finally said after switching clothes. "Let's go."

"Take the garbage cart and mop with you," Huer suggested. "It'll add that needed whiff of realism to your disguise."

"Good idea."

"I'll go first," Huer said, and his image silently slipped "through" the closet door. Kemal waited a moment, then the message "All clear" came up on the uplink's small viewscreen, and he followed Huer out into the corridor.

The digital personality's image was nowhere to be seen. Kemal glanced down at the hand-held uplink. "Left," it said, and Kemal trundled off in that direction, pushing the garbage cart in front of him.

He came to a fork in the corridor, followed Huer's directions, and turned left again. He went on perhaps another fifty feet, then the uplink's screen started to blink, "Careful, careful, careful . . ."

Up ahead, an armed security patrol was marching smartly down the corridor. There was nothing Kemal could do. If he ran, he definitely would give himself away. He just had to try to gut it out.

He lowered his head, almost like a turtle withdrawing into its shell, and plodded on toward them.

"Hold it right there," the squad's sergeant said.

Kemal stopped, outwardly stolid and patient, inwardly shaking.

"Let me see—" the sergeant began, then the unseen speakers mounted in the ceilings started blaring again.

"Intruder alert! Intruder alert! All security teams, third level! Repeat, all security teams to the third level!"

"Let's go, men!" the sergeant shouted, and they wheeled and ran off, leaving Kemal with a huge, heartfelt sigh.

Huer sparkled into existence before him and grinned. "How was I?" he asked.

"Great! You sounded so much like Dalton that you almost fooled me."

Huer nodded. "I thought I'd slip into the computer system and run interference for you." He pointed down the corridor. "Go that way. Turn left, right, and left again, and you'll come to an airlock. I've already checked, and there's an adequate supply of pressure suits. The airlock was sealed, but I've already taken care of that through the computer net. The rest of your trip might better be accomplished via the surface. No one will suspect you of trying to reach the docking facilities from the outside."

"Right, Doc."

Huer nodded and blipped out of sight. Kemal got behind his garbage cart and pushed it as if a platoon of clone-warriors were hot on his trail. Within moments he'd reached the airlock that Huer had promised. There were five pressure suits in the antechamber. He donned one as quickly as he could and gathered up the helmets of the other four to prevent any possible pursuit. He opened the airlock door and took the helmets in with him. He waited impatiently for the airlock to cycle, then rushed out onto the asteroid's surface, abandoning the extra helmets as he hit the vacuum.

He took a moment to orient himself. The landscape was starkly beautiful, with the jagged cliffs and abrupt shifts in plane of a world that lacked the ameliorating effects of climate. The docks, he decided, must lie to his left. He turned and was nearly blinded by a flood of artificial light. The glare was coming, he realized, from the light towers that energized the crystals. The Sun Flowers, the freight handler had called them. Kemal had come straight through the asteroid and out the opposite side. The Sun Flowers were located right where he'd thought they'd be.

The airlock was set right on the lip of the bowl-shaped depression in which the lighted field lay. From this distance, however, Kemal could make out few details in the blinding light.

"Visor," Kemal said, "polarize to max. Full magnification and focus. One hundred yards."

The scene blurred, seemed to rush speedily upon him, then leaped into startlingly fine-grained focus.

Kemal held his breath at the dazzling beauty of the Sun Flowers. No two were exactly alike, and each was truly a breathtaking work of art. The light that bathed them was transformed into glowing pastel shades that dripped like liquid color from their hundreds of cubist petals. They presented a startling contrast to the stark black-and-white landscape in which they were set, like the dream of a mad artist.

It was difficult to believe that something so beautiful could be so deadly, thought Kemal. In a way, they were like lovely animals whose flesh was poisonous to the touch. But these objects were more than poisonous. They could be positively disastrous in the wrong hands—such as Gordon and Dalton Gavilan's.

Kemal roused himself as if from a dream. He couldn't stand around and gape at the thirty-or-so crystals, no matter how awesome they were. There was still the little matter of making it to safety. He turned and oriented himself once again on the landscape. As he'd first thought, the spaceship docks should be to his left, just over the horizon. He began to move, swiftly but carefully, over the dangerous rocky surface using the thrusters of his suit's space belt.

It was then that he realized the ground was vibrating under his feet.

He turned, looked over his shoulder, and saw a great black hole opening in a distant cliff across the crystal field from him. He suddenly realized what would come out of it: the same skimmer that had blown Malik Ferdenko into his constituent molecules.

"Chameleon mode," he snapped as he faded back into shadow. The colors of the pressure suit began to shift and fade, blending in with the grays and blacks and browns of the background.

The skimmer nosed out of its hanger like a great prehistoric carnivorous beast. It paused, casting about for prey. Kemal froze in the shadows, afraid to move, lest he call attention to himself.

Great, he thought, just great. Either they'd had the airlocks monitored and saw him use this one, or else the skimmer was simply going out on precautionary patrol. He watched it drift silently away from him and let out a breath he hadn't even realized he'd been holding.

The skimmer apparently was just patrolling. At least it hadn't zeroed right in on the airlock Kemal had used to exit the research station. He still had a chance, if he was quick and careful . . . and lucky.

He flitted through the shadows like a mouse trying

to escape a monstrous cat, heading for a jagged ridge to put between himself and the skimmer. He didn't dare look back at the machine as he fled from it. He had to give all his attention to the treacherous rocks beneath him. A sudden fall and a puncture in his suit, and he was just as dead as if he'd been vaporized by the laser.

He finally slipped over and behind the rock ridge, congratulating himself on making it to safety, when the suit's readouts suddenly went crazy. There was intense heat that pushed the suit's refrigeration coils to the max. Even so, Kemal would have broken into a soaking sweat had he not been of Mercurian blood. He glanced backward and saw that a chunk of the sheltering ridge behind him was gone. It had vanished as if something had taken a round, smooth bite from it.

The skimmer, a silent, deadly bird of prey, was heading right for him. The parabolic dish in front of it was rotating, aiming the deadly Sun Flower directly at him.

He reacted almost without thinking. The pressure suit he was wearing had been designed for use in ship maintenance and repair, so its space belt had pressurized gas thrusters strategically placed around the hips. Kemal slammed down on them, full thrust. They hissed into life, throwing Kemal like a human javelin, clear of the asteroid's negligible pull of gravity.

But he hadn't had time to balance the controls. He went spinning out into space like a human pinwheel.

The stars flashed around him like particles in a kaleidoscope, alternating with madly whirling, split-second views of the asteroid's surface.

Despite his years of training and experience as a rocketjock, Kemal was struck by a bad case of vertigo and had to fight down the sudden sickening urge to vomit. He clamped his lips together stoically and swallowed the harshness that rose in him. It traced a burning path back down his throat as he fought the hand controls of the thrusters to stabilize his flight path.

It took only a moment, but by the time he'd succeeded in bringing himself under control, he already was well clear of the asteroid. He was so distant that it was only a featureless rock at his feet. The skimmer was a bright insect crawling on its surface.

Kemal felt a sudden surge of relief wash over him like a cleansing wave. The skimmer remained hovering close to the asteroid's surface, apparently acting as a watchdog for the remaining Sun Flowers. It wouldn't come after him. He had no idea of the laser device's range, but in any case, the persons operating it had to track him to use it, and he doubted that they could find a man-sized target at such a great distance.

All he had to do now was call Huer on the uplink unit and have the doctor relay the call to Barney, waiting somewhere out in space on the *Free Enterprise*. Then he'd be home free.

He reached for the uplink device and stopped, cursing aloud. He'd put the damned thing in the hip pocket of his coveralls. There was no way he could reach it through the space suit. And for now, it was set only to receive messages from Huer. He couldn't broadcast an alarm through it.

Kemal would have slapped himself on the forehead in frustration if he could have reached it through the helmet.

Great, he thought, just great. What now?

He could try calling on the suit's radio, but he saw that it had only one channel, a channel no doubt being monitored very closely by the station personnel. They would definitely have the advantage in the race to his helplessly floating body.

But he wasn't exactly helplessly floating. He still had the space belt's thrusters. He could return to the asteroid's surface and continue on with his attempt to reach the docking area. It was still risky, but maybe his best chance. Besides, once inside the station, he could call Huer. The doctor would immeasurably increase his chances of making it.

Kemal looked down at the asteroid, floating through space at his feet, and calculated rough trajectories in his head. It was a simple task for a man who'd been flying since he was eight. He thumbed the thruster button and air spurted from the hip jets. He started on a long loop that would bring him back to the asteroid, but the jets died.

"Now what?" Kemal said aloud. He punched buttons on the control plate set into the suit's right forearm, and the thruster's fuel readout came up on the visor screen. It read zero.

Kemal groaned with frustration. That was the problem with dressing on the run. He hadn't had enough time to check the suit's service status. This one apparently hadn't been serviced at all. He'd been lucky that it'd had enough pressure in the thrusters to allow him to escape the skimmer. Lucky—

A sudden thought struck Kemal. If the suit was low on thruster pressure—

He quickly called up the oxygen gauge and stared in dismay at the readout. He had six minutes of air left in his tank.

Kemal was too stunned to even swear. Had he, he wondered, traded a quick, fiery death for a slow, lingering one?

CHAPTER SIXTEEN

Kemal had only one recourse. He knew that he had to swallow his pride, call for help from Rising Sun Station, and hope for the best.

He flicked on the helmet mike with his chin.

"Spaceman in distress," he said, "spaceman in distress. This is Con Smythe calling." He figured that he'd keep up the deception of his false identity as long as possible. "Marooned in space roughly one hundred miles from Rising Sun. Please acknowledge."

There was a moment's silence, then the voice of the station's communications officer came crackling through his headset. "Con Smythe, this is Rising Sun. What is your situation?"

"I'm drifting with empty thrusters. I've got—" he

checked the gauge—"approximately five minutes of oxygen left."

"Are you the spy that our security has been tracking through the station?"

Kemal swallowed. "Yes."

There was a long silence from Rising Sun, then the com officer's voice came back on. "Sorry, Smythe. We are unable to scramble a rescue vehicle that would reach you in time."

Kemal swallowed anger and outrage. He could tell from the com officer's tone of voice that he was lying.

Anger washed over Kemal, leaving him icily calm. He sensed Dalton's hand in this. His cousin was cruel but also calculating to a fault. He probably had decided that it wasn't worth the time, effort, and expenditure to rescue someone he considered an enemy . . . even if he was family.

Kemal glanced at the oxygen gauge. Four minutes left.

"I know you're lying, Rising Sun," he said calmly.

"Sorry, Smythe," the radio operator repeated. Kemal could tell from the tone of his voice that he was shaken, and that he was just following orders. "There's nothing we can do at this end."

"I understand," Kemal said. "Just tell Dalton Gavilan, if he isn't listening in already, that this will come back to haunt him someday. Someday he'll pay for his decision to abandon a marooned spaceman. Tell him that someone will repay him someday, somehow."

There was another long silence, then the operator

said in a strained voice, "I will pass on your message, Smythe. Rising Sun Station signing off."

Then there was nothing.

Kemal stared off into darkness for a moment, then glanced at the oxygen gauge. He clicked it off. There was no sense in torturing himself by watching the seconds of his life tick away.

He had read once that time was a subjective thing, that the internal clock ticking in a person's head ran as quickly or as slowly as he or she wanted it to. Right now, he had no desire for it to run fast. He wanted to live. He'd done a lot in his life, but there was much more to do. With no clocks to define time, with only the slow, awesome majesty of the universe spread like a glorious tapestry before him, perhaps he could make his last few seconds stretch into minutes, or even hours. Perhaps in the time he had left he could live a full, long life even if it was only in his head.

There was no sense in raging against those who had abandoned him. He didn't want to spend the last part of his life consumed by useless hate. He felt his thoughts turn, without conscious direction, strongly and irrevocably to his origins, to the home world that he'd lived on so briefly, to the family that he'd barely known.

He couldn't remember his mother at all. No one talked about her. He knew, even when young, that there was some sort of scandal associated with her name. He had never pried into it. He just accepted the fact that she was a blank in his life. He never really missed her, because he couldn't miss what he never had.

His father, though, was a different matter. Kemal had only been four when his father suddenly had died, so he couldn't remember Ossip Gavilan very clearly. But fragments of memories had haunted him all through his childhood. They sometimes still did.

Kemal remembered his father's voice, his pleasant masculine scent. He remembered tottering by his father's side, his little hand engulfed in the great, gentle paw that was Ossip's hand. He remembered being tickled by those hands. He remembered laughing and running and catching a bright red ball that his father threw to him. He remembered, as clearly as a tri-dee drama, the day his uncle Gordon had come to his room, awakened him up from a sound sleep, and told him simply and without any attempt at sugar-coating that the prince's father was dead, and that Kemal would be leaving for school on Mars the very next day.

It was a terrible memory that still came back as clear and vivid as reality during dreams that still haunted Kemal. And because he was four years old and there was nothing else he could do, he'd gone off to school on Mars as his uncle had wanted.

Later, when he was old enough to return home, he never stayed on Mercury for long. There was always some cause somewhere in the system to take up. NEO and its rebellion against RAM's domination had been just the latest.

Kemal was always running away from home, from

the remnants of a family he hated, from the heritage he was afraid to embrace.

The realization that his father may not have died accidentally should have occurred to him years before. Kemal thought now that it probably had. He had just buried it in his subconscious, where it would occasionally surface in awful dreams in which Ossip called for help Kemal couldn't give.

That was why, Kemal now knew, he'd stayed away from Mercury all those years. That was why he'd thrown in with NEO instead of going home and fighting his own personal battles.

He was afraid that he would uncover the facts concerning his father's death. And he was afraid that he wouldn't be able to exact justice for it.

It was the height of irony, Kemal thought, to come to these realizations when it was too late to do anything about them. If he could, he would now go home. He would investigate Ossip's death. He would strive to take his place as the rightful Sun King of Mercury and lead the planet for the benefit of all its people, not just a select few.

But it was too late for all that.

It felt warm in his pressure suit. Warm, heavy air seemed to congeal like gelatin in Kemal's laboring lungs. He could draw no sustenance from it. He was too tired to fight it. Too tired to do anything. He closed his eyes.

Dying wasn't as bad as he thought it would be. It didn't hurt at all. There was a heavy pressure, like a great weight pressing down on his chest, but that was all.

Soon, Kemal thought, he'd be able to see his father face-to-face and ask firsthand what had happened to him.

A deep stillness engulfed Kemal. He floated inside it, womblike, until there was a sudden jar that shook him like birth trauma. He opened his eyes, blinking against a harsh light. His father loomed above him.

"Smythe," his father grumbled, shaking him like an earthquake, "wake up."

He remembered his father's voice to be different, somehow deeper.

"I said, wake up, damn yer!"

There was sharp pain from a ringing slap to his cheek. Kemal shook his head, clearing it somewhat, though he still was groggy and bewildered. His eyes finally focused.

"Mom?" he asked.

The squat figure looming over him grinned. "Yer all right!" Mom Quillan said, and cuffed Kemal playfully on the side of the head.

"We heard yer on the space-com and scrambled the *Widow*. What's going on here, Smythe?"

Kemal took a deep breath. He tried to sit up but didn't have the strength. He looked at Mom Quillan's seamed, concerned face staring down at him and smiled. It was time for the truth, both for her and for himself.

"My name isn't Con Smythe," he told the astonished freight captain. "It's Kemal Gavilan, Prince Kemal Gavilan of Mercury."

"Mercy me, dear boy," she said, laying a concerned hand gently on his cheek. "Yer havin' delusions brought on by lack o' oxygen to the brain."

Kemal laughed. He felt the strength returning to his body now. He sat straight up.

"No, Mom," he said, "my brain's clear for the first time in years. I know now what I have to do." His voice was strong and full of determination. "I'm going home."

CHAPTER SEVENTEEN

Kemal almost had forgotten how awesome the sun looked when viewed from Mercury.

Covering a full degree and a half of arc in the sky, the sun was nine times bigger than it appeared from the Earth, nearly *sixteen* times bigger than it appeared from Mars. A blazing molten ball that dripped fire like smoldering blood, it hung in the sky like an angry wound in the fabric of heaven. Seeing the sun again from so close, Kemal could well understand how the ancients worshiped it as a god.

Barney, though, had a more prosaic outlook.

"Hot as hell," the pirate said.

Kemal nodded. Down below them, the planetary surface was a living advertisement for Dante's *Inferno*. There was nothing soft or gentle about it—no textures, no surface features. The colors were all dark and violent, except for the blinding whites and flashing silvers that pained the unshielded eye. The surface features were all craggy craters and sharp-edged planes dissected by sheer-sided gullies and knifelike ridges that had never been terraformed— smoothed by the ameliorating effects of air or water.

Although easily the most inimical environment ever colonized by humans, Mercury lacked such nice-ties as atmosphere, water, and plant and animal life. The ancients had thought that Mercury had always presented one side toward the burning face of the sun, the other toward outer space. Even though it was ultimately discovered that Mercury did rotate at a different rate than it revolved, climatic conditions weren't noticeably improved. During the day, surface temperatures rose to nearly eight hundred degrees. During the night, they dropped to a frigid four hundred below.

It was, in its own way, as hellishly beautiful as it was deadly. Kemal was surprised to realize how much he'd missed its uncompromising starkness.

He'd thought long and hard about it during the trip sunward from the Asteroid Belt in the *Free Enterprise*.

His mission to uncover the origin and genesis of the laser device had started out as another of his cru-sades. It had turned personal when Lilith had died in his arms. It had turned even more personal when Dalton had unexpectedly turned out to be the com-mander of Rising Sun.

The relationship between Dracolysk and the House of Gavilan still was unclear, but it seemed that Dracolysk had supplied the material for the station. Mercury—not necessarily Kemal's family—had supplied the crystals, and Dalton seemed to have been in charge. Who really ran the show? the prince wondered.

Kemal vowed that he'd find out soon.

All interplanetary traffic coming into Mercury docked at Caloris Station, a surface spaceport that could accommodate any size spacecraft. Caloris was strictly functional, totally utilitarian. It's spare, almost severe design and utter lack of ornamentation gave no hint of the wealth controlled by Gordon Gavilan. He saved all his ostentation for Hielo—also known as Mercury Prime—his orbital home circling between the Mariposas, the enormous energy collection stations that were the source of his riches.

Barney wiped away the sweat trickling down his broad forehead as he and Kemal hiked the short distance from the *Free Enterprise*'s berth to Caloris's customs facilities.

"Remember," Kemal said in a low voice, "this is my show. I let you handle things out in the Belt. Let me take care of things here. I know this world and its customs."

Barney grumbled again but nodded.

"Good," Kemal said in the same low voice. "Here we are."

"Next," said a bored functionary behind the customs service counter. He didn't even look up as Kemal and Barney approached.

Kemal reached into his tunic pouch and pulled out
his Class AAA Mercurian diplomatic passport. The
document was decorated liberally with gold scroll-
work, purple ribbons, and rosettes of every imagina-
ble color. It was so thick that it made an audible thud
when Kemal slapped it on the counter in front of the
clerk.

The startled customs agent stared at it as if it were
a poisonous serpent. Such passports were reserved
only for the highest upper crust of Mercurian society.
The customs agent probably had never seen one before in his career.

"If you would be so good," Kemal said in his haugh-
tiest tones, "please clear me immediately to Mercury
Prime." He checked his thumbwatch negligently. "I
would like to have luncheon with my uncle, Gordon
Gavilan."

The clerk lifted his staring eyes from the impressive passport to Kemal himself. Kemal, minus the
disguise he had worn in the Belt, wore his finest tunic and trousers ensemble. It was indigo, trimmed in
the cloth of gold and royal purple reserved only for
the Sun King himself and his closest family members. A snarling Barney, standing a respectful pace
to Kemal's rear, had polished his body armor until it
shone. Together they were a living representation of
power and majesty the likes of which the clerk had
never seen, nor was likely ever to see again.

"Yessir," he mumbled, glancing down at the flor-
idly lettered passport again, "Prince Kemal. Shall I

call ahead and inform him of your arrival? Or," he added hastily, "would you rather I not?"

Kemal feigned indifference. "Well, I had hoped to surprise him. . . ."

"I *should* call to obtain proper clearance, you understand."

"Barney," Kemal said, stepping aside.

Snarling, the space pirate stepped up to the counter while the clerk's eyes got wider as the full impact of Barney's size and savagery sunk into him. He winced as Barney's hand whipped to his belt, and shrunk back as it came shooting forward and slammed down on the counter with the impact of a jet pistol. The countertop jumped but held together. When Barney removed his hand, a small, clear pouch of Mercurian konigs—coins worth twenty credits apiece—was sitting there in plain sight.

But not for too long.

The clerk's hand quickly shot out, covered it, and pocketed it before any onlookers could even realize what had happened.

"Well, if you want to surprise your uncle, I guess that's all right with me." He smiled with false sincerity as he stamped Kemal's passport with a flourish and handed it back past a still-scowling Barney. "I'll clear you through to the spaceport of Mercury Prime."

Kemal nodded bored thanks.

"I hope your stay is long and enjoyable, O Prince."

Kemal nodded again and waved languorously at Barney.

"My man here is lacking certain documentation." He gestured again at Barney, who placed another pouch on the countertop. It disappeared as quickly as the first.

"What you've shown me is . . . sufficient," the customs official said.

Kemal and Barney moved away from the counter.

"My man?" Barney asked.

"Relax," Kemal said. "I told you that I know how this place works. The oaf behind the counter thinks you're my servant. Therefore, you have no significance. Therefore, it's all right to look away and let you enter Mercury Prime without a passport. As long as he's properly recompensed, of course."

"Rigmarole," Barney growled in a low voice. "Why a bribe? The oaf'll pocket it and report to your uncle anyway."

"Exactly," Kemal explained. "Politics on Mercury is a game of intrigue. There are circles moving within circles within circles. I never had the patience or the inclination to play the game before. But, now," he continued, his voice turning grim, "I do. It wouldn't hurt to let my uncle think I was still a little naive as to how things worked around here."

Barney nodded his mohawk-topped head. "I see. I think."

"There was no way we were going to 'surprise' my uncle with a sudden arrival. He controls things on Mercury much too tightly. But if we let him think that we think we've surprised him, then we lower his estimation of us."

Barney nodded. "Always let your enemies underestimate you. Then they'll be surprised when you go in for the kill."

Kemal nodded. "Exactly. And I *really* want to surprise my uncle this time around."

Barney grinned, a feral baring of his fangs that had no humor in it whatsoever.

* * * * *

Mercury Prime, the hereditary home of the Gavilans, hovered into view on the Mercurian shuttle's viewscreen. A cylindrical orbital station established by Bahlam, the first great Sun King, its outer surface was intricately carved with friezes and bas-reliefs depicting heroes and scenes from history and mythology. Many of the most prominent figures in the reliefs had the faces of Bahlam and the succeeding Sun Kings who had patronized the artisans work after Bahlam's passing.

"Incredible workmanship," Kemal said as they approached the docking port.

"Busy," Barney grunted. He preferred his art to be more austere. And he definitely preferred it in more valuable materials than stainless steel and bronze.

"Wait until we get inside," Kemal promised. "I'm sure you'll see something to your liking then."

Barney's eyes lit up.

"But remember, we're not here on a looting expedition. You can look, but don't touch."

Barney growled wordlessly.

There was an unexpected welcoming committee waiting for the two when the shuttle arrived at the docks. Gordon Gavilan's younger son, Tacitus "Tix" Gavilan, was waiting for them. Although a few years older than Kemal, Tix radiated an aura of uncertain youth despite his prematurely thinning hair. He was tall, thin, and slightly stooped with a pale, nervous manner. His speech was quick but filled with sincere depth. He was highly intelligent, with an aptitude toward art and interior design. Kemal liked him and embraced him warmly and willingly as they met at the entrance gate.

"C-c-cousin Kemal!" Tix said with a slight stutter, flipping his long hair out of his eyes with a characteristic nervous gesture. "It's been so long! Welcome home!"

"Too long," Kemal acknowledged. He held Tix at arm's length and regarded him critically. "How'd you know we were coming?"

A nervous smile lit his cousin's face for a moment, then was gone. "Oh, word spreads, C-c-cousin, quickly on a station the size of Mercury Prime. Someone informed security you were coming. I happened to overhear and wanted to greet you first."

"Does uncle Gordon know I'm here?"

"I suppose so," Tix said.

Kemal smiled to himself. He'd been right about his uncle's security apparatus. Hopefully his apparent naivete would help screen the depths of his newfound cunning from his uncle. "Well, Tix," he asked his cousin, "how have things been for you?"

"The same, C-c-cousin, the same. I've been redoing F-f-father's bedroom in Early French Royal. You should see it!" He stopped his rush of words as he seemed to notice Barney for the first time. "But I'm being rude, K-k-kemal. Who is your friend?"

"You can call him Barney," Kemal said with a wry smile.

"Barney? Not the pi—" he paused, evidently afraid that he would insult Barney by calling him a pirate.

Barney, however, was nonplussed. "Pirate," he affirmed. "Do I look like a fool accountant?"

"No, eh, of course not. You look just like a . . . a man of action."

"Barney and I," Kemal said confidingly to his cousin, "have been business partners. Of a sort."

"Really?" Tix's eyes grew as big as saucers. "F-f-father will be so impressed."

That's part of the plan, Kemal told himself. He wanted his connection with Barney to make it look as if he were no longer a hopeless idealist. He had to impress upon his uncle that he was now a 'practical' man—and Barney was one of the most practical men in the entire system. He had to impress his uncle with his connections, but not too much. Kemal had to seem still a little out of his depth, still a little naive, still a little too trusting. Otherwise, Gordon would never feel comfortable enough to let him in on whatever was happening on Rising Sun Station.

"Is uncle Gordon busy?" Kemal asked as he and Tix walked side by side down the corridor, Barney looming a short pace to the rear, attracting more than a few curious glances as they passed other Mercurians in the corridor.

"He's in a meeting," Tix said, "of the Mariposa governors. It should be over soon."

"And Dalton?" Kemal asked casually.

Tix waved an agitated hand. "My b-b-b-bro-brother is off Mercury Prime. On some kind of mission. You know how h-h-h-he is."

Kemal only nodded. There was certainly no love lost between himself and his cousin Dalton. There hadn't been even before Dalton allowed Kemal to linger near death in deep space. Kemal now would cheerfully strangle the damned strutting cock with his own hands. He knew that Tix and Dalton had never gotten along, either, but relations between them must have deteriorated since Kemal had last been on Mercury. The mere mention of Dalton's name caused his younger brother to stutter almost uncontrollably, and also started a nervous tic jumping in his left cheek.

"Will you be home for long this time, K-k-kemal?" Tix asked.

"Maybe," Kemal said quietly. "It all depends on Uncle."

Tix nodded and glanced back at Barney. "I'm sorry to be neglecting you, Mr. Barney. I hope you're not too bored."

"Bored?" Barney rumbled. He shook his head wordlessly as he stared about the corridor. It was obvious that he was more dazed by his surroundings than bored.

"Oh, yes," Tix said, glancing around them. "Like the interior design? I did it, oh, two years ago. This whole section of Mercury Prime has been devoted to mythic themes. This is the Egyptian corridor."

Kemal, already having been exposed to the exaggerated excesses of the home of the Sun Kings, hadn't given their surroundings a second thought as they passed from the utilitarian spacedock area to the Gavilan manor proper. Barney, though, probably had never seen so much precious ore and valuable ornamentation in his entire life. Which was saying a lot.

Life-size statues of all the Sun Kings, from Bahlam the first down through Gordon, were set in niches along the corridor, flanked by intricately ornamented obelisks glorifying their reigns. The statues were cast of solid gold that had been collected from the streams of molten metal that ran like water during the hottest part of the Mercurian day. The obelisks also were gold, inlaid with silver and precious jewels and crystals from all the worlds of the system.

"Nice place," Barney said with curt understatement.

Kemal turned back to him and said out of the corner of his mouth, "Don't get any ideas."

Barney just looked at him.

They found Gordon Gavilan on the golden Sun Throne in the audience room, a glass of strong Venusian brandy already half-empty on the long dining table before him.

Gordon was the largest of three Gavilan brothers.

Ossip, Kemal's father, had been the oldest. Gordon, who'd taken Ossip's place after his death, was the middle brother. Garrick, short, stout, and ineffectual, was the youngest. Kemal didn't know him very well—not that he knew Gordon all that well either—but Garrick was a real cipher to Kemal. He supposed Garrick was off somewhere in the Solar System developing his own family fortune.

Gordon was broadly built with a deep chest and wide shoulders. He had put on weight since Kemal had seen him last, and the furrows in his brow had deepened, as if he frowned a lot.

He didn't seem to notice them enter the capacious audience chamber. It was a huge, mostly empty room with a high ceiling lost in the darkness. Gordon sat at a long dining table set in front of a series of tall windows in the chamber's far wall. The table had multiple candelabra and formal place settings for at least forty people, but Gordon was the only one present in the room.

The windows had off-white draperies blowing gently in a breeze created by a concealed wind machine and looked as if they opened onto a range of distant mountains smothered in virgin snow. A herd of deer came stepping through the drifts and browsed on snow-laden tree branches as Kemal, Tix, and Barney watched. The breeze ruffling the curtains was scented with pine and the fresh, cool sharpness of mountain air.

It looked so good that it almost seemed real.

It was just a holographic projection, however, designed to ease minds that otherwise had to content themselves with endless metal corridors, artificial chambers, and stale, recycled air. Mercury Prime was too small to have an eco-chamber, or else the Sun Kings just considered one a ridiculous waste of space. In either case, they had to satisfy themselves with untouchable tri-dee pictures instead of the real thing.

Tix cleared his throat after a moment, and Gordon looked up at them for the first time.

"Look who's come to visit, F-f-father," Tix said.

"What a surprise!" the oldest Gavilan said in his deep, hearty voice, though he looked more troubled to see Kemal than surprised. Kemal had been on Mercury Prime twice as an adult. The first time, he'd been under twenty-one, and Gordon had held the club of his inheritance over his head to try to get Kemal to the betray the nomadic surface dwellers called the Dancers. Kemal had resisted his uncle's efforts that time, and since he'd reached his age of majority, Gordon could no longer threaten him with loss of his inheritance.

Kemal's second trip to Mercury had been even less pleasant. During the Martian Wars, Gordon Gavilan had tried to make an alliance with RAM. Kemal had already joined NEO on the other side, and in an effort to control his nephew, Gordon had had Kemal kidnaped and thrown into the Mercury Prime dungeons. Kemal had passed an unpleasant period there as Gordon's jailer tried to break his mind with insidious drugs that were meant to sap his will and destroy his spirit.

Kemal, however, had stood up to the torture and ultimately was released from the dungeon when Buck Rogers had captured Dalton Gavilan and forced an exchange of prisoners.

It was all too evident that Gordon was unhappy to see his nephew home on Mercury Prime, where he could be causing trouble. He much preferred that his nephew fritter his time and energy away on some distant backwater such as Earth, where the trouble he could cause Mercury—that is, Gordon Gavilan—was minimal.

Kemal put a smile on his face that was as insincere as his uncle's.

"I hope we're not interrupting. Tix said that you had a meeting . . ."

Gordon Gavilan brushed Kemal's polite protestations away. "Finished it, Nephew," he said. A wolf-like smile creased his face as he thought back on it. "The damn fools of the Mariposa governing board thought they were being sly, thought they could trick me out of my proper share of revenue. Well, I showed them exactly where they stood, showed them if they didn't listen to me, they'd be down on the surface frying eggs on their foreheads with the damned Dancers if they didn't give in." He nodded his head in satisfaction. "And they did. They gave in, by damn."

"Congratulations, Uncle," Kemal said. He looked around the audience chamber. "It's good to be home. You don't know how much I've missed Mercury Prime."

The last part of his statement, at least, wasn't a lie.

Gordon looked at Kemal carefully. "Come, you and your friend . . ."

"Black Barney," the space pirate responded.

"Yes. Black Barney. I thought I recognized you. You and your friend sit down."

Kemal watched as Barney squeezed himself into a decorative, spindle-legged antique chair that had come all the way from Earth, where it once had been the property of kings. Louis the Fourteenth of England, Kemal thought. The chair creaked alarmingly at Barney's weight, but it managed to hold together. The pirate picked up a solid platinum fork from the place serving set before him and eyed it critically. He polished it on his sleeve and looked at it again.

"You're just in time for dinner. A little brandy with your meal?" Gordon asked.

Barney looked up from his intense scrutiny of the cutlery. "Ginger beer," he said. "Boar's Head Brand."

"Ginger beer? Well, of course." Gordon picked up the little golden bell that sat on the table by his elbow and shook it once, precisely. A servant, garbed in the Gavilan colors of yellow, black, and gold, appeared as silently as if he'd materialized out of thin air. Gordon gave him Barney's order, and he bowed a precise two inches.

"Make it two," Kemal said.

"That sounds good," Tix put in.

The servant bowed again, said, "Very good, sirs," and glided away on silent feet.

"Well," Gordon said when they were alone, "what

brings you back home, Kemal? I hope you're planning on a long stay."

Kemal sat back in his chair, keeping his smile to himself. The verbal fencing match was about to begin. "Oh, I am," he said. "In fact, I was thinking about making it permanent."

"Permanent?" Gordon's eyebrows rose in astonishment. "What about your work with NEO?"

"Those savages," Kemal said, dismissing the New Earth Organization with a wave of his hand. He sat up straight and looked intently at his uncle. "I realized a hard truth, Uncle. There was no future for me with them. What do I care about rebuilding their planet? What do I get out of it? The chance to spend my life toiling on a backward ball of mud that lacks all the amenities of life?" He shook his head. "No. That's not for me. I have to start looking out for myself. I discovered that when I met Barney here, toward the end of the Martian Wars. He opened my eyes to the reality of the universe. We've been . . . working together since and have cut a few highly successful . . . business deals."

"I see," Gordon said, nodding.

Kemal could see his uncle mulling over his speech. It hadn't, he knew, convinced his uncle of his sincerity of rejoining the family. Gordon was too crafty and too suspicious for mere words to change his mind. He would require action of some sort, action that showed definitively that Kemal had shed his NEO connections and was willing to work for the good of the Gavilans again. Kemal simply had to discover the precise deed he needed to perform to convince his uncle of all this.

The silent waiter reappeared carrying a tray with their drinks. He slid a gold-rimmed crystal goblet full of ginger beer in front of Barney, who raised it to his lips and downed it in one gulp.

He looked hard at the servant. "You call this a glass?" he asked.

"Most people do, sir."

"Not me," the pirate growled with silken menace in his voice. "Bring me a man-sized glass." Barney looked hard at Gordon. "Of this cheap brand."

"It is the only one we stock, sir," the servant said. He placed drinks before Kemal and Tix and wafted off in silence again.

Barney looked at Kemal. "I should get one of those for the *Free Enterprise*," he rumbled.

"A butler?" Kemal asked.

"Why not?"

"Why not, indeed," Gordon said. "Take him if you want. He's yours."

Barney shook his head. "Too quiet. Don't like my crew sneaking around."

"Put a bell on him," Kemal suggested.

Gordon broke out into a roar of laughter. "Put a bell on him," he repeated. "That's funny. You never used to have a sense of humor like that."

He still didn't, but Kemal had to pretend a lot of things in order to convince his uncle to take him back into the family.

"I've never had a lot of things that I'm going to

have. My own servants, my own palace, perhaps, someday, my own planet," Kemal said, purposely planting a notion of overweening ambition into his uncle's mind.

Gordon looked mildly uncomfortable for a moment, then smiled again. "Well, boy, you know you're welcome here while you look around, get your feet on the ground, and find something you'd like to get into."

Kemal toyed with the stem of his gold-rimmed goblet carefully. It was time to show a few of the cards he was holding. "Oh, I've found something already."

"You have?" Gordon asked, taking a sip of brandy from his own goblet.

There was no sense in being bashful about it. He had to let his uncle know what he wanted in an open, direct manner. Only if he got Gordon to focus on Kemal's own supposed greed and ambition would he even have a chance of hiding his true motive from Gordon's suspicious gaze.

"Sun Flowers," Kemal said quietly.

Gordon sputtered, choking on the brandy. "Sun—Sun Flowers?" he asked.

Kemal smiled. "Don't play coy with me, Uncle. I've been out in the Belt. I know what's going on out there on Rising Sun Station."

"Well." Gordon smiled weakly. Kemal could sense that he had thought about lying for a moment then decided to come clean and acknowledge the truth of at least a little of what Kemal had said. "Well, you have done your homework, haven't you."

Kemal only nodded.

"And what do you want with Rising Sun?"

Kemal leaned forward intently, suddenly deciding to shoot for it all. "I want to head the project."

Gordon smiled widely and shook his head. "My, you have gotten ambitious lately. Well, I can't say I blame you, but that's impossible. Quite impossible. Dalton is in charge," he said, confirming Kemal's awful suspicions of the depth of his family's involvement with the laser device. "And he's been doing a fine job for me. A very fine job. I couldn't consider replacing him." Gordon looked at his nephew closely. "Couldn't even consider it. Unless . . . of course . . ."

Kemal immediately saw what his uncle was getting at. He wouldn't replace Dalton as head of Rising Sun unless Kemal could give him something in exchange. Something that would make the deal worthwhile for him. It couldn't be wealth. Gordon already had more than he needed. It couldn't be power. Kemal had none to give. It had to be knowledge, then. But as far as he knew, he knew nothing his uncle needed to know.

"What do you need, Uncle?" Kemal asked quietly.

Gordon leaned forward intently. "You've been out to Rising Sun. You've seen the crystals?"

Kemal nodded.

"The Mercurian Sun Flowers were first discovered in the Phidian lowlands. They had interesting thermoluminescent powers, the ability to collect and focus light. Some of our scientists—the leading technicians in the entire system when it comes to dealing with the properties of sunlight—saw how they could possibly be used as the focal point of a lens of almost unimaginable power. But the weakness was in the crystals themselves. After long experimentation, our scientists decided the crystals couldn't carry a sufficient power load. The project was discarded." Gordon paused and took a long pull from his brandy glass. He burped, then wiped the back of his hand across his lips and continued speaking. "Right about then, some interesting geegaws started showing up on the system's art markets."

"The Sun Flowers," Kemal put in.

"Right," his uncle confirmed. "They were similar to the crystals we had seen, but when our scientists tested them, they discovered that they were bigger, better, somehow more pure. Their crystalline structure could carry loads that disintegrated inferior crystals. They were the perfect instruments to serve as the focal point of the laser device. Imagine our surprise when we discovered that they were being sold to off-world art collectors by the Dancers."

"The Dancers?" Kemal echoed.

Gordon nodded precisely. "And they won't let anyone know where they're getting them."

Kemal suddenly knew what his uncle wanted: full access to the Sun Flowers. And he knew that the Dancers trusted Kemal. He knew that if they revealed their secrets to any outsider, it would be Kemal.

Kemal's stomach churned. How could he betray Duernie and the Dancers? She had risked her own life by coming to Mercury Prime to rescue him when he'd been imprisoned in its dungeons. She'd suffered imprisonment herself for him. How could he reveal her people's greatest secret to their worst enemy?

He hesitated. But he also couldn't allow Gordon—and Dalton—to control a weapon that could devastate the entire Solar System. He *had* to make sure that didn't happen.

The secret of the Sun Flowers would come out eventually, he told himself. Kemal knew his uncle well enough to realize that he would find a way to crack the Dancers' secret, whether through fear, bribery, or intimidation. And Gordon would then leave the Dancers with nothing.

If Kemal were involved in the affair, however, he could make sure that somehow, someway any betrayal of the Dancers would only be temporary. He could see that they would ultimately retain their rights to the Sun Flowers. He would have to.

"What if," Kemal said, keeping as calm an expression on his face as he could while he dangled the bait before his uncle, "someone could ensure an almost limitless supply of the crystals—an almost limitlessly cheap supply."

"You mean," Gordon asked, "that this someone would be able to bypass the Dancers and obtain the Sun Flowers for us on his own?"

"Exactly," Kemal said, nodding.

"Then I'd say that I had a new project manager."

"I thought you would," Kemal said with a smile that went no deeper than his lips.

* * * * *

The taste of imminent betrayal was as bitter as bile in the pit of Kemal's stomach. The twelve-course meal he had just eaten hadn't helped any, either. Barney had liked it, though. He'd finished everything and even had seconds on some dishes. But Barney was as much an eating machine as he was a fighting machine. Kemal was only human. He could only pick at the items on his plate by the time they'd reached the sixth course, which had been fish. Kemal thought of Carp as he'd eaten his portion, wondering how the Belter would have reacted to being served such a dish. Gordon, though, had matched Barney plate for plate, delicacy for delicacy.

It wasn't the overabundant, rich food that fueled Kemal's discomfort, not entirely. He was finding it difficult to bear the thought of betraying the trust that he had fought so long to win from Duernie. She'd been very suspicious of him when he'd first returned to Mercury, but he'd proved to her that he was no Gordon Gavilan. He proved that he cared for people other than himself, that he wanted freedom and well-being for all the people of Mercury and not just more power for the Gavilans. In the end, she'd come to believe in him enough to risk her own life in a futile attempt to rescue him from the Mercury Prime dungeons.

The fact that he'd won her respect, as grudgingly as it'd been given, had been one of the great triumphs of his life. He desperately wanted not to lose it now.

Kemal pleaded weariness after dinner, which was only a half-lie. He had to get out of his uncle's presence. He had to be alone to think things out and convince himself that he wasn't a traitor. He went to his rooms, unused since his brief return to Mercury right before his twenty-first birthday.

Although the household staff apparently came in to dust every now and then, as far as Kemal could remember nothing was out of place. Nothing had been subtracted or added, or even moved. Nothing apparent, that is. Knowing his uncle, there probably were plenty of hidden spy-eyes. But that was all right. They were hardly going to catch him in a compromising situation all by himself.

This suite of rooms—playroom, bedroom, and bathroom—had been his since birth, so there were artifacts left untouched since he'd first left Mars when he was only four. The children's furniture had been removed, of course, when he'd come home as a graduate from the Ulyanov Academy, and been replaced with an adult bed and adult chairs and tables. But all his toys remained, now put up on shelves or stashed away in closets.

He wandered around the suite, trying to draw on those few misty childhood memories. They were as elusive as ghosts, and as tantalizing. He sat down before the table on which his old computer sat. He remembered learning to read and count on it.

On impulse, he switched it on. A prompt appeared on the monitor, and Kemal typed in his password, a simple password that a child would know. It was the first thing he had ever learned to spell, long before he had mastered the difference between upper- and lowercase letters.

"kemal."

The password pulsed on and off for a moment, then the screen went blank. Kemal frowned, wondering if the ancient monitor had blown a tube, but then a picture started to form on the screen.

It was vague at first, blurry and unfocused. Colored mists swirled like smoke puffing from a magician's sleeve, then started to coalesce into a face, a strong, handsome face that Kemal remembered from suppressed dreams. It had a high forehead, strong jaw, and noble, bladelike nose.

It was his father, Ossip Gavilan.

Kemal stared, mesmerized. The image on the computer screen seemed to shudder then collect itself. Its piercing eyes focused on Kemal. He wanted to get up and run away and hide from the knowledge in those eyes, but he couldn't. He was rooted to the chair in half-wonder, half-fear.

The image then spoke in a voice that Kemal remembered echoing in the corridors of his dreams.

"My son. Is that you, Kemal?"

Kemal's heart tried to escape from the cage of his chest.

"Father?" he whispered.

The ghost on the computer screen nodded. "It is I. Wait. Wait and I shall come to you."

The screen went blank again as Kemal sat shaking in his chair. He rubbed at his eyes, but the screen remained blank. He let out a deep, gusting sigh. He had imagined it. It had been some kind of weird hallucination caused by too much rich food and an overwhelming sense of guilt over betraying the Dancers' secret.

He pushed away from the computer and stood just as his father's ghost materialized in front of him. Kemal groaned and took a step back as the misty specter held out its hand placatingly.

"There is nothing to fear, my son," it said. "I'm just the remnants of a program your father put into the system years ago, scant days before his death. He had heard whispers, you see, that someone was plotting his murder. He put me into the Mercury Prime computer system as a safeguard and a watchdog over you. I've been wandering in the system since then. Sometimes I've been glimpsed, sometimes they've come after me with their eraser programs, but I've outwitted them all through the years.

"No one talks openly of me now, no one admits to my existence, but I think they fear me. When they talk of me, it is in whispers, and they call me the ghost in the machine."

Kemal felt a vast sense of relief wash over him as he realized that he wasn't being confronted by the accusatory spirit of his father. At almost the same moment, however, he remembered the possibility of his room being bugged.

"Can you be picked up by spy-eyes?" he asked the digital personality.

The image shook its head. "I have total control over

this room, though my programs are very weak outside these walls. Otherwise, I would have helped you
when you were imprisoned in the dungeon. Gordon
Gavilan has indeed planted spy-eyes all around us,
but they see only what I want them to see. Right now,
to them, you're sleeping."

Kemal nodded. He knew now that it was time to utter the awful truth he'd been denying to himself all
these years.

"Then, you—my father—were murdered."

The holographic image inclined its head gravely.
"I'm afraid so," it said.

"Who did it?"

The image sighed, making a sound like a wind rus-
tling the leaves of graveyard trees at midnight. "I
don't know. I was created days before Ossip's death.
He had only suspicions, no truths. I have pondered
the suspicions the long years I have spent in the Mercury Prime computer system but have come to no
conclusions. I have scoured the net ceaselessly, but
whoever committed the murder was clever. He left no
clues behind for me to uncover."

"But you still have your suspicions," Kemal asked
in a low voice.

The ghost in the machine nodded. "Of course. I
daresay you have them, too."

Kemal did. Who had benefitted the most from his
father's death? Who was ruthless, consciousless,
filled with avarice beyond measure? Who had tried to
manipulate Kemal's life, from the age of four up,
keeping him off the scene and out of the way so that

he could run Mercury as if it were his own private estate?

His uncle. Ossip's brother. Gordon Gavilan.

Kemal couldn't say the words, though the image of his father nodded as if he knew what Kemal was thinking.

Fratricide was a terrible crime, but how many times had it been committed down through the centuries when there was a kingdom at stake? wondered the prince.

Although there was no proof to back it up, Kemal felt in his heart that Gordon had killed his father. Gordon, the man for whom Kemal was about to betray the only people he loved on Mercury.

He sat on the edge of the bed and put his head in his hands. The image of his father came over to stand by Kemal's side, but his ghostly hands could not touch, his whispered words could not comfort.

CHAPTER EIGHTEEN

Mercury was a planet of savage contrasts. Kemal was reminded forcefully of that as he and Barney left Caloris Station in a small jetcar, arranged for them by Gordon, and headed out across the surface.

It was a planet of dead black and blinding white, of freezing cold and blistering heat. Of orbiting palaces of unbelievable gilded decadence to deep, sweltering caverns where men would kill for a sip of cold water. Mercury had it all.

Kemal and Barney were skimming over the day-side, where surface temperatures were approaching eight hundred degrees Fahrenheit. The jetcar's viewscreens were polarized to the maximum and the air conditioner was cranked to high, but Barney was still sweating. He was trying to keep an eye on several control systems that were all threatening to shut down at once because of the killing heat. He was flustered, too, at Kemal's naturally cool disposition in the heat.

"You have to go down there?" Barney asked dubiously as he looked out at the tortured landscape.

Kemal nodded again. "Have to. We have to get in touch with the Dancers and find out where they're getting the Sun Flowers."

"They live in that hell?"

"That's right. They don't have stationary homes but live in caravans that travel the surface of the planet, keeping mostly in the dusk, right on the edge between dark and light."

"For a crummy bit of nothing?"

Kemal looked down at the landscape below them. There were no plants, no water, not even any air to take the edge off its harshness. Nothing could live unsheltered on the planet. The Dancers, though, were willing to risk their lives to live on it because it gave them the one thing they cherished most: freedom.

"Because," Kemal said, "it's *their* crummy bit of nothing."

"If I was them," Barney muttered, "I'd find a better place to hang my hat."

"They're satisfied with what they have." Kemal said, almost amazed himself at the simple truth of his statement.

The Dancers were high-tech nomads with little in

the way of material things to call their own. But they were fiercely proud of what they had, and fiercely defensive of it as well. They had no desire to take what belonged to others—but anyone who tried to take anything of theirs had better be aware of their deadly "laser knives." They had no compunction against defending their belongings, their vehicles, and their land rights to the death.

"There," Kemal suddenly said as he pointed. "A lead stream."

A glowing thread of molten ore wound its way down a lobate scarp into the plain below. The scarp, a shallow scalloped cliff, was an example of one of the more common surface features found on Mercury. The scarps were gigantic wrinkles formed in the planet's crust as its iron core had cooled and contracted uncounted millennia before. Such cliffs frequently bordered the relatively smooth plains that separated the meteor impact craters that peppered the surface of Mercury much as they did the lunar surface. This particular example was a rather small scarp, less than half a mile high and probably only a few hundred miles long. The lead ore ran down it like a river trickling to the dry sea of the smooth plain below.

"If we follow it, we'll eventually come to a Dancer caravan. They find ore streams for the surface Miners, then test them to make sure it's worth rolling one of the Miner arcologies to the site."

"This Duernie you're looking for will be with them?"

"If not, they'll be able to take me to her."

"All right," Barney growled. He still was obviously very dubious, but this was the best plan they could come up with.

Barney skillfully piloted the jetcar above the stream of pure molten ore. It was easy when he didn't have to worry about sudden wind shifts, updrafts or downdrafts, but the unrelenting heat made instrument readings unreliable. Barney had to do some fine seat-of-the-pants flying as they followed the meandering ribbon of liquid metal as it wandered from the scarp to the plain below.

"There," Kemal said after a few moments, "Dancers."

Their shiny pressure suits made them look like odd, glittering insects scattered about the dark, dead plain. They were grouped around the metallic stream as if they were drinking from it. Of course, they were just testing its purity, but Kemal couldn't shake the image of robotic bugs from his brain.

"Going down," Barney said. "Can't stay on the surface long—this jetcar's not built for it. Suit all right?"

"Sure," Kemal replied more confidently than he really felt. This was the best sun suit they could find in the Belt, but it hadn't been manufactured with the hellish properties of Mercury in mind. Nevertheless, if Kemal was to pull off his meeting with Duernie, he had to look authentic.

"Your cremation," Barney said with a shrug of massive shoulders. "Tell me where to send your ashes."

Kemal shook his head. "Nowhere," he said. "I'm already home."

Barney touched down, and Kemal popped out of the jetcar's small airlock. Despite the cooling capabilities of the sun suit, the heat was like a slap in the face as Kemal climbed down onto the Mercurian surface. The beads of sweat that would immediately have formed on a Terran's forehead and back did not form on the naturally resistant Mercurian's. The awful heat did penetrate the thickly insulated soles of his boots, though, and he soon felt as if he were standing on a bed of coals. He sprinted across the landscape, heading for a pool of dark shadow that promised temporary relief. Once he reached the shadow, he checked the temperature gauge running on the faceplate of his helmet. The temperature had plummeted a hundred degrees in the shade, to a balmy six thirty-five.

Break out the cold drinks, he thought, I've found paradise.

A line of static roared in his earphones. He could make out only a few words among the noise.

". . . to go," Barney said from the jetcar. "Good . . . take . . ." and the space pirate lifted off.

Kemal waved, but he didn't know if the pirate could see him in the shadows. The Dancers, about a mile distant, certainly could. He watched them scurry about the lead stream, reminding him again of robotic ants whose nest had been kicked over. At first he'd thought that he'd have to hike over to the Dancers, but they were already scrambling toward their vehicles, two of which headed his way, while the others took up defensive positions in case this was all some kind of elaborate trap on his and Barney's part.

The Dancers, he thought, hadn't changed much. Still as paranoid as ever. On the other hand, considering his uncle Gordon's rapacious nature, just because they were paranoid didn't mean that someone wasn't after them.

He sat in the shade and dreamed of tall, cool pitchers of Terran iced tea until the Dancer vehicles arrived.

The first was a small desert tractor, built for no more than two people. A scout, it consisted mainly of an engine, treads, and insulation. The other was bigger and had gunnery ports. It's weapons, though, were shipped to avoid exposing them to the awful exterior temperatures until the drivers were sure that Kemal posed a threat. So far, and Kemal considered this to be a fine piece of good luck, it seemed they weren't entirely sure that he was an enemy.

He stood as the scout tractor wheeled within ten yards of him, then held his hands out, palms upward, in the universal gesture of peace and disarmament.

"Hello," he said into his radio mike. "I'm Kemal Gavilan. It's vitally important that I see Duernie right away. She knows who I am and knows that I am a friend to the Dancers."

The inhabitants of the armed tractor were silent, but the scout answered in a burst of static.

"All right," a voice said through the annoying buzz of interference caused by the excruciating high temperatures. "Come aboard. We'll take you to her."

Kemal entered through an open door on the side and squeezed into the storage space behind the two-man tractor's seats. It was a tight fit. His knees were pressed together and bunched up near his chin, his shoulders were pressed up against the tractor's walls, and his head was hunched over.

The Dancers he was riding with were not a loquacious duo. Dancers rarely were. Something of the loneliness and severity of their home world entered each Dancer's soul at birth, making them as quiet and uncompromising as the airless Mercurian landscape. Kemal knew better than to badger them with questions about their destination or complaints about his accommodations. The trip would end when it ended, and to the Dancers, discomfort was just an ordinary part of life that had to be endured.

By hunching down into an even more compressed and uncomfortable position, Kemal could see through the tractor's front viewscreens. Although it increased his discomfort, it relieved the tedium a little to watch the hellishly beautiful scenery roll by.

Eventually, just when it seemed that all his leg muscles would cramp from lack of circulation, a huge shiny structure came into view, and Kemal knew that he had reached the end of his cramped journey.

The Dancers were surface nomads, continually traveling the Mercurian landscape in caravans that consisted of half a dozen to two dozen closely related families. They kept to the twilight as much as they could, where temperatures were moderate, at least for Mercury. They did send scouting parties, like the one Kemal had stumbled across, out into the light or sometimes even into the Dark, for various specific purposes, but those were just splinter groups, not entire caravans consisting of men, women, and children.

The Dancers' vehicles were their homes, though each caravan also contained a large trailer that was used on the rare occasions when the Dancer community met face-to-face for certain political or social functions. The meeting trailer was what Kemal had first seen as the tractor approached the Dancer caravan.

One of the Dancers sitting in the front of the tractor picked up the radio and said into it, "This is Alec, calling Duernie. Duernie, please respond."

There was a moment of silence. She must have replied, because the Dancer started speaking again, but Kemal couldn't hear her voice because it was channeled directly into the Dancer's earphones.

"We have a visitor for you. Says his name is Kemal Gavilan." There was another silence. "I don't know," the Dancer then said. "He was dropped off by a jetcar out on the fringes of the Caloris Range." More silence. "All right. Whatever you say." The Dancer turned to the driver. "Heard her?" he asked.

The driver grunted laconically, drove past the mobile meeting hall and half a dozen personal vehicles before pulling to a halt in front of one halfway down the caravan line.

"There she is, Gavilan," the Dancer spoke without turning back to look at him. "Duernie'll be waiting for you on the other side of the airlock of her vehicle. Good luck."

Kemal grumbled his thanks. Knowing Duernie's propensity for having a short fuse, he knew that he needed more than good luck. He needed extraordinary luck.

* * * * *

He was right. Duernie did not seem exactly happy to see him again.

"You manage to find your way back into my life every few years, don't you, Kemal Gavilan?"

Duernie sounded, and looked, annoyed. She could have been beautiful if she would lighten up on the frown lines—which habitually creased her forehead—and the pucker of her mouth. But she hadn't changed any since the last time Kemal had seen her.

"It hasn't been that long," he protested.

"It has here," she said in what clearly was meant as a rebuke. "You never think like a Mercurian."

He suddenly realized what she meant. It had been several Mercurian years since he'd seen Duernie last. Of course, a Mercurian year was only eighty-eight Earth days long, so it hadn't really been a very long time. But the real rebuke, he knew, was that a real Mercurian would think in terms of Mercurian years. A real Mercurian would think in terms of Mercurian time and temperature, needs and desires. He didn't. He never had.

She sighed. "Same old Gavilan. Caught between two worlds—or is it three now?"

"My heart has always been on Mercury," he protested.

"Has it?" she asked.

He looked at her. She was tall and thin, with no extra flesh. Few Dancers could afford such a luxury. Her skin was darker than Kemal's own bronze color. Her hair and her eyes were dark.

"You know it has," he said softly.

She looked away from him. When she looked up after a few moments, a hint of a flush suffused her fine, high cheeks.

"Why have you come back now?" she asked.

Kemal sighed. He couldn't tell her right out what he needed from her. Not just yet. He had to approach the subject slowly and work himself up to where he'd be in the position to betray her and her people. The thought made him vaguely ill.

"What do you know about the crystals called Sun Flowers?" he asked.

She looked surprised at the question. "Why?"

Kemal hesitated. He couldn't lie to her, but now was not exactly the time for the whole truth. "I've run into some of them out in the Belt and been given information that indicates they might come from Mercury. But I'd never heard of them before."

She nodded. "That's because the Dancers just discovered them less than three years ago."

"Then," Kemal asked, "the crystals are a Dancer invention?"

"Well," Duernie corrected, "I wouldn't exactly say invention. More like a discovery."

Kemal frowned. "Then they're a natural phenomenon."

"More or less," Duernie said. "A Dancer named Madog discovered the fissure where they grow when he was out scouting for new ore deposits. For a long time he kept them a secret. Our artists and scientists are still studying them and have budded some. So far, the best growths have been natural. The best we can figure is that the precise temperature and morphological conditions of this little fissure have caused the Sun Flowers to grow only in this one particular area on the whole planet."

"Can you take me to see them?"

Duernie glanced at him. "I suppose," she said. "The location's been kept a secret because we don't want it overrun by greedy outside developers. We've been selling off some of the crystals to get much-needed money, but there's a strong segment of the Dancer community that wants to preserve the whole valley and leave them in their natural setting." She gave him a quick, shy smile. "But I suppose we can trust you with the secret. After all, you've proven your friendship in the past."

She was referring to the time Gordon Gavilan had called Kemal back to Mercury just before his twenty-first birthday. Gordon had evolved a scheme whereby he would put the Dancers under the thumb of the Warrens, the underground cities that were one of five social groups that formed the Mercurian planetary council—the Warrens, Dancers, Musicians, Miners, and Mariposas. Kemal had foiled that plan, thereby allowing the Dancers to maintain their own social, cultural, and political identity in the tapestry of Mercurian society. He had met Duernie during that adventure, when she'd rescued him from a Warren city that had kidnaped him to get him to accede to its political demands.

"How have things been since my absence?" he asked Duernie, just to get off the subject of the crystals for a moment.

"As always," she said. "We continue to be poor but proud, and independent, though the Warrens still try to put us under their thumb. Your uncle," she said, gazing at Kemal as if to gauge his reaction, "uses the excuse of Earth's rebellion to try to draw the reins of power tighter into his own hands. He acts more and more like an autocratic despot rather than the head of a diverse planetary council."

"Ah, yes," Kemal said, eyes narrowing. "My uncle. I've yet to pay my respects to him."

"You haven't seen him yet?" Duernie asked.

Kemal looked at her. "No," he lied. "I thought I'd first make a more pleasant visit."

He couldn't be sure, but he thought he saw her blush under her tanned skin as she looked at him and smiled. He wanted desperately to take her into his arms and tell her all the things he felt about her, but he couldn't do it. He didn't have the right, not when he was going to betray her and her people to the man she despised most in the system.

CHAPTER NINETEEN

Betrayal burned like bitter gall in the seething cauldron of Kemal's stomach as he sat in the front seat of the tractor next to Duernie. She looked uncharacteristically happy. She smiled and chatted animatedly as she drove over the treacherous Mercurian landscape. Kemal realized in a flash of insight that it was his presence that made her happy. He had finally succeeded in breaking past her reserve. She liked him, liked his company. Maybe it was even more than that.

Great, Kemal thought. Just great. Why now of all times?

"When are you going to pay your respects to your uncle?" she asked. "Hey—" she tapped him on the thigh "—you listening to me?"

"Sure," Kemal said. He turned to her and tried to put a smile on his face. He was sure that she could see the falseness of it, even if she gave no outward sign. "Maybe I'll see my uncle and my cousin Tix sometime tomorrow. Dalton is off somewhere, thank god."

Dalton was off in the asteroids, he wanted to tell her, using your beautiful crystal flowers to create a weapon capable of vaporizing a man in his tracks.

But he couldn't say it. He swallowed the truth, where it sat like a burning stone in the pit of his stomach.

"Your uncle's been quiet lately. Has he really mellowed, or is the old tyrant up to something?"

"Oh, you know my uncle," Kemal said. He couldn't tell her the truth, but he vowed to himself not to lie to Duernie. "I wouldn't trust him as far as I could throw him. On Jupiter."

Duernie laughed, then fell silent as she concentrated on driving. They were about to negotiate a particularly dangerous bit of landscape, which, on Mercury, was saying a lot.

They were in twilight, heading toward the dark. The merciless sun was busy burning the other side of the planet. The heat it had baked into this side during the long, terrible Mercurian day was slowly dissipating into space. The metal streams were cooling, solidifying in their spillways like gleaming ribbons. Tiny bits of rock flaked off the surface of the towering cliffs, popping away as they cooled.

Temperature change was virtually the only thing that affected the surface of this airless, waterless world. That and human hands, present now in the small tractor trundling through the gathering night, its headlights throwing off beams of light like lances into the increasing darkness.

"When were the Sun Flowers found?" Kemal asked as Duernie maneuvered their tractor around the edge of a sudden, unexpected chasm that ran as sharp and jagged as a sword cut through the planet's surface.

"About fifteen years ago," she said, almost absently, concentrating on driving.

Kemal juggled figures in his head. About one Earth year, he thought, about half a Martian year.

"It was Madog who found them," Duernie said after a few moments of silence, "exploring the south fringe of the Phidian Basin for new mineral deposits. He came upon them during twilight, about this time, and was so enthralled by the sight of them that he almost stayed too long. It got so cold that he would have frozen in the heart of the dark. In desperation, he moved his tractor closer to the crystals and discovered that they radiated warmth as well as the light they had captured from the sun. They saved his life."

"He was the one who started to harvest them?" Kemal asked.

Duernie shook her head. "For a long time he told no one of his discovery. He was an old man when he felt death approaching. He took his son Caradog to see the crystals. When his father died, Caradog brought one back to the caravan," Duernie told him. "It was the most beautiful thing any of us had ever seen. We knew their value. One of our number, Ubrahil Carrera, managed to obtain the mining rights to the sector. We decided that they could be sold as works of art, but to keep their value high and conserve them, we decided to limit the number we'd sell."

"How many have you harvested so far?"

Duernie shrugged. "Oh, forty, maybe. Less than fifty."

Dalton Gavilan had had maybe thirty on Rising Sun Station, Kemal knew. Gordon must have gone through a score of corporations and fictitious art collectors to put together his stash without the Dancers realizing the extent of it.

"How much are the flowers worth?"

Duernie shrugged. "How much does one pay for priceless beauty? We ask for a lot of money, and we usually get it. One to five million credits apiece, depending on their exact size, shape, and ability to disperse color. We've added more than a hundred and sixty million credits to our treasury. That's brought our people a lot of things we've needed. A lot of gear and medicine and supplies. And such financial security will also help ensure our independence from the Warrens."

Seeing the fierce pride on Duernie's face made Kemal realize that he couldn't go through with his deception. He couldn't take such a resource away from the Dancers and hand it over to his uncle. They deserved it infinitely more than Gordon Gavilan did.

But before he could confess anything, the tractor edged around the base of a lobate scarp that towered more than a mile into the airless sky. It formed one wall of a small box canyon that was hewn into the southern edge of Phidian Basin like a knife slash cut by the hand of an immeasurably huge giant.

There, bunched together at the end of the canyon, thrown carelessly about like a trove of priceless jewels scattered on velvet cloth, were hundreds of shimmering lights.

Kemal's breath caught at the sight. These Sun Flowers, still extant in their natural setting, where they had found the optimal conditions of light, soil, and chemical nutrients, put the ones he had seen on Rising Sun Station to shame. They were pedigrees compared to mongrels, champions compared to culls. They were bigger, brighter, more magnificent in color and form. Behind the garden loomed a dome, a pale mirage beyond the glory of the crystals.

As Kemal and Duernie got closer, the crystals sparkled more brightly with every rich and living hue of the spectrum. There was flaming scarlet and gentle cerise, royal purple and vibrant indigo. There was orange and yellow and blue in all possible values. And green. Green sparkled like emeralds, like fields of new, fresh grass, like the deep, plush richness of a billiard table.

Green. Kemal had never seen green on the hellish landscape of Mercury before. He had never thought he would.

"Incredible, aren't they?" Duernie said in a small, hushed voice. "I've never seen colors like those before."

Kemal realized that she was speaking the literal truth. Mercury was a colorless world of black and white and gray. Duernie had never been off-planet to see the cerise deserts of Mars or the azure oceans of Earth. True, there were holograms and tri-dee images and pictures and tapes of every conceivable form and quality, but the Dancers were a poor people with little to spend on such frivolities. The Sun Flowers, he realized, were probably the brightest, most colorful, most beautiful things she and the others had ever seen in their lives.

He couldn't take all that away from them.

"Wait until you see them up close," she said in the same awed voice as she engaged the small surface crawler's gears and they edged forward. "Words can't describe the colors. We never would have sold even one of the flowers if our own economic need hadn't been so desperate."

Kemal turned in his seat to face her and put his hand on her right forearm. "Listen, Duernie," he said urgently. "Stop the tractor immediately. Turn back. Turn back at once."

She looked at him, puzzled. "Why?"

"There's no time to go into it now. Just turn the tractor around and I'll tell you as we head back to the caravan."

She frowned. "All right."

Kemal sighed and sat back in his seat. How could he tell her, how could he even begin to broach the subject of his treachery?

"About the Sun Flowers," he began as she carefully

reversed the tractor and swung it in a long, curving arc to start back the way they'd come. "They're not just objects of beauty. They have some other . . . unusual properties."

"Our scientists are working on that," she said. "We know that they can store and focus light in odd ways."

"Your people aren't the only ones investigating the Sun Flowers," Kemal told her. "Someone else has already discovered that they can be used as the focal points in a weapons system capable of unbelievable destruction."

She stared at him as if he were mad. "Who, Kemal?" she demanded. "Who's been working on these weapons?"

"My uncle," Kemal admitted. "Uncle Gordon and cousin Dalton."

"And you—" she began, angry spots of color burning in her high cheekbones.

But she never finished her sentence. The crackle of static from the tractor's radio receiver interrupted her, followed quickly by a deep, authoritarian voice.

"Dancer surface crawler, this is Sun King Jetcar One-A, House of Gavilan. Heave to. Surface crawler, heave to. We have no wish to fire upon you, but we will if we must. Please heave to."

Duernie glared at Kemal and let out a string of curses. He wasn't sure if they were directed at him or the jetcar flashing overhead. She grimly hung onto the wheel and stomped down on the tractor's accelerator.

"Heave to," the skimmer insisted. "We have you covered and you have no chance to escape."

Duernie craned her neck and desperately looked out the tractor's forward viewscreen. In the air above them was a squad of jetcars painted in the distinctive pattern of the House of Gavilan. Kemal realized that his uncle must have placed a tracer on him somehow. His uncle hadn't totally trusted him to betray the Dancers—and he'd been right. But now everything had been taken out of Kemal's hands.

There were at least a dozen jetcars buzzing around the vicinity like giant, bloated flies. All were faster than the tractor, all were more heavily armed and armored. The speaker was right. They had no chance to escape.

Duernie slammed on the brakes with such ferocity that Kemal bucked forward in his seat and hit his knees painfully on the dash. She turned and glared at him. Sorrow caught at Kemal's throat at the burning hatred he saw in her eyes.

He opened his mouth to explain his actions, to try to tell Duernie why he had to betray her and her people, but no words would come. She stared at him, realizing the full extent of his betrayal, perhaps even more deeply than Kemal did. The period of prosperity for the Dancers would never arise now, and, even worse, their chance at economic and political independence had probably disappeared.

"You, you . . ." she had no words for what she wanted to tell Kemal. He could no longer meet the hurt, angry look of her eyes but looked away as she

sputtered in rage. Some of the jetcars were heading
for the heart of the Sun Flower canyon. Others still
hovered nearby, their occupants keeping an eye on
the Dancer crawler.

Kemal realized that he had to tell her, he had to
somehow find the words to let her know why he had
betrayed the Dancers to his uncle. He took his courage firmly in his hands and looked up to meet her
searing gaze.

"Duernie—" he began, but he could get nothing
more out.

Her hand moved swifter than he could block it, if
he'd wanted to, lashing out and catching him powerfully across the cheek. The slap resounded loudly in
the close confines of the crawler, and her palm left its
mark, a burning red welt of pain and anger, on his
cheek.

"*Never,*" she said, in a dangerous low voice, "never
say my name again, *Gavilan.*" She spat his last name
as if it were a curse.

He looked away, then quickly back to her. The tears
in his eyes were only partly from the stinging pain of
her blow. She met his gaze steadily, but there were
tears in her own eyes as well.

"I should kill you, Gavilan," she said, "but I can't."
She lifted her shoulders and let them fall in a hopeless shrug. "It is my shame. My shame that I love a
man who cannot be trusted. A man who sells out the
only friends he knows for a Gavilan's power and
gold."

"D—" he began, but then stopped. "I—wait!"

He shouted the last word as she whirled her seat around and bolted into the small airlock that was the rear compartment of the crawler. Kemal was too slow to catch her, and once the airlock door slammed shut and began the cycling procedure, it couldn't be opened again until the cycle was complete.

It took only a few moments. When it opened again, he caught a glimpse of Duernie in a sun suit, leaping swiftly across the rugged Mercurian terrain. He moved to go after her, but the voice coming over the crawler radio stopped him cold.

"Halt, Dancer," it ordered. "Halt, or we'll fire!"

Kemal grabbed the radio controls. "This is Kemal Gavilan," he shouted into the mike. "Let her go! Let her go, dammit!"

There was hesitant silence from the jetcar patrolling overhead, then a reluctant, "All right, if you so order."

"I do," he said wearily, then slumped back in his chair. He looked out the crawler's side viewscreen. Duernie was nowhere to be seen. She'd already vanished into the hellish landscape that was the only home she'd ever known. She was lost to his sight.

She was lost to him forever.

CHAPTER TWENTY

The formal Gavilan dress uniform was stiff and uncomfortable. It reminded Kemal of the dress parades from back in his academy days, but either he had grown less tolerant of high, stiff collars, tight necks, and constricted waists, or else this uniform was even worse than the one he'd endured as a cadet.

But he needed it. He needed every ounce of authority he could muster if he was to face down his cousin Dalton for control of Rising Sun Station, something he was sure Dalton wasn't going to give up very easily.

Gordon Gavilan had been ecstatic when his team had returned with the location of Sun Flower Canyon, so ecstatic that he'd barely noticed Kemal's glum countenance.

"This will do it, my boy," he said as he poured over the aerial photos of the region brought back by the jetcar squadron that had been on Kemal's trail. "This will provide us with a nearly unlimited supply of the crystals."

"You're not going to cut the Dancers out entirely, are you?" Kemal asked.

His uncle looked at him almost suspiciously. "Not going soft on us, are you, boy?"

Kemal's self-disgust flared into anger that Gordon interpreted as righteous indignation. "I just think that it might be best to pay the Dancers a cut of the crystals' worth. In that case, they wouldn't be able to claim that we've stolen them."

"Hmmm," Gordon rubbed his square jaw. "You may be right. Tell you what. We'll give them, say, ten thousand credits for any crystal we take. That's a fair price."

That's not anywhere near a fair price, you greedy weasel, Kemal thought to himself, but it would have to do. He couldn't push it any farther and raise Gordon's suspicions as to his real motives.

A pleased Sun King then signed a written commission for Kemal to take command of Rising Sun Station.

"From Dalton's last report I gather that their work is almost done anyway. Your main mission will be to shut down operations and bring the solar laser back to Mercury. But," Gordon emphasized with a wave of the document that he'd just signed, "even though

you have this, I don't expect you'll have an easy time
with Dalton. He's a headstrong one," Gordon continued with more than a touch of pride. "Takes after his
father. He's bound to give you trouble. In a way, this
will be a good test for him. See how closely he'll follow my orders."

And it's a test for me, too, Kemal realized. You want
to see if I'll be able to handle your swaggering son.
Well, I think I'll surprise you. I'm ready to play your
games of deceit and deception now, and I'm going to
play them harder and tougher than you ever thought
possible.

Kemal had a long time to think about things during the voyage from Mercury to Rising Sun Station.
He had command of his own House of Gavilan
cruiser, the *Sun Spot*, traveling in tandem with Barney's *Free Enterprise*.

Barney had a reputation throughout the system for
ruthlessness and toughness. Kemal knew that Gordon was more than a little impressed—and also more
than a little surprised—that his heretofore straight-
laced and idealistic nephew was working with the pirate. He figured that Kemal somehow had become
corrupt—like all the other Gavilans—to the pirate's
level of greed and rapine. Kemal suspected that Gordon had never guessed that the opposite was true,
that Barney, mainly through his association with
Buck Rogers, was now willing to do the right thing—
as long as there also was a little bit of profit in it for
him at the end.

All the deep cogitation in the universe, however,

failed to soothe the sorrow in Kemal's heart when he thought of what he had done to Duernie and the Dancers. He knew that he had to betray them in order to gain his uncle's trust. He knew that the greater good was at stake here, that he had to weigh the needs and desires of a small group of people against the damage that could be caused by the laser device in the hands of an unchecked tyrant. He knew that he had simply done what had to be done.

But he still felt like a rat.

And he still had to face Dalton in—he checked his thumbwatch—a little less than an hour's time. That he would enjoy. He promised himself that.

He looked himself over in his cabin's mirror one last time. The uniform as a perfect fit. Not a thread, not a hair was out of place. His face looked as if it had aged over the past few weeks, and indeed perhaps it had. Some of the youth, some of the lightheartedness had gone out of it. He looked as grim and hard as a sword blade. His experiences in the Martian Wars had been the base on which he'd built these last few weeks. He had grown, painfully but immeasurably. Dalton had a great reputation for blunder and bluster and arrogance, but he was about to meet his match.

Kemal marched from his cabin to the bridge of the *Sun Spot*, where he took over the command chair from his second mate, Kal Hawker, a veteran sailor grown old in the service of Mercury and the Sun Kings.

Hawker surrendered the chair without comment as

Kemal came on duty early. Kemal wanted it known from the set of his face that something was up. Just what, he wasn't about to disclose. He didn't want Dalton to hear of his arrival too long beforehand and have an opportunity to prepare a defense against him.

"ETA Rising Sun Station?" Kemal asked his helmsmen in calm, even tones.

The helmsman checked their position. "Thirty minutes, sir."

"Wait until they query to identify us," Kemal ordered.

The communications chief raised an eyebrow. "That's not customary procedure, sir."

"I'm aware of customary procedure," Kemal said in the same even voice.

"Yes, sir," the com chief replied. He glanced at Hawker, who looked steadily back, as if to say, I don't know what's going on, either.

The cruiser approached Rising Sun Station as the minutes ticked away in a tense silence that Kemal seemed utterly indifferent to. The events of the past few weeks, from Lilith's death to the discovery of his father's murder to his forced betrayal of the Dancers, had changed him. He had been to the forge and emerged tempered like fine steel, bendable but not breakable.

The helmsman counted down their approach at Kemal's request. Moments after the crewman had announced "ETA ten minutes," the ship's com unit came alive.

"Rising Sun Station to unknown ship, you are violating private space lanes. Please identify yourself and state your purpose."

Kemal turned to the communications officer. "Sound and picture, please," he ordered, then he swiveled the command chair back to face the viewscreen. "This is the cruiser *Sun Spot*, outward bound from Mercury, Prince Kemal Gavilan, commanding. I have come under the orders of Gordon Gavilan to take command of Rising Sun Station. Please acknowledge."

The jaw of the station's communications officer dropped wide open. "Say again, *Sun Spot*."

Kemal permitted himself a tight smile and repeated his orders.

"You, uh, you have confirmation, sir?" the com chief asked.

Kemal held up a computer microdisk, then reached out and handed it to his own communications officer. "Transmitting confirmation right now. I also have hard copy signed by Gordon Gavilan, Sun King of Mercury."

He had been sure to mention his uncle's title, to give his pronouncement the weight of formal authority.

"Uh, yes, sir. Uh, Commander Dalton is sleeping now, sir."

"Then wake him. Have him in the control room when I arrive." He turned to his own com chief. "End transmission," he ordered, and the screen went blank.

Kemal stood and looked at Hawker. "You may have the chair again."

The old second officer looked at him. "You probably don't know Commander Dalton very well," he told Kemal. "He's not going to like this. He's really not going to like this."

Kemal permitted himself another smile.

"I know him better than you think," he said as he left the bridge.

* * * * *

Hawker, in fact, turned out to be a master of understatement.

Dalton was waiting, as Kemal had ordered, in the control room. Dalton Gavilan was a big man, bigger than Kemal. He was powerfully built, with a thick chest and wide shoulders. Although only in his early thirties, the frown lines on his forehead already were deeper than his father's. His dark eyes were wild and sinister, as was the black mustache that curved down over his narrow-lipped mouth. He looked slightly disheveled, as if he'd just woken up, and more than a little outraged.

"What is this nonsense?" he stormed at Kemal as the younger man entered Rising Sun's control room, followed by Hawker and several junior officers.

Kemal smiled. "Nice to see you again, Cousin, after all these years."

"Can the sentiment, Kemal. What do you mean by waltzing in here and announcing that you're taking over?"

"Just what I said. I'm taking over."

"By whose authority?" Dalton roared.

"By the authority of Gordon Gavilan, Sun King of Mercury. Your father."

Kemal held out the signed orders and slapped Dalton in the chest with them. Dalton stared at them as if they were some kind of poisonous reptile.

"What kind of trick is this?"

"No trick," Kemal said. "It's politics."

"Politics," Dalton grumbled, unconvinced. He took the papers from Kemal and began to scan them. He looked up after a moment, still steaming but more visibly under control. "Not that I don't trust you, Cousin," he said, patently not trusting him, "but I'll have to go over these thoroughly. Just to be sure that the best interests of the House of Gavilan will be properly served."

"Certainly," Kemal said with a smile one cut above a sneer. "I am sure that the interests of the House of Gavilan are foremost in your mind. Particularly when they coincide with your own."

Dalton's eyes narrowed. He was uncertain if he'd just been insulted, so he decided to ignore what Kemal had said.

"I shall relinquish control of Rising Sun Station when I'm convinced that these papers are authentic and that they do call for a change in command."

"Very well," Kemal said. "Do what you want with them. I have copies in case this one somehow gets damaged or lost."

This time Dalton was sure he'd been insulted, but he visibly forced himself to calm down. He brushed by Kemal with a snarl and an ungracious, "Make yourselves comfortable."

"Thank you," Kemal said to Dalton's back as the commander stormed out. Kemal looked around the control room, ignoring the frank stares of the station personnel as they appraised him. Not too many people dared bait Dalton Gavilan the way he had, and even fewer got away with it. He immediately went up in their estimation. Dalton Gavilan had not been a popular commander.

"Tell me," Kemal asked the station's communications chief, "do you tape all incoming and outgoing radio messages?"

"Sure," the chief said. "Security reasons. Our commander—that is, our ex-commander—was a real stickler for security."

"How long do you keep the tapes before destroying them?"

The chief scratched his head. "I don't think we ever destroy them. We've got them all stored on the main computer's hard disk."

"By date?" Kemal asked.

The chief nodded. "Yup. Day and time."

Kemal smiled. "Your commander told me to make myself comfortable. To do that, I'll need a computer and a copy of those files."

The com chief nodded. "Yes, sir."

Kemal smiled. Dalton's fetish for detail might prove to be his undoing.

CHAPTER TWENTY-ONE

Kemal asked for a computer in a private place because he didn't want it spread about just yet what he was looking for. The com chief led him to a unit in a quiet corner of the rec room and hung over his shoulder as Kemal switched it on. Kemal turned and smiled at him.

"That's all for now, chief," he said.

"Sure you don't need my help?"

Kemal shook his head.

"Nothing else I could do for you?"

Kemal shook his head again.

"Okay. Just holler if you need anything."

"I will."

The com chief backed off, nodding his head and smiling widely, if a bit fixedly, at Kemal. Kemal couldn't decide if the man was trying to do his job or just sucking up to the new commander. Either way, he was glad to get rid of the man.

The blinking prompt brought his attention back to the monitor. Dalton, he was sure, wasn't fool enough to keep the records in an open file. He probably had them blocked with passwords and security files. That was no problem for Kemal, though, not as long as Huer could be called in.

"Doctor?" he said with a low voice into his uplink unit.

Huer, correctly assessing the situation, didn't materialize holographically. Instead, he logged in on the computer screen.

"Hello," suddenly appeared next to the prompt. "What do you need from the old doctor this time?"

"I'm sure you remember our last visit to Rising Sun," Kemal typed onto the screen.

"I certainly do," Huer responded in print.

"Track down the communication records for that day. I want the recording of my distress call and Rising Sun's response. I want further documentation to show that the com officer was lying when he said they couldn't send a rescue vehicle in time to save me. And I want documentation showing where the lie originated."

"With Commander Gavilan."

"Undoubtedly." Huer knew as well as Kemal that Dalton had ordered Kemal abandoned. But Kemal wanted hard evidence. He wanted to be able to document what a rat his cousin was, then expose him to the entire system.

"Working," Huer wrote. There was a pause, then the message continued. "By the way, I have named the new element in the Sun Flowers 'Dancenium.' " He suffered a pang over Huer's reference to the dancers, even as he warmed at the scientific compliment the digital personality had paid them.

Kemal reached over and turned off the set. Huer was on the case. There was nothing for him to do but wait. He decided to make a private visit to Dalton's quarters. There was a lot he and his cousin had to talk over.

Dalton's quarters were near the docking facility. Kemal buzzed the door, identified himself, and it swished open automatically. Kemal looked around as he entered. At least Dalton hadn't used his command position to enrich himself personally.

His quarters could best be described as spartan. There was a utilitarian desk, a utilitarian chair set, a utilitarian bed, and a utilitarian wardrobe, and not much of anything else. There were no decorations, no ornamentation, no photographs of loved ones or objects. Dalton's rooms were those of a man totally defined by his job. Without the job, without the position of authority that he held, he was nothing. He was a walking shell, thought Kemal, a body with no reason to exist.

For a moment that made Kemal feel sorry for his cousin. Then he remembered what a rotten bastard Dalton was, and all his sympathy went out the window.

Dalton was sitting in his utilitarian chair behind his utilitarian desk, scowling at the sheaf of papers he'd received as if he still couldn't understand the meaning of their contents.

"The words aren't going to change," Kemal told him, "no matter how many times you read them."

Dalton transferred his scowl from the papers to Kemal. "Why?" he asked. "Why did my father replace me with *you*, of all people."

Obviously, the thought of anyone replacing him was difficult for Dalton to bear. The fact that it was Kemal replacing him made it almost unendurable.

Kemal smiled. "Maybe," he said, sticking a figurative knife into Dalton, "he realized that I was more useful to him." He gave the knife a twist. "Maybe he realized I was the better man for the job."

Dalton shot to his feet. "You no-good, worthless weakling," he spit through clenched teeth. "If I could, I'd teach you a lesson you'd never forget!"

"You're right, Dalton," Kemal said quietly. "*If* you could."

He had finally goaded his cousin too far. Dalton roared in anger and launched himself across his desk. He had ten years' experience and twenty pounds of muscle on Kemal, but Kemal was ready for him. He knew he could taunt Dalton into doing something foolish, but he hadn't realized that his words would turn his cousin into a raving madman.

He calmly stepped aside of Dalton's flying charge and his cousin smashed into the chair set in front of the desk. The chair and Dalton both careened into the wall, but Dalton was back on his feet in half a moment, showing much quicker reflexes than Kemal thought possible.

"I'm going to break you with my bare hands," Dalton ground out, then charged at Kemal again.

Kemal stepped back and launched a side-kick that caught Dalton in the stomach. The force of the kick lifted Dalton off the floor and again into the wall. Dalton grunted in surprise and pain but managed to grab Kemal's ankle before he could pull away.

He twisted savagely and Kemal writhed. Dalton shoved Kemal heavily into the opposite wall. As the larger man barreled into him, pain lanced through Kemal's knee as if it'd been transfixed by a knife. Something had torn loose inside the knee joint, and it hurt like the blazes.

Kemal couldn't afford to worry about that now. Dalton was straddled before him and bringing up a huge fist to smash his face. The fist descended like a hammer ready to pound a nail, but Kemal blocked it with crossed forearms. Dalton tried to punch him again, but this time Kemal caught his wrist and twisted it as hard as he could.

Dalton howled in pain and tried to pull away, but Kemal held onto his wrist like a terrier fastened to the throat of a rat.

"You bastard," Dalton panted.

Kemal twisted harder. They both heard a loud snapping sound, and Dalton screamed and tried to push off the wall and away, but Kemal still wouldn't relinquish his cousin's wrist.

The broken ends of Dalton's ulna grated against each other, and he shrieked like an animal. Kemal finally let go of the wrist. He pushed Dalton away, rolled, and came up into a crouch, his magnetized boots once again firmly on the floor, his body ready to spring.

Dalton lurched up to his knees and held his right arm tightly against his chest. "You broke my wrist, damn you!" he ground out. "I'll get you for that, you—"

He never finished his threat. The computer console on his desk pinged loudly and a voice trying very hard to be calm came over the air. "Commander Gavilan, Commander Gavilan, sir, we're trying to locate Commander Gavilan—eh, that is Commander Kemal Gavilan. Is he with you?"

Dalton lurched to his feet and glared at Kemal. He leaned over the desk, wincing in pain as he tried to cradle his broken wrist against his chest. "I haven't relinquished command yet, damn your eyes. I'm still in charge here!"

"Yes, sir!" the communications man said, the panic growing in his voice. "Sir, a squadron of ships is approaching Rising Sun Station. They refuse to identify themselves."

"How many ships?" Dalton snapped.

"Five or six. They're getting very close—"

The com chief's voice was drowned out in a sudden explosion that shook the entire asteroid. Dalton slammed his good hand down on an alarm klaxon that hooted throughout the station.

"This is Commander Gavilan," he shouted into the com unit, "Commander *Dalton* Gavilan. Rising Sun Station is under attack. Go to your battle stations! Repeat! Battle stations!"

The asteroid shuddered again as another charge slammed into it. Dalton yelped in pain as his arm was jarred, and then he glared sullenly at Kemal.

"We'll settle this later, Cousin. It seems that we have more pressing matters to occupy our attention."

Kemal thought quickly. It would only confuse things and impede their defense if he pressed Dalton about taking over the station. It would be best, he decided, to let Dalton retain control for now. They could finish their personal feud later—if they managed to beat off this unexpected, unknown enemy.

Kemal nodded decisively. "All right. I'll scramble the *Sun Spot*, and we'll see what I can do from space."

"Good idea," Dalton said grudgingly, and Kemal turned to run from the room. "Cousin," Dalton called out after him.

Kemal paused on the threshold of the room.

"Be careful," Dalton said.

Those were the last words he expected to hear from Dalton's mouth.

"I want to finish you off myself after this," Dalton said through clenched teeth.

Kemal smiled and nodded. That was more like the Dalton Gavilan he knew.

* * * * *

The crazed activity in Rising Sun Station reminded Kemal of an anthill that had just been kicked over by an unseen giant. Men were scurrying here and there, some purposefully, many at random.

This was, Kemal realized, primarily a research station. Although they occasionally had to deal with spies and intruders—as Kemal knew quite well from firsthand experience—most of the men stationed on the asteroid were scientists, technicians, and workers. There were only a few military men on the rock, and although they seemed to know what they were doing, they definitely were in the minority.

Kemal felt as if he were a salmon fighting against the current as he tried to reach the spacedocks. Most of the station personnel headed in the opposite direction, into the guts of the rock, where they'd be better protected against attack.

Kemal gave up after a few minutes of pushing and shoving, and ducked off into a small side-corridor that had a lot less traffic swarming through it. He caught his breath for a moment, then spoke to the empty air.

"Huer," he called aloud, and the digital personality materialized at his side within the moment.

"You were right," Huer told Kemal. "I've got the evidence against Dalton. It's all there in the tapes as the com officer insisted on getting a formal order to maroon you. There's no doubt that Dalton knew he could have rescued you, but was just going to let you die."

Kemal nodded. "Great. Save a copy of all the relevant data. Right now, we've got something else to worry about," he added as the station was rocked by another explosive salvo.

"Oh, yes," Huer said. "I noticed that something was going on."

"I've got no details, but apparently the station is under attack by a small fleet of five or six ships. It sounds to me like pirates," said Kemal.

"You don't think Barney's impatience got the better of him, do you?" Huer asked.

Kemal shook his head. "I wouldn't like to think so, but I just don't know. I want to scramble the *Sun Spot* to see if we can take out some of the attacking ships, but I can't reach it through the panic in the corridors around the docks."

Huer nodded. "I'll relay your orders."

He blipped off, and Kemal paced through the small side-corridor, tallying his options. They were few and far between. In the face of an utter lack of intelligence about the enemy, he just didn't know what moves to make.

An attack on the station, he realized, had been bound to come sooner or later. If he and Huer had discovered the existence and location of the laser device, there were probably others in the system with equal—if not superior—intelligence capabilities who would be very interested in getting such a weapon for their very own.

Kemal found the timing of the attack very interesting. It couldn't have come at a worse time for Rising Sun, with two men fighting over command. Perhaps, he wondered, the attackers had inside information. Perhaps they knew that such a disruption was taking place and that this was the optimal time to launch their assault.

If that were the case, Black Barney and his crew definitely would be under suspicion.

But it couldn't be Barney, Kemal told himself. They were bound by blood and steel, and of all the clone-warriors, Black Barney was the least likely to break his vow. The pirate had his faults, but faithlessness wasn't one of them.

Unlike you, a small voice told Kemal. He felt a twinge of guilt but knew this wasn't the time to indulge himself. He would worry about Duernie and the Dancers later.

He looked around the side-corridor. He felt utterly useless where he was. He had to do something to help defend the station. Unless this was a simple smash-and-grab raid with a squadron of pirates looking for loot at random, the focus of the assault definitely would be the Sun Flowers and the laser device. That would be where the fighting would be the most intense.

That was where he had to go.

Kemal stepped back out into the corridor. It was quieter. The traffic had subsided considerably. He'd probably have no difficulty making it to the *Sun Spot* if it hadn't taken off already. He stood there, indecisive, wishing Huer would let him know how things were going.

As if reading Kemal's mind, the computer persona

suddenly appeared before him.

"It was too late to send the *Sun Spot* out," Huer reported. "The raiders hit the docks first. The *Sun Spot*'s damaged. The station's own cruiser has been destroyed."

"Damn!" Kemal said. "Do you have any other information?"

Huer nodded rapidly. "I went on a quick scout. The Rising Sun was initially bombarded from space, which destroyed most of its offensive capabilities. The raiders then landed boarding parties at three separate points. There's hand-to-hand combat in the corridors near the dormitories, the labs, and the airlocks leading out to the Sun Flowers. The raiders seem to be mercenaries. They're a mix of gennies and various human races. They seem to be a tough, disciplined lot, and they outnumber our security forces."

"Who's winning?" Kemal asked.

Huer shook his head. "It doesn't look good for the good guys."

"Who're the good guys?" Kemal muttered under his breath, taking off down the corridor at a run. He ignored as best he could the pain lancing through his knee at every step.

If things were as bad as Huer described, only one weapon could possibly turn the tide.

The laser device.

CHAPTER TWENTY-TWO

The sounds and smells of combat lay heavily in the corridors of Rising Sun Station.

The hiss of energy weapons mingled with the eerie moan of bolt rifles being fired on full automatic, and the loud, snapping explosions of rocket pistols and shaped-charge grenades. Punctuating these sounds of destruction were the all-too-human moans of the injured and dying.

Kemal passed a knot of casualties as he cut through the station's lab section. All the wounded and dead were Rising Sun personnel. All were workers and scientists, noncombatants, cut down with unbelievable savagery by the unknown raiders.

Kemal dropped down to one knee, and cradled the head of one of the few survivors, whose body was curled up in pain. "What happened here?" Kemal asked.

"Raiders broke in," the woman gasped. "We didn't resist, but the one in charge ordered his men to kill us as he took the plans for the laser."

"The one in charge," Kemal asked, "what did he look like?"

"Cyborg," the woman said. "Artificial legs. Had a patch over his left eye."

"I've seen a man like that before," Kemal told Huer.

The digital personality nodded. "Yuri, on Barbarosa. Dracolysk rears its head again. They're trying to get sole control of the laser device."

Kemal didn't know what could be worse, the laser device in the hands of his family, or in the hands of Dracolysk.

Kemal nodded. "Look," he told Huer, "you go to the *Sun Spot*. See if you can get some medical attention for these people. I'll go on to the Sun Flower airlock."

"Be careful," Huer said. He put out his hand almost wistfully, as if wishing he could touch Kemal.

"I will," the Mercurian promised. "Help is coming soon," he promised the wounded woman, then he eased her head back to the wall and rushed on through the wrecked lab.

He drew his laser pistol as he ran, his blood boiling at the needless savagery inflicted upon innocent noncombatants by the raiders. He personally would see that they paid for their barbaric actions, paid in the coin they understood best. Blood.

As he approached the airlock that led to the asteroid's surface, he could hear the sounds of combat echoing through the station's corridors. He slowed his pace from a reckless run to a cautious crawl as he saw a knot of raiders clumped in the mouth of the corridor leading into the airlock's dressing chamber.

Barricaded in the chamber was a group of security men, fighting a hopelessly outnumbered battle against the superior numbers and firepower of the raiders who had them pinned down.

Dalton Gavilan was leading the Rising Sun defenders. He'd been wounded at least twice, seared across the forehead by an energy beam and stitched across the chest by a couple of bolt rounds that had managed to penetrate the armored smart suit that he wore. The wrist that Kemal had broken was taped haphazardly to his chest, and he was covered in sweat and blood.

But he was in his element. Grinning like a death's-head, he fought side by side with his men, his terrible cries rallying them against almost impossible odds.

Kemal decided he'd try to do something about evening them just a little.

He hefted his laser pistol. It would be next to useless against the raiders' armored smart clothes, and he needed something that would do more than pick them off one at a time anyway. He needed to make a quick impact on their numbers, or else Dalton and his security squad were dead men.

Then it struck him. A pistol could be useful—if he could find the right kind and chose the correct target to use it against.

He ran back down the corridor to one of the bodies he'd seen earlier. Clad in the black and gold uniform of a Sun King guard, the magnetic clamps of its metallic utility belt held the body securely to the floor. There Kemal found what he was looking for, a rocket pistol with enough ammunition to cause the intruders problems. He took it and quickly returned to the battle scene.

Kemal kneeled and aimed, not at the raiders, but over their heads. The pistol's clip was nearly full. He discharged the entire load as quickly as he could into the steel and naked rock of the corridor ceiling right above the raiders.

Each tiny projectile exploded as it hit. While gravity could not carry the shards toward the attackers, the concussive blasts alone sent chunks of rock and metal flashing down on them. Dust flew and sparks rained down on the raiders like burning bits of hail.

The raiders were battered and confused. Dalton saw his chance and took it. With a berserk scream he charged his suddenly confused foes while they tried to recover from the hail of rocks and molten metal that had fallen upon their heads. Dalton's men followed him.

There were a few moments of screaming, yelling chaos, and by the time Kemal reached the fray, it was all over. Dalton and a few surviving security men stood among the bodies of the dead raiders.

An odd light danced in Dalton's eyes.

He's actually enjoying this, Kemal thought, then

the light died when Dalton recognized his savior.

"It's you," he grunted.

Kemal nodded. "No need to go all mushy on me. We have to get out to protect the Sun Flowers."

"That's what I was trying, when these bastards jumped us."

"There's nobody to stop us now," Kemal pointed out.

"I'm afraid there is," said a silken, sly voice that Kemal recognized—and hated.

They whirled and looked back up the corridor. Standing there, surrounded by a knot of mercenaries armed to the teeth, was a slyly grinning Hugo Dracolysk. In the fore of the mercenaries was a smiling Yuri, whom Kemal had last seen in Malik Ferdenko's apartment on Barbarosa. This time, Yuri had on both cyborg legs and was pointing a bolt rifle right at Kemal, Dalton, and the few remaining Rising Sun security personnel who could stand on their feet.

"Your spies were right, Yuri," Dracolysk said to his henchmen. "It is the bastard who destroyed our arcology. This was definitely worth the trip out to the middle of nowhere." He turned to Kemal. "I told you I'd pay you back for what you did on Ceres," he said. "And this seems like the perfect time to carry out my promise."

"You've been working for us, Dracolysk," Dalton ground out.

Dracolysk laughed. "Working for you? Hardly. More like letting you get our work done for us. Letting you go through the grind of experimentation and development, of trial and error, while you perfected your device. Oh, we've been supplying you, as your father and I agreed, but we've also been monitoring you. And now that you have a working device, I think it's time that Dracolysk stepped forward and took over as I had intended all along."

"Liar." Dalton spat. "You cheat—"

"I prefer to think of myself as a rather sharp businessman," Dracolysk said. He looked at his henchmen. "Yuri, take care of our disaffected partners, will you?"

"My pleasure, boss," Yuri said with an evil grin.

He raised his rifle and aimed it. Kemal and Dalton stood shoulder to shoulder, both too weary to protest, too proud to do anything but face death straight on.

The lights on the airlock door right behind them started to blink, and Yuri uncertainly lowered his rifle as the airlock door swung open.

That was a mistake.

Out of the corner of his eye Kemal saw a towering figure in black armor filling the door to the airlock, and he dove to one side, yelling "Duck!" at his cousin.

Dalton reciprocated as a blur of motion burst past them, screaming like the damned. Yuri brought up his bolt rifle and fired, but the barbed projectiles glanced harmlessly off the figure's armored pressure suit.

"Barney!" Kemal yelled, then the space pirate was among Yuri and the Dracolysk mercenaries.

Foot-long daggers sprang from the sheaths implanted in Barney's forearms, cutting through his pressure suit from the inside as if it were tissue paper. He slashed left and right, and Yuri went down in a welter of blood.

Dracolysk screamed in terror as Barney closed over him like a tidal wave. Dracolysk mercenaries fell on Barney's unprotected back, and Kemal rose to his feet to go help him as Dalton grabbed his arm.

"Let them fight it out," Dalton screamed. "We have to get to the solar laser."

Kemal hesitated only a moment, knowing his cousin was right, and hating it. His heart told him to help his friend, but his brain said that they had to get to the solar laser and protect it from the raiders.

"All right," Kemal spat, following his cousin into the airlock chamber and closing the door after them. The last thing he saw was a pile of moving, thrashing bodies, and Barney's blood-stained wrist daggers showering dark red droplets of blood over everything as they swung time and again.

Kemal got into his pressure suit first, but he let Dalton lead the way out of the airlock. Under no circumstances was he going to put his back to his cousin for the rest of the fight. That simply would put too great a temptation in Dalton's path.

All suited up, Kemal went out again onto the surface of Rising Sun Station. When he peered around Dalton and the other security men, the view was not quite as spectacular as it had been the first time he'd seen it.

The Sun Flowers had been smashed. All of them were destroyed, broken into tiny crystalline shards that shed multicolored light like blood. Kemal and the others went down into the bowl-shaped depression where the crystals had been kept, Dalton swearing monotonously and unimaginatively the whole time. Footprints and jet pack markings weaved among them, signs of the now-vanished culprits who had vandalized the crystals so thoroughly that only fist-sized fragments remained suspended in space.

Kemal sifted the shattered crystal shards near him through a gloved hand. The pieces sparkled like jewel dust, burning with internal light that faded even as he released them.

Suddenly, the ground started to vibrate.

"Damn," Dalton shouted, "the skimmer hanger is opening!"

Once again a black hole gaped open in the side of the nearby cliff, and the skimmer slipped out of its mooring, the dish antenna mounted on its front casting through the vacuum like the snout of some blind beast.

"It's got us, damn it, it's got us dead," called Dalton.

There was nowhere to run, nothing to do. They stood out in the open, naked and vulnerable, as the skimmer trundled toward them.

Kemal clenched his teeth so tightly that his jaw ached.

It couldn't end now, it just couldn't. He had his father's murderer to uncover, the Dancers to pay back, and the laser device to recover.

It couldn't end now.

The skimmer came so close that they could see the

silhouette of the driver's bulk, huge and dark, through the vehicle's opaque bubble windshield. The driver was a huge man with a plastic-and-steel crest crowning the top of his head.

It couldn't be Barney, Kemal thought. He's got to be still inside. But then he realized that he'd never gotten a clear look at the figure who had charged like a berserker out of the airlock. It could have been Barney, but it also could have been Quinto, or Stalin Khan, or Sattar Tabibi, or any one of half a dozen of their clone-brothers whom Kemal had never seen before.

The skimmer stopped, the dish antenna with its glowing Sun Flower pointed directly at the small party of defenders.

Kemal looked at his cousin. "I'm glad," he said, "that all this happened while you were still in charge."

Dalton looked at him but said nothing.

The skimmer then surprised them all by slowly and gracefully rising from the surface and into space.

Kemal and Dalton and the others looked up. Hovering a half-mile above their heads was a small cruiser, its cargo bay doors gaping as a thick cable neared the laser device. A magnetic clamp reached the skimmer, gripped it firmly, and drew it back into the cargo bay's depths.

The mohawk-crested figure sitting behind the skimmer's controls waved once, then was gone.

CHAPTER
TWENTY-THREE

Kemal never knew if the clone-warrior who stole the laser device was being merciful and letting them live, or if he just couldn't figure out how to work the controls to vaporize them.

At any rate, Kemal almost wished he had been killed.

He fired off a terse report to Mercury about the situation on Rising Sun Station, then started the process of putting the pieces back together.

There wasn't much they could do. Casualties had been heavy among station personnel, especially among the security forces. No living raiders had been captured. Apparently they'd abandoned their attack after their leader, Hugo Dracolysk, had been killed in the air-lock corridor. His body, and that of his henchman, Yuri, had been found in the corridor among a pile of slain mercenaries. The few security personnel who had witnessed the savage brawl said that the damage had been done by a clone-warrior who they thought was Black Barney, the pirate, who had then dragged himself away, bleeding from half a dozen wounds.

Hugo Dracolysk's head was missing. One of the security men swore that the pirate had ripped it off Dracolysk's body and bore it away as a gory souvenir.

Dalton and Kemal, by mutual unspoken consent, decided to postpone their confrontation. It was all right with Kemal. The killing had burned the fire out of him for the moment.

The *Sun Spot* was damaged but repairable. All the while his Mercurian crew was working on it Kemal hoped that Barney would show up at the station, but the space pirate remained out of touch. Not even Huer could find him, which worried Kemal tremendously.

It took some time, but they managed to limp home to Mercury Prime. Kemal was not looking forward to meeting with his uncle. Even though Dalton still had been nominally in charge of the station when the disaster had hit, Kemal felt responsible for it. He felt as if he'd failed at every turn.

He was incredibly surprised, however, when the *Sun Spot* was greeted with the pomp and circumstance usually reserved for conquering heroes. Gordon Gavilan, resplendent in his finest garb, greeted Dalton and Kemal personally, with warm hugs and kisses on their cheeks to the wild cheers of the assembled crowd.

It was some hours before the hubbub died down and Kemal and Gordon were able to meet in Gordon's personal audience room to talk about the mission.

"I thought you'd be . . . less pleased than you seem, Uncle," Kemal told Gordon candidly.

The Sun King simply beamed at his nephew. "Why? You showed your loyalty to the House of Gavilan. Even Dalton had to admit that you exhibited great courage. You helped foil that damned Dracolysk's attempt to snatch the solar laser for himself. I think you've passed all the tests I've laid before you. I think that I can welcome you back with open arms into the House of Gavilan."

I'm not sure you'll be all *that* trusting, Kemal told himself. I'm still going to watch my back around you, and especially Dalton.

Still, things could be worse. He had managed to insinuate himself back into his family, where he could keep an eye on things, repair his relationship with Duernie and the Dancers, and lead the attempt to recover the laser device. If he stayed on that project, he would somehow find a way to dispose of the weapon. Things could be worse.

Still, he wondered why his uncle seemed so downright cheery about the events at Rising Sun.

"Rising Sun was nearly destroyed," Kemal said aloud. "The Sun Flowers were destroyed, and the solar laser was stolen. Surely that's something of a setback to your plans."

Gordon waved a large hand, brushing it all away as if it were nothing. "I wouldn't worry about all that," he said. "The work at Rising Sun was finished. They developed the weapon in secrecy, and that's all I ever wanted from the place. As to the Sun Flowers, well—" he winked conspiratorially—"we know where we can get plenty more of those, don't we?"

"But the laser itself," Kemal protested.

"Pfui," Gordon said. "It was nothing. Just a toy. A mere working model."

"Working model?" Kemal said with a sinking feeling.

"Here," Gordon said, "let me show you something."

He went to a cabinet, unlocked it, and took out a sheaf of plans.

"Take a look at these."

Kemal did. They appeared to be sketches of a solar laser similar to the one built on Rising Sun Station, but the scale was tremendous. It dwarfed the Rising Sun laser by a hundredfold.

"This thing looks like it can burn down planets," Kemal said in a small, horrified whisper.

Gordon seemed not to notice his tone. "Exactly right, my boy," he beamed. "Exactly right."

There on Mercury Prime, orbiting the hottest planet in the Solar System, Kemal felt a cold chill run down his spine. He managed a weak smile as his uncle laughed and laughed and laughed.

BUCK ROGERS XXVc

THE 25TH CENTURY BOOKS

THE INNER PLANETS TRILOGY

Book Two:
PRIME SQUARED
M. S. Murdock

Having discovered his own family's plans for a colossal laser device, Kemal prepares to head back to Earth to inform NEO. The prince learns, however, that Ardala Valmar has snared a prototype of the weapon. Kemal is compelled to stay and destroy the greater of two evils—his family's nearly completed full-scale model. The Mercurian prince maneuvers through one double-cross after another, trying to keep his uncle, the reigning Sun King, from uncovering his true allegiance. Available in November 1990.

Book Three:
MATRIX CUBED

Kemal unravels instability in the Sun King empire and finds himself thrust into daunting circumstances. His problems are compounded by the fact that others—including RAM—may have developed remarkably similar laser projects. Available in May 1991.

COUNTDOWN TO DOOMSDAY

THE FIRST SCI-FI ROLE-PLAYING COMPUTER GAME BASED ON TSR'S NEW **BUCK ROGERS**® XXVc™ GAME WORLD. NOW SSI LETS YOU JOIN BUCK AND HIS ALLIES IN THE FIGHT TO FREE THE SOLAR SYSTEM!

Available Fall 1990: IBM, C-64/128, AMIGA.
Visit your retailer or call 1-800-245-4525 (USA or Canada) for VISA/MC orders. For SSI's complete catalog, send $1.00 to:

STRATEGIC SIMULATIONS, INC.™
675 Almanor Ave. Suite 201
Sunnyvale, CA 94086

FANTASY ADVENTURE

The Dark Elf Trilogy
R. A. Salvatore

New Trilogy Begins in 1990!

Homeland

Travel back to strange and exotic Menzoberranzan, the vast city of the drow elves, and follow young Drizzt Do-Urden's adventures as he grows up in the vile world of his dark kin. Available in September 1990.

Exile

Forced from Menzoberranzan, Drizzt and his magical cat, Guenhwyvar, must fight for a new home in the labyrinths beneath Toril's surface. He also must find peace with peoples normally at war with his kind. Available in December 1990.

Sojourn

Drizzt reaches the glorious surface of Toril and resolves to live beneath the stars. Little does he suspect the adventures that lay before him in Icewind Dale. Available in early 1991.

DragonLance® Saga

PRELUDES II

RIVERWIND, THE PLAINSMAN
PAUL B. THOMPSON AND TONYA R. CARTER

TO PROVE HIMSELF WORTHY OF GOLDMOON, RIVERWIND IS SENT ON AN
IMPOSSIBLE QUEST: FIND EVIDENCE OF THE TRUE GODS. WITH AN ECCENTRIC
SOOTHSAYER, RIVERWIND FALLS DOWN A MAGICAL SHAFT—AND ALIGHTS IN A
WORLD OF SLAVERY AND REBELLION. ON SALE NOW.

FLINT, THE KING
MARY KIRCHOFF AND DOUGLAS NILES

FLINT RETURNS TO HIS BOYHOOD VILLAGE AND FINDS IT A BOOM TOWN. HE
LEARNS THAT THE PROSPERITY COMES FROM A FALSE ALLIANCE AND IS PUSHED TO
HIS DEATH. SAVED BY GULLY DWARVES AND MADE THEIR RELUCTANT MONARCH,
FLINT UNITES THEM AS HIS ONLY CHANCE TO STOP THE AGENTS OF THE DARK
QUEEN. AVAILABLE IN JULY 1990.

TANIS, THE SHADOW YEARS
BARBARA SIEGEL AND SCOTT SIEGEL

TANIS HALF-ELVEN ONCE DISAPPEARED IN THE MOUNTAINS NEAR SOLACE. HE
RETURNED CHANGED, ENNOBLED—AND WITH A SECRET. TANIS BECOMES A
TRAVELER IN A DYING MAGE'S MEMORY, JOURNEYING INTO THE PAST TO FIGHT A
BATTLE AGAINST TIME ITSELF. AVAILABLE IN NOVEMBER 1990.

B·O·O·K·S

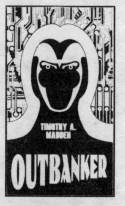

Outbanker
Timothy A. Madden

Ian MacKenzie's job as a space policeman is a lonely vigil, until the powerful dreadnaughts of the Corporate Hegemony threaten the home colonies. On sale in August.

The Road West
Gary Wright

Orphaned by the brutal, senseless murder of his parents, Keven rises from the depths of despair to face the menacing danger that threatens Midvale. On sale in October.

The Alien Dark
Diana G. Gallagher

It is one hundred million years in the future. When the ahsin bey, a race of catlike beings, are faced with a slowly dying home planet, they launch six vessels deep into space to search for an uninhibited world suitable for colonization. On sale in December.